RISING
OF 6 THE
SHIELD HERO

Aneko Yusagi

THE RISING OF 6 THE SHIELD HERO

Motoyasu Kitamura

Itsuki Kawasumi

Characters

Eclair

Rishia

Naofumi Iwatani

Ren Amaki

Raphtalia

Filo

"Can I . . . Can I be stronger? Will he respect me someday?"

"Rishia, I'll help you. I'll help you until you are strong enough to help yourself.
We can do it!"
That was how I really felt.
We'd been through the same things. We'd been framed, called weak, and condescended to.
I saw myself in Rishia, and I was going to make sure
that Itsuki understood how wrong he had been.
"Come with me!"
I reached out a hand to her. She hesitated, then took it.

Table of Contents

Prologue: Cal Mira Superstitions

The rhythmic sound of the crashing waves was soothing as I gazed at the blue ocean and sky.

"The beach is so peaceful. It's hard to believe that the ocean is so rough out there."

"Mr. Naofumi, isn't there still a storm raging off shore?"

We were at a resort island called Cal Mira, but we weren't there to relax. The island was in the middle of an activation phenomenon, so we'd come to reap its benefits.

The activation event was something similar to what happens in scheduled MMORPG events. It was a set period of time where the amount of experience points received by players was dramatically increased. So while the phenomenon was occurring, we would receive much more experience than usual for the same amount of battling.

Experience points seemed like such a strange idea, but I'd gotten used to it. This was a completely different world, after all.

"See? If you squint way out at the horizon, you can just make out some black clouds."

"Hm . . ."

I strained to see them, but it was so far away that I couldn't be sure. I guess I did see a dark line over the ocean.

The waves looked higher out there too. The breeze was wet.

"Raphtalia, you seem to know a lot about the ocean."

"Well, I am from a fishing village. I have a sense for these things, I guess."

"Oh yeah."

Why were we relaxing and watching the waves roll by? Well, we did have a fair amount of time to kill until we could act on the next phase of our plans.

To explain what I was doing in a completely new world, I should explain from the beginning.

My name is Naofumi Iwatani. I used to live in Japan as a member of a normal, modern society. I used to be a university student with otaku tendencies.

One day I stumbled into the local library to kill time and found an old-looking book called *The Records of the Four Holy Weapons*. I started flipping through it and before I knew what was happening I lost consciousness and woke back up in a new world, apparently summoned there to serve the role of one of the characters that had been described in the book: the Shield Hero.

The book had told the story of a disastrous phenomenon called "the waves of destruction." These waves were threatening to destroy the world. Standing against it were four heroes, each summoned from another world, each wielding a legendary weapon.

The weapons were the sword, spear, bow, and of course the shield.

Sure, the shield doesn't really count as a weapon *per se*. Nevertheless, that's the role I was summoned to play.

But the book wasn't complete. The text continued just until the section detailing the Shield Hero, and from that point on all the subsequent pages were blank.

And that's pretty much how I ended up here.

Anyway, this world was very different from my own. People here accrued levels and experience points, as if it were a game.

Whenever you battled and defeated monsters, you were awarded a certain amount of experience points, which would raise your abilities and level.

They called this system "status magic." Whenever I concentrated on it, I could see my various status attributes and their values spelled out before me in mid-air.

It was an interesting world. It rewarded you in direct proportion to your efforts.

But the Shield Hero was really a defense specialist. I was only able to defeat monsters indirectly.

If I didn't have party members to battle with, I was severely limited in what I could achieve. It was essentially impossible for me to defeat a monster on my own.

But it wasn't all bad. The Legendary Shield had a whole host of abilities and skills that I could use.

The Legendary Shield itself grew more powerful by absorbing monsters and various materials, and it could transform into other powerful shields.

So the plan was to level up and grow as powerful as I could before the waves came.

Unfortunately, it didn't really work out that way. The country that summoned us, Melromarc, clung to a historical vendetta against the Shield Hero.

Because of the persecution I experienced, I was unable to recruit party members of my own. Eventually I was able to recruit someone, but just when I thought I'd earned her trust and appreciation, she betrayed me. I was framed for a crime and sent out into the streets penniless and alone.

It was a very dark time, but I eventually found a party member—actually I purchased one. She was a slave when I bought her, so she didn't really have a choice in the matter. Nevertheless, together we were able to face the first wave of destruction and come out of the ordeal alive.

That doesn't sound very good, and it wasn't. But it is the truth.

The slave's name was Raphtalia, and she was only a young girl. I purchased her for a paltry sum and forced her to fight monsters on my behalf.

"What should we do next?"

"We can't go out into the open ocean until the storm blows over, so I guess we'll just kill time here on the island."

The girl next to me on the beach, the one who now cared for me sincerely, was Raphtalia.

She appeared to be around 18 years old, but in truth she was younger than that.

She was a demi-human, a type of person that existed in this world. There were different races of demi-human, among which she was a *tanuki-type*.

If you think of her as a girl with tanuki ears and a puffy tanuki tail, you'll be pretty close to what she looks like.

She had a symmetrical face framed with smooth red hair. Her skin was white and fine like porcelain.

Ten out of ten people would call her beautiful.

Demi-humans grew differently from normal humans. Even if they were young children, their bodies grew in proportion to their level, not their age. Because Raphtalia started battling with me when she was only a small girl, her body grew into a young woman nearly before my eyes. This unique way that demi-humans grew up meant that she was actually younger than she appeared to be.

When the first wave of destruction washed over the world, it took Raphtalia's village and family with it. In the ensuing chaos, she was captured by slave traders and forced into servitude, leading to an extended period of darkness in her life.

In the end I bought her as a slave, and the rest is history.

After I was betrayed, framed, and persecuted, I lost the ability to trust others.

But I was eventually able to put my trust in a slave, knowing that she had no option but to tell me the truth and could never betray me.

It may seem ridiculous, but Raphtalia was eventually set free from her life as a slave—then she voluntarily became a slave again to earn my trust. I might have lost faith in humanity, but I wasn't so far gone that I could witness such sincere devotion and remain unmoved.

Now she is my most trusted ally.

She was a very serious person.

Her sense of purpose was her highest priority—one that she never forgets. When my temper gets out of control and my language gets rough, she's always there to reel me back in.

Because of the loss and suffering she experienced during the first wave, she was extremely dedicated to fighting them.

She didn't want anyone else to endure the hardships that she'd been forced to suffer through.

To put it plainly, I respected her very much.

"Filo."

"Whaaaat?"

I called out to Filo. She was just down the beach, swimming and playing in the water.

"We're going to head over to the market. What do you want to do?"

"I wanna keep swimming!"

"Fine. Swim all you want."

"Okaaaay!"

Filo was the second friend I'd made, after Raphtalia. She was a monster and a young girl at the same time.

We received a stipend from the crown after surviving the wave of destruction, and I used the money to participate in a lottery game where you choose a monster egg from a crate for a set price without knowing what kind of egg you are going to get. Filo was the monster that hatched out of the egg, but for some reason she eventually acquired the ability to transform into a young human girl with small angel-like wings on her back.

When she was in human form she looked like a blonde-haired, blue-eyed girl of ten.

Her hair was glossy and smooth. Her eyes were clear and blue like the sea, her skin white like snow. She looked like a foreign pop idol who ran around barefoot, a snapshot of carefree youth.

One look at her face and you knew that she was as naïve and carefree as they come.

Her innocent face and expressions and her absurd, playful antics always cheered me up.

Sometimes she took things a little too far and could be irritating, but even that could be endearing.

Her real form was a filolial queen. Filolials were giant bird-like monsters with a penchant for pulling heavy objects (like carriages), and when raised under certain mysterious conditions they can mature into filolial queens.

She was much bigger than I was when in her filolial queen form, and she looked something like a mix between an owl and a penguin.

Filolials were giant birds, but for all the power they held in their legs, they were unable to fly. It might help to think of them as this world's equivalent of ostriches.

Her feathers were mostly white, though there were patches of pink here and there.

There was one other thing immediately noticeable about her that differentiated her from other filolials: she had a giant feather crest that rose vertically from the top of her head.

When she was in human form it manifested as a huge cowlick in her hair. It was very distinctive and memorable. It was her trademark.

She looked like she was around ten years old, but if you didn't take her seriously you'd end up in a lot of pain.

She was very quick on her feet and much stronger than she looked. I'd grown to trust her with my life.

As for our levels, I was at level 73, Raphtalia at 75, and Filo at 76.

Those two were my only party members, and my only real friends.

To be honest, I was starting to think that I needed to recruit someone else.

If this were just a game, then we should have been able to overcome any difficulty just by leveling up enough to overpower the enemy. But this was reality, albeit a different one than I was accustomed to. No matter how high our levels got, we were eventually going to need another pair of hands.

"How should we prepare for the next wave?"

"I think we need to find another party member."

"What about Melty-chan? She proved herself powerful during the time we spent together."

"Melty? Sure, she's powerful enough. But I don't think we can just commandeer her for our own purposes."

Melty was Filo's friend and also the princess of Melromarc.

A lot had happened and we'd ended up fighting with her for a time, during which she had demonstrated what a powerful fighter she could be. But the waves were dangerous, and it didn't make sense to put the heir to the throne in the line of fire.

Oh, that reminds me. I mentioned that I had been framed for a crime. Melty actually had a lot to do with that.

But to explain I need to back up and tell you a bit more about the country that summoned me to this world: Melromarc.

Melromarc had a religious vendetta against the Shield Hero.

The national religion was called the Church of the Three Heroes, and they worshiped all the heroes aside from the Shield Hero.

So the citizenry had always equated the Shield Hero with villainy and deceit.

Now you might be wondering why a religion like that would even exist.

The roots lie in Melromarc's widespread human supremacy and the oppression of the demi-humans that accompanied it.

As you might expect, there were countries that embraced the opposite of that philosophy. There were demi-human supremacist countries out there too, places where humans faced unjust discrimination.

Melromarc had a long history of war with one of those countries, where the demi-human population had long worshiped the Shield Hero among the other gods of their pantheon.

When I was summoned to Melromarc, the king who was serving at the time immediately discriminated against me, then saw to it that I was framed, prosecuted, and sent out into the streets penniless and alone.

But a royal conspiracy alone isn't enough to explain everything that happened next.

The world was currently under the existential threat of the impending waves of destruction—there was no time to spend dilly-dallying over how to treat the Shield Hero.

The true ruler of Melromarc was not the king, but the queen. The queen sent Melty as an intermediary between myself, the Shield Hero, and her father, the king.

Melromarc was traditionally a matrilineal country—all the true power lay with the queen.

When all this happened, the queen was traveling around on diplomatic missions to try and rally the disparate nations of the world against the threat of the waves.

It was a particularly perilous time for diplomacy. Realizing the threat of the waves and the need to call on the heroes, an international agreement had been reached. The heroes would be summoned by a mutually agreed upon country. But in the queen's absence, the king had teamed up with the Church of the Three Heroes and summoned the heroes to Melromarc without conferring with the international body. Understandably, this act of defiance angered the rest of the world, and the queen had her hands full simply trying to prevent the outbreak of war, which seemed imminent.

Were it not for the efforts of the queen in those dark days, Melromarc would probably no longer exist as a sovereign nation.

At the time, Raphtalia and I had no way to know what was really going on. After surviving the first wave we slowly saved money by selling various trinkets. That was the only way to secure the funds necessary to update our equipment from what we'd started with, which wasn't anywhere near powerful enough to ensure our survival.

Our traveling merchant life was boring but had plenty of

advantages. Of course, I hid my identity as the Shield Hero and instead called myself the saint of the bird god, because Filo was pulling my carriage and she really stood out in a crowd. Citizens actually started to respect the saint of the bird god.

We were eventually able to secure better tools, materials, and equipment through my mercantile efforts. In the end, we managed to become at least as powerful as the other heroes.

But the Church of the Three Heroes didn't like the idea that I was traveling free under a pseudonym.

The other three heroes had caused some trouble on their travels, and it was starting to foment doubt among the populace. Realizing that its status as the national faith might soon be shaken, the church decided to become an active player in the events unfolding in Melromarc.

They concocted an elaborate plan to tarnish my reputation further. I was accused of kidnapping the very princess that the queen had sent to repair the strained relationship between the king and I: the heiress of the throne, Melty.

The crown sent the other three heroes to bring us back in while we fled from them in an attempt to prove our innocence.

Along the way we ran into all sorts of trouble. We battled the very same nobleman that had once imprisoned and tortured Raphtalia. And we had to take down a massive monster that he had released from its magically sealed prison.

There's more. We ended up running into the queen of the

filolials after that fight, and finally, after the smoke had cleared, the church decided to dispense with its shadowy operations and came after us directly. They called it a holy war, and they were out for blood.

In the end I was forced to use my last resort. The cursed, dark side of my shield contained an unbelievable power, and I used it to destroy the head of the church itself: the high priest. At last, my innocence was proven to the people.

The queen returned to the country and heavily punished her husband, the king, and Melty's bitch of an older sister— the one who had originally framed me. She had their names officially changed to Trash and Bitch.

At long last, things were as they should have been from the very start. I was considered equal to the other three heroes, and my actions were officially supported and sanctioned by the crown. Finally, we were free to dedicate our efforts to fighting the waves.

Or so I thought. It wasn't long before new problems started showing up.

"Why did they have to be our enemy? I wanted to invite them to join our party."

"I know how you feel. They were very powerful and kind. They were the kind of people we could have depended on."

". . . Yeah."

On the ocean voyage to the Cal Mira islands we had

coincidently shared a room with two other adventurers: L'Arc Berg and Therese.

L'Arc seemed really nice, like a dependable older brother type of guy.

He was very experienced in battle, he was considerate, and he was fun to be around. To be honest, I didn't hate him.

Therese was very skilled with magic, and because my party didn't have a lot of back-row support, she was a very valuable asset during the time we spent together.

Both of them had been extremely powerful in comparison to other adventurers I'd met.

But in the end they turned out to be compatriots of the enemy we'd met at the end of the third wave of destruction: a mysterious woman named Glass.

During our exploration of the islands we found an underwater temple. Venturing inside, we found a dragon hourglass, which was a mysterious object that counted down the time until the next wave of destruction appeared. The wave came, and after a large battle, we fought an Inter-Dimensional Whale, which was the wave's boss monster. Immediately after the monster fell, L'Arc and Therese turned on us.

The battle was one of attrition and ended with their retreat. I don't know who would have won if we had continued to fight.

So we survived another wave, but the mystery at the core of the phenomenon had only grown deeper.

When L'Arc and Therese retreated, they disappeared into the dimensional rifts that occurred during the wave. I tried to follow them, but we were too late.

What *were* the waves?

When I first arrived in this world, I thought they were a phenomenon where endless waves of monsters poured from dimensional rifts. But after listening to the things L'Arc and Glass had said, I wasn't so sure they were a natural phenomenon anymore.

They had to be something else. L'Arc and the others had made it clear that their end goal was specifically to kill the heroes.

"There's no point in worrying about it. Let's go kill some time at the market."

"Good idea."

We were stuck on Cal Mira for the time being.

The storm at sea would calm down eventually.

The massive monster boss we'd defeated out at sea had already been hauled back to the island.

The monster was an Inter-Dimensional Whale.

The thing was so massive that I wasn't going to be able to use any of it for materials until the villagers on the island managed to break it down a bit—and apparently that was going to take a while.

"Look, Mr. Naofumi, they're selling accessories."

"Oh yeah?"

I looked over at the shop she was indicating and could hardly believe my eyes.

"What the hell?!"

The prices were absurd. I get that merchants want to get what they can from their customers, but there have to be *some* standards! I glared at the shopkeeper.

Had he set the prices up to say . . . double the market value, I could have overlooked that. You have to expect that sort of thing in tourist areas. But did he really think he was going to get away with charging *four times* the market value?

"Hey."

"Yes, yes! Step right up! What can I do for you?"

"Don't you think your prices are a little high?"

I pointed to a necklace hanging from a rack behind him.

Dummy Sapphire Necklace (Magic +)
quality: poor (concealment) normal

Had we been in Melromarc, every one of his items would be considered terrible in their price class.

The guy had even used concealment magic on his items to hide their inferiority. If you didn't look closely, you would have thought they were pretty good.

But the prices were set so high that he was charging prices

higher than even the most expertly crafted accessories could command. *Four times* higher. I'm all for getting what you can out of customers, but there has to be a limit.

I looked over his other accessories to make sure that his pricing was consistently crazy—it was.

He could scam people if he really wanted to, but I wished he would do a better job of it.

"Please understand. The prices are the result of our isolation. These islands are very far from the main continent, so the prices need to be a little higher to pay for their shipment."

"A little higher? Is that why you've used concealment magic on them?"

"Well, this is a business. Importing the materials costs me quite a lot."

I didn't like the look on his face. He was going to try and play innocent.

He thought I was just another complaining customer, and he waved his hand to send me away.

I could have called for the queen. Or I could have used my hero status to give him a lecture. But I decided to talk to him as a fellow businessman instead.

"Have you ever heard of this guy?"

I flashed the accessory dealer certificate that I had.

It was a real certificate. I'd received it through some connections I'd made when I was pretending to be the holy saint of the bird god.

The guy that had given it to me was very well established in the community—a famous man. His seal of approval had an impressive effect on everyone I showed it to.

The dealer immediately reacted to the paper. He twitched, a wince of sorts. Then he took it and carefully read it, pouring over all the minute details. As he did, the color drained from his face.

"I can think of some people that might be interested in hearing about your business practices. I'll be sure to remember you."

"W . . . Wait just a second!"

In a split second he bounded over his table of wares and threw himself at my feet, petitioning for mercy.

"What do you want? I'm a busy man."

"I took another look at the prices and realized that I had accidentally attached the wrong price tags! I'll change the prices to what they were originally supposed to be, so please wait just a moment!"

"Nah, don't bother. I'm not doing anything but having a chat with some of my friends back on the continent."

"W . . . Wait! Please! I'm going to sell them at a 30 percent discount!"

"30 percent off those prices? I don't know about that . . ."

"No, 30 percent off of the proper price! Of course!"

"Thanks, but no thanks."

"Wait! 50, no . . . 60 percent off!"

"I wonder where my friend is these days? I'll have to look him up when I get back . . ."

"S . . . 70 percent!"

"I'm pretty sure he was part of the national merchant's guild . . . "

"80! 80 percent off!"

"I'll tell him that there was this guy who used concealment magic on terrible items and that he sold them for 400 percent the market value. Can you believe it?"

"90 percent! I'll give you a 90 percent discount!"

That was probably about as good as I could hope for.

"Sold."

There was nothing worse than building a business on intimidation and power. This guy would use people's mortal fear to try and turn a deal. I was pretty sure that if the merchant guild found out about him they would shut him down.

That's fine with me. He deserved whatever he got.

"I'm not telling you that you have to take slim margins and sell tons of stuff. You just have to be reasonable. In the end you only harm the industry—you only harm yourself."

I would have said the same thing to a merchant who sold his products at substantially under market value.

It might look like what they were doing was good and nice, but in the end it only accelerated deflation. Lower prices weren't always the best option.

If there were merchants that wanted to charge substantially over market value, they needed to be in competition with another merchant. That was the only way to stabilize prices.

Considering how far Cal Mira was from the mainland, it was only natural that prices would be somewhat higher.

From my time in the market, it didn't look like there was any other business that was really in direct competition over accessory prices. Either this guy was chasing them out of town or he was cornering the market in some other way.

If there were no other shops offering competition for the same articles, then he could just raise the prices to whatever he wanted, and customers would have no choice but to buy from him.

And if that happened, the association of merchants would lose the trust of the people.

"If you're going to turn a profit, at least make sure the customer is smiling when they hand over the cash."

"What do you mean?"

"Think about it. We're in the middle of an activation event, aren't we?"

"Well, yes . . ."

"Then why don't you spread a rumor? You could say that accessories formed with ore from the islands raise the level up rate for the wearer. Or something like that."

"What?"

"Don't you get it? You just have to spread the rumor. You don't have to actually improve the efficacy of the item. You only need to spread the superstition. Think about it. Everyone that has come here to level up is excited about leveling up. They already want to buy something to help them."

It was the same concept behind local good luck charms and amulets.

Even if they didn't actually have an effect, the wearer *felt* like they did.

"I think I see what you mean!"

I'd used that strategy in the past, and it had worked for me.

If I heard that a village needed medicine, I went and sold it to them. If they need pesticides, I went and sold it to them. I did the same with food. The price was higher than it probably should have been, but the customers went away happy nonetheless.

In the end it isn't the price that matters—it's the satisfaction that the customer feels when the deal is done.

The merchant seemed excited by the idea. He nodded and stood back up.

"You understand the rest, right? You keep an eye on what the customer thinks they want to pay, and then you try to get a little bit more. As long as you do that, the customer will leave satisfied. Then they believe in the superstition that they are leveling faster than they would have without it. They tell their friends all about how well it works, and then more customers come to you."

I didn't know if he could actually expect such a dramatic effect or how long the effect would last. But it would probably work for a while.

During the activation event, the experience points awarded for battle were higher than usual. So the adventurers on Cal Mira would already be leveling up faster than they were used to. Once they noticed the effect, they wouldn't be able to tell what was the result of the activation event and what was due to the accessory. Then they would buy into the rumor that the island ore was somehow special—and they'd be happy about it.

If that went on for a while, then the number of people using the accessory would grow, and that in turn would lead to wishful thinking, leading even more people to believe in the power of the accessory.

"I'll try your suggestion right away!"

The merchant handed me the necklace I had been looking at. Then he closed up shop and got to work.

"Whew."

I did a great job with that one. In the end, I'd gotten the necklace for free.

"Mr. Naofumi . . ."

Raphtalia looked disappointed. She sighed and slapped her palm to her forehead and moaned.

I guess it did kind of look like I picked a fight just to cheat the guy.

"He deserved it. He disrespected the very idea of business."

"I understand that, and yet I feel like we've just led him to shadier practices."

"True, but that's just how people work. They love superstitions."

The queen came walking over and called out to me.

"What are you doing in a place like this, Mr. Iwatani?"

"What's the matter?"

"The preparations for the meeting are complete. The other heroes are waiting."

"Okay."

I guess I'd gotten wrapped up in the conversation. Time had slipped by faster than I'd expected.

The queen led, and we followed. We were heading for the castle-like inn that we'd been staying in since we'd arrived in the islands.

We arrived at the inn and followed the queen up a flight of stairs.

"The other heroes' party members are waiting in another room. What would you like Ms. Raphtalia to do?"

"Um . . ."

The last time we'd had a meeting of the heroes it had been

back in Melromarc castle. During the meeting, Raphtalia had gotten in a fight with some of the other heroes' party members.

It wasn't really her fault. A certain few of them were really selfish and cruel, and they were prejudiced towards demi-humans.

Just because the national ruler publicly declares something bad doesn't mean that the racism inherent in society just vanishes. People were mean to her just because she was in league with the Shield Hero, never mind that she was a demi-human.

"At the moment, the majority of the heroes' compatriots are wandering around the island freely. Still, I can have a room prepared for Ms. Raphtalia, if you would prefer that."

The queen meant to imply that the easiest solution would be for Raphtalia to take this as free time and go somewhere else to avoid unnecessary conflict.

Raphtalia had figured that out as well. She nodded.

"I understand. I'll just be off then."

"I'll call for you if we need you. Just do whatever you like until then."

"Alright."

I parted ways with Raphtalia, and the queen led me into the meeting room where the other heroes were waiting.

Chapter One: The Seven Star Heroes

I was led up the spiral staircase just like in Melromarc tower and into a high room with an impressive view over the country.

The other heroes were already there, sitting around a table and waiting for my arrival.

"So you finally showed up, eh?" the Sword Hero, Ren Amaki, blurted out.

He was a 16-year-old swordsman that liked to dress in black.

His hair was cropped short, and his face—or actually his whole aura—gave off an intelligent, cool, and collected sort of vibe.

If you ask me, he faked it all. He just wanted people to think he was cool.

For example, I'd just recently found out that he didn't know how to swim and was terrified of the water. So my guess was that he just tried to keep his pathetic side hidden.

He had been summoned from an alternate version of Japan, just like me.

In Ren's Japan, they had a type of game called "VRMMO," which apparently was a combination of virtual reality and internet gaming. He'd explained that the players could completely immerse themselves in an online world. I sort of thought that maybe he had just come from my Japan, only in the future.

From the interactions we'd had, I gathered that he was able to exercise some degree of common sense. Still, I only say that in comparison to the other heroes.

"Where have you been?" demanded Itsuki Kawasumi, the Bow Hero.

He had naturally curly hair and looked like a sensitive, artistic type of guy.

In reality he had an overactive sense of justice and was pretty hot-tempered.

His favorite thing to do was to travel around the country in disguise, hunting down bad guys and making sure they were properly punished.

He liked to exercise his authority as a hero to right the wrongs of the world.

He was like a famous general commander character from a period drama.

From where I stood, he just looked like an arrogant prick—but I couldn't deny that some unfortunate people had benefited from his self-righteousness.

The problem was that his party members worshiped him with religious fervor, which naturally only fueled his arrogance more.

Knowing that they basically worshiped the ground he walked on, Itsuki himself made no effort to change their behavior. That's another thing about him that rubbed me the wrong way.

"I bet you were out picking up chicks, weren't you? They probably threw themselves at you after that last battle," chimed in Motoyasu Kitamura, the Spear Hero.

"Is that all you think about?"

"Motoyasu, let it go this time."

"Yeah, we're all tired of your shtick."

Motoyasu was the most handsome of us four heroes. His hair was pulled back into a ponytail. I guess you called it a ponytail?

I'm a guy, but I can admit that he was pretty good-looking. He looked pretty easy-going, not uptight at all.

If you were just going to hang out normally, then I guess he was fine. I mean you probably wouldn't hate him or anything.

He sure was stubborn though. Once he decided what he believed, nothing would change his mind.

Apparently he was supposed to be the most loyal of the heroes. That was true in a way, but he was also an idiot that never doubted his "friends."

He was also a full-time womanizer. Whenever he had a second to spare, you could bet he'd use it to hit on a girl.

He'd hit on both Raphtalia and Filo the first time he met them.

I'd heard that he was walking around Cal Mira hitting on girls too. I didn't doubt it for a second.

The bitch that framed me was one of his party members, so of course he believed her completely. To this day, he still thought that I tried to rape her. But lately the queen had forced Bitch to show her true colors time and time again, and it seemed like even Motoyasu was starting to take notice.

All three of the other heroes had been summoned from alternate versions of Japan, and all three of them had played games that very closely resembled the world we now found ourselves in.

Ren had played a game called Brave Star Online, through the VRMMO system that was used in his world.

Itsuki had played a game called Dimension Wave, which he has said was a console game.

Motoyasu's game had been called Emerald Online, and it was an MMO.

But I had never played a game resembling this world; I had read about it in a book called *The Records of the Four Holy Weapons*. We'd all learned about this world in different ways, but what that meant was still a complete mystery.

"I was just watching the ocean from the beach."

I took a seat.

"Yeah, well. The storm is still raging out there, so we can't leave yet."

"I guess we could use the time to level up and collect drop items? Any other ideas?"

"Not really."

At least they seemed to understand that we were stuck on the island for the time being.

"So? What's the meeting for?"

"Don't you know?"

The reason we'd all been called to the meeting was obvious.

I'll just be blunt about it: the other heroes were too weak to be of any use.

When the battle with L'Arc and the others began, L'Arc had used a single restraining move against them to keep them from interfering. He'd only had to use it once. The three of them all fell instantly and stayed out for the remainder of the fight.

It had been some kind of lightning-themed combo skill, I think.

They were hit by the attack once and were instantly paralyzed for the whole battle.

Luckily, L'Arc had never intended to kill them. It had been the sort of attack that you often see in anime or manga—the sort intended to knock someone out without causing any permanent damage or threatening their lives.

If they were so weak that they were knocked out of battle by a single hit, then they were never going to stand a chance of victory.

L'Arc and Therese were both very powerful. I had spent a long time leveling and powering up, and I really thought that the attacks they were using were strong enough to kill me.

I had used a shield with a very high defense rating in the battle. It had skills that had enabled me to keep L'Arc in place. I blocked his attacks and prevented him from dodging ours while Raphtalia and Filo kept up the offensive.

But L'Arc and Therese had plenty of cards up their sleeves.

For example, just when I thought that I had him cornered, L'Arc's scythe started to glow. He brushed my shoulder with the tip.

I had a really high defense rating, and I'd been able to withstand L'Arc's attacks up until that point, but not that attack. That one had really hurt.

Luckily, it hadn't been enough to knock me out of the battle, but he'd found an attack that was extremely effective against me. You might say he'd found my weak point and gone straight for it.

It was the type of attack that turned my defense rating into a liability—a defense rating attack.

It worked by dealing damage based on your defense rating. The higher your defense, the more damage you would take. It was a very rare sort of attack, but I'd seen it before in a game.

This whole world seemed to operate just like a game, so I'd realized that it was a possibility that such an attack might exist.

Still, I certainly hadn't expected to get hit with it right in the middle of a life-or-death battle.

For a shielder like myself, whose greatest strength is their defense rating, an attack like that can be fatal.

There was another problem. I could have switched to a shield with a lower defense rating as a way to get around the defense rating attack, but then I wouldn't have had a strong enough defense rating to survive their normal attacks.

He really had found the most effective means of fighting against us. For a moment, I thought we were done for.

Then I realized that I could use skills that I had, like air strike shield and shooting star shield, to prevent their attacks from reaching me. That would make their attacks completely ineffective. Still, the existence of their defense rating attacks turned the tide of the battle, and we were put on the defensive.

For the most part, I could use my skills to defend myself. But then I was left with no way to deal any damage to them.

Even if I teamed up with Raphtalia and Filo to get some attacks in, L'Arc still had Therese on his side. I couldn't figure out what to do, but then things got even worse.

Glass showed up right in the middle of the battle.

Glass also had an attack that was very effective against me, though for the opposite reason. She had a defense rating ignoring attack.

Both L'Arc's defense rating attack and Glass's defense

ignoring attack were very effective against me. With both of them there, it felt like there was no need for the Shield Hero to participate in the battle at all.

Just when things were looking their worst, we put up an impressive fight and were able to beat the three of them back.

Glass was exhausted and depleted of energy, and it looked like we might win. But then L'Arc pulled out a bottle of soul-healing water and dumped it all over Glass, immediately restoring all of her SP.

I don't even want to remember what happened after that.

I'd been able to withstand all attacks aside from the defense rating and defense ignoring attacks, but the newly-restored Glass came flying at me with new attacks that were now much more powerful than I was capable of defending against.

Her attacks were unbelievably fast and strong.

They were so quick that Raphtalia and Filo, despite all the leveling up we'd done, weren't able to follow them at all.

And then, for whatever reason, Glass and the others just retreated. The battle was put on hold.

I'd like to call it a draw, but it wasn't really like that. We weren't going to be able to defeat them, and they ran away for some other reason.

If we ran into them again, we would probably lose.

Which brings me to the main problem. If the other heroes were so weak that L'Arc had been able to defeat them in one fell swoop, what would have happened if they'd been challenged by Glass?

The answer was as clear as day. They'd all be dead in a second.

I'd heard that if the heroes died, the waves of destruction would grow stronger. If I could do anything to avoid that outcome, I had to do it.

Besides, if the other heroes could start to manage for themselves, then the burden of fighting Glass and the others wouldn't fall solely on my shoulders.

I looked over at the queen and she nodded in response.

"Very well, let us begin the second meeting of the heroes. I, Milleria Q. Melromarc, will moderate the discussion."

All three of them reclined dramatically.

"Discussion, eh?"

"What's left to discuss?"

"Naofumi's the only one here who hasn't been forthcoming."

I was already getting irritated with them.

"I've already told you this, haven't I? You were all correct about the power-up methods. All I did was what you three taught me to do. That was how I became strong enough to battle through the last wave."

We'd already had a meeting like this once, before we'd all come to the islands. We'd talked about the various ways to power-up our stats and weapons.

Our weapons had special abilities and power-up methods that weren't available to other adventurers. That was why the heroes could become stronger than other people.

But when they all started talking about the power-up systems they used, it turned out there was very little overlap. Each one of them had a completely different idea about how it worked. The "meeting" devolved into name-calling and stubborn insistence on their own methods and ended up being called off before we came to any sort of consensus.

But afterwards I tried each of the methods they'd detailed using my shield, and it turned out that they had all been correct.

Melromarc used shadows to deliver messages, so I sent them all what I'd discovered. They refused to believe me. In the end none of them were powerful enough to be of any use during the wave of destruction.

There was a catch though. The power-up methods I discovered only worked if you truly believed that they were going to work.

If you held on to any lingering doubts when you tried them, the weapon wouldn't respond.

Our weapons, it seemed, were able to turn our emotions into power. If you didn't believe in the power-up method that another hero explained, the icon that enabled it wouldn't even appear in your menu.

"There you go—lying again! Isn't it obvious that Naofumi

just found a way to cheat the system? Just fess up already!"

"Yeah! You cheater! You better stop lying to us!"

"You haven't even told us about the power-up methods that you use! What a coward! Did you do all this just to ruin Whore's life?"

They were so ridiculous it was hard to stay mad at them. They were too stupid to merit any real anger.

"So you decided not to believe all the things I've already told you, and you keep insisting that I cheated to get ahead? Is that it?"

All three of them nodded in unison.

"And besides! Your party members have also powered-up! It's unbelievable! You expect us to believe that all that is because of your shield?!"

"I already told you how that works. Raphtalia and Filo both level up faster than normal because of maturation adjustment skills that I unlocked. I also told you that when we finally participated in the class up ceremony, Filo's cowlick responded and some kind of special class up occurred."

"It's true. I was there to witness it," the queen explained. "From what I saw, that is exactly what happened. Something unique occurred when Filo and Raphtalia underwent the ceremony, and it seems to have affected the extent to which their abilities improved."

The queen had just confirmed by story, but the three

heroes continued to glare at me suspiciously. Why did I have to be interrogated?

"Look, guys. Have you ever thought about this from my perspective?"

"What?"

"Why would I want to do that?"

"I have. I wanted to figure out how you discovered this cheating method. We need to know that."

They were impossible to talk to, but that didn't change the fact that I needed them to be stronger than they were.

It wasn't necessarily that I thought I was the best, but during the last battle I'd realized—painfully—just how serious of a predicament we were really in.

"Just think about this. I can't attack. All I can do is defend, right? So how do I benefit from cheating to get more powerful than the rest of you?"

"Well."

The three of them looked around the room and at each other. They appeared to be at a loss for words. They must have been desperately trying to think of something that would sound reasonable.

"But you DO have a way to attack!"

Itsuki leapt to his feet and jabbed his finger at me.

Was that his burning sense of justice coming to the rescue? Nothing was more irritating than a self-righteous idiot.

"Are you talking about iron maiden and blood sacrifice?"

"Yes! You have those two powerful attacks, so that should give you a reason to want to pull ahead of the rest of us!"

I really didn't have very many ways to go on the offensive.

One of them was a counter effect that my shield had. It could respond to an attack from an enemy with a counter attack of its own.

So I could use a shield with spikes all over it and that would hurt an enemy if they punched it. But did that really count as an offensive attack?

It was strictly a passive way to do damage.

Then there were the two skills that Itsuki had mentioned: iron maiden and blood sacrifice. Those skills were only accessible when I was using a cursed shield, the Shield of Wrath.

But both of those skills came with problems of their own.

I sighed heavily and turned to answer Itsuki's accusation.

"Iron maiden works by first using shield prison to enclose the enemy, then using change shield (attack) to activate iron maiden. Doing so uses all of my SP. You have broken through that attack once yourself, so you should realize there is a serious flaw in the attack."

"Is there?"

I was so irritated with them I could hardly think straight.

Ren tapped his chin with a fingertip, apparently deep in thought. Motoyasu just went on glaring at me.

Finally, reaching a conclusion, Ren opened his mouth.

"The preparations for the attack take too long."

"Exactly. If the enemy breaks through the shield prison, then I can't continue with the sequence. Of course I could just try to use the skills as quickly as possible, but that doesn't do away with this fundamental flaw."

So using iron maiden required a long and elaborate set up on my end of things, which made it easy enough for an attentive enemy to break the sequence.

"You've broken that skill sequence yourselves. You should know this."

Even if I were able to run the whole skill sequence, it wouldn't work if the enemy were able to break the shield prison and escape—or worse, if the enemy just broke the iron maiden itself.

The iron maiden didn't move very quickly, so if another enemy scored a direct hit against it, it was always possible to break the attack.

"Then what about blood sacrifice?!"

"Have you already forgotten? When I use that I have to bear the brunt of an essentially fatal attack. *If* I survive it, then I end up with a curse that drops my stats by a full 30 percent."

By the time the wave of destruction was actually bearing down on Cal Mira, I'd managed to recover most of my stats, but it wasn't like I could just push myself to the brink of death every time I got in a fight. The recovery was taxing and took a long time.

"Those are the only methods of attack available I've got, both of which are burdensome and ask way too much of me in payment. Even the Shield of Wrath comes with its issues. I can't just use it whenever I want, you know?"

The shield was cursed. Using it eroded my very soul.

"But there were others, too! What about that attack that throws black flames everywhere?!"

"That's only a counter attack. And that skill is tied to the Shield of Wrath, so I can't just use it whenever I feel like it."

Every time I used the shield it had an effect on me. It felt like I was going to be swallowed by rage and misery.

So every attack I was capable of using on my own was tied to the cursed shield series. There was no proper method of attack open to me.

If they wanted to call that cheating, fine. They could call it whatever they liked.

But they were missing the point. The actual problem had yet to be addressed.

It was like they bought a game but skipped the tutorial and didn't read the instruction manual. Then when they realized that a method they knew from another game worked, they stuck with it and never bothered to check to see if there was a better way. They were the worst kind of gamers.

They weren't using the right power-up method, so it only made sense that their progress would bottom out halfway through.

"Besides, the Shield of Wrath seems to have its own power-up method that I don't understand. None of your methods work on it, and I can't get it to unlock any other skills."

As for the Shield of Wrath, whether it's iron maiden or blood sacrifice, it seemed like nothing I did would unlock any additional abilities.

"Do you get it yet? I really don't have any proper attack abilities of my own."

"Liar!"

Motoyasu screamed at me. I didn't see any other way to make them understand, so I stood up, walked over to him, and punched him in the face.

I slowly pulled my fist back and then returned to my seat.

Motoyasu looked like he couldn't believe what just happened. He was holding his cheek.

It hadn't hurt him at all, I could tell. That was exactly what I was trying to tell them.

"Do you get it now? It seems like you all think I've somehow weaseled my way into an enormous amount of power, but don't you see? No matter how high my defense stat grows, my attack stays the same. I'm never going to be able to attack."

Motoyasu hadn't taken any damage.

"Now, if *you* wanted to try attacking *me* yourselves, I might be able to make you regret that. Want to try?"

Finally, I got what I'd longed for all this time: all three of them shut up.

Still, they were looking at me as though they couldn't process what had just happened.

"It doesn't matter how far ahead of you three I get. It doesn't help me at all. If only one of you had managed to power-up the way that I have, don't you think that battle on the sea would have turned out differently?"

I already explained this, but the three of them were knocked out right along with the other adventurers and knights by L'Arc and Therese's combo skill at the start of our battle. They just stayed unconscious for the entire fight.

"You all like to call this sort of thing a losing event, like we were never supposed to win it. How many losing events do you think happen in a row?"

"Dammit . . ."

Ren murmured to himself, annoyed.

Itsuki and Motoyasu's hands were curled into fists.

"You all need to get it through your heads. L'Arc . . . L'Arc Berg, Therese, and Glass came here specifically to kill the heroes. Luckily for you, they thought I was the only real hero, so they focused on trying to kill me. If they figure out who you really are, they'll come after you next."

And then what would happen? I actually already knew the answer.

Fitoria, the queen of the filolials, had told me.

"I heard that the waves get stronger if a hero dies."

If one of them died in battle, it would only make my life harder.

I couldn't afford to let that happen.

"If that's the situation that we are in, how do I stand to benefit from overpowering you three?"

"Obviously, you want to be stronger than us so that you can claim to be a *real* hero! You want all the glory for yourself!"

"Give me a break."

Itsuki was getting dumber and dumber.

"I cannot believe the words of a man who strives for nothing other than his own self-satisfaction!"

"Stop making stuff up and then believing it!"

I could have said the same thing to myself, but it was still true. Deciding things in haste will only make your life harder in the long run.

That's why I decided to believe in my friends as much as I could.

If I didn't, then I'd never make it out of this alive.

Of course, I still have a healthy amount of skepticism, but I've realized that if you doubt everything, you'll never get anywhere.

"'You aren't the protagonist of this story.' That's what you said when Bitch framed me. Isn't that right, Motoyasu?"

Motoyasu had been agreeing with Itsuki, so I addressed him.

"Think about where we find ourselves and tell me, who's the protagonist here? Ren, you think about it too. One of us is trying to get everyone together to fight against the waves of destruction while the other heroes just sit around and call him a cheater. Who do *you* think is the protagonist of this story?"

It looked like I finally struck a nerve. All three of them cast their eyes down at the table.

I don't think I ever said that I wanted to compete for protagonist status. All I wanted to say was that we needed to be realistic about how to deal with the problems we were facing.

"If you think I'm cheating, fine. I'll tell you how I did it. I actually used the power-up methods that you taught me. There! That's all!"

". . ."

They all continued to sit there in silence.

"You know what I really want? I'd like to be able to fight for myself a little. Sure, Raphtalia and Filo are both really strong, but at the end of the day that's still only two people. If I want to have some more offensive power, isn't it ideal to team up with you three? You are the heroes, after all."

It felt wrong just saying it. I could hardly imagine having to team up with them.

"You know, it kind of seems like you are condescending to us, even though we're doing all we can to become as powerful as we can."

I sighed.

I really couldn't stand listening to them talk.

"Ren, you just said that I wouldn't be forgiven. Whose forgiveness did you think I needed?"

". . ."

Well, he clearly thought highly of himself.

He was acting like a server administrator or something.

"You idiot. Who do you think needs to be doing the forgiving here?"

He cast his eyes noncommittally at the tabletop.

Had he just realized how ridiculous he sounded? Had he just let himself get emotional for a second?

"Just how powerful do you think you are? Give me a reason to listen to the dribble you speak. Should I assume that you still have some secrets you haven't shared?"

He sighed and looked away.

I guess he hadn't been serious. He'd just let his emotion slip for a second.

I'd met people like him before.

It was like you were playing an online game and came across someone with a rare, powerful weapon. Because they had the weapon they were able to fight monsters and bosses that would normally be inaccessible to someone of their level. People would see that and think they were cheating, so they would run to tell the administrators.

I knew about it because I used to be the manager of a pretty big guild. We had a stash of rare items reserved for anyone that aligned with us.

"It's time to open your eyes. I've been telling you the truth this whole time. I know it sounds sentimental, but it's true— you have to believe in the system to make it work. Belief is our power."

"You like this? Do you like sitting there and lecturing us?"

They never let up, did they?

I glared at them.

"You're weak enough to warrant a lecture or two. Stop acting like weaklings. Playtime is over."

I figured they would respond to the taunt, so I tried to push them into considering the conversation more seriously.

"What?!"

"I refuse to speak with you further!"

"You coward!"

They all jumped to their feet and started shouting in unison.

Then the queen used her magic to form a massive ball of ice and dropped in on the center of the table. It was very loud and heavy.

"Control yourselves! Is this any time for infighting?"

"Whatever. Why should we listen to someone who would team up with a cheater?"

Ren glared angrily and the floor, and the queen seemed to have had enough.

"My country will do all it can to help you heroes become as powerful as necessary to battle the waves. Please regain your senses."

It was really unbelievable. How long were they going keep this temper tantrum up?

I sympathized with the queen.

"Let's set your various power-up methods aside for the moment. I'd like to discuss the enemies we encountered during the last wave."

"Good idea. Maybe one of you encountered characters like them in the games you'd played back in your own worlds."

The book I'd started reading at the library, the *Records of the Four Holy Weapons*, hadn't contained any information regarding the true nature of the waves—which rendered it pretty much useless in this situation.

But the other heroes might have known something that I didn't.

"So tell us. Have you ever run into anything like those three in one of your games?"

"No."

"Me neither. That man fought with a giant scythe. I've

never met a character that fought with a weapon like that."

"Yeah. I've heard of them before but never seen one. They're pretty minor as far as weapons go."

L'Arc had used a scythe. I couldn't argue with how strange that had seemed at first.

"Why don't you tell us about them? It seemed like you got to know them pretty well before the wave came."

"After you three took over all the rooms on the ship to Cal Mira, we got stuck with the bill and had to share a room with those two. We got to talking and agreed to spend one day on the islands leveling together."

"So you didn't know them very well?"

"No."

"When you were leveling with them, did anything seem . . . strange?"

"Actually, yes. L'Arc's giant scythe acted like our legendary weapons do. He was able to absorb monsters and items into it."

"Didn't you think that was odd at the time?"

How was I supposed to know what was normal in this world?

The other three were supposed to understand how everything worked, and yet little things surprised them all the time.

Had they been in my position, I'm sure they would have done the same thing I did, which was to ignore the mystery until it became a problem.

"I don't know much about how things work in this world. I thought it was weird though, so I asked him about it. He acted like it was a relatively normal thing, so I didn't press the issue."

"Is that true?" Itsuki asked the queen.

"No. Only the heroes wield weapons with those properties."

"Is there any other type of weapon that might mimic the actions of the legendary weapons?"

"No. I've never heard of weapons that can appear to absorb monsters and produce their dropped items."

Hmm. So apparently L'Arc and the others had thought it was normal, but they were using weapons of a sort that don't exist in this world.

"Their weapons sound very strange indeed."

"I agree. There are only supposed to be four holy weapons, so where would they have gotten a scythe like that?"

"You mean you haven't heard of the other seven legendary weapons?"

"What?" the three heroes all shouted in surprise.

"There are other weapons? Does that mean that there are other heroes too?"

Why were there constantly new, and potential major, bits of information being dropped on us like this? It was exhausting to keep up with it all.

I'd never heard of anything like that!

"Allow me to explain."

The queen's eyes sparkled. Based on the way her eyes lit up when I told her about the filolial queen, I figured she was probably excited by legends. Melty had once told me that the queen used to travel around the country looking for ancient relics.

"The most famous legend in these lands involves the four holy heroes, but there is another famous legend about the seven star heroes."

"Seven star heroes?"

"Yes. Just like the four holy heroes, there are seven other heroes that each carry a special legendary weapon."

There were *seven* of them?

If all of these weapons were different types of weapons, then this world was even more like a game than I'd come to expect.

In RPGs you'd often meet characters in the latter half of the game that would use different weapons, weapons you would eventually have a need for.

But judging by the other heroes I'd met since I arrived here, I wasn't sure I wanted to meet any more.

I'd yet to meet a single decent one.

"Trash and the church made a real mess out of my country. But Melromarc abandoned any attempt to claim partial ownership over the seven star heroes long ago. We may have shut our eyes and ears to some of the particulars since then."

"Whoa . . ."

"The seven star heroes and the four holy heroes are intimately connected, as they are both known as legendary heroes . . ."

They went on explaining the legend for a while.

"So there are seven other heroes that were summoned here just like we were?"

"There are that many people from other worlds here?"

"Sounds like a better deal than only having four people in charge of saving the whole world."

The other heroes looked away when I said that.

"Not exactly."

"No?"

"The seven star heroes are often looked upon with admiration by normal adventurers. There are seven star heroes that are summoned to this world, but it is also possible for a normal adventurer to become one."

So you didn't have to be summoned to become a seven star hero. People from this world had become heroes in the past?

I guess there were some reasonable people to choose from. Maybe.

If they were choosing new heroes, I'm sure they would try to pick people who were actually heroic, right?

"The weapons are used in a summoning ceremony. But in the event that the summoning fails, the weapon itself will be available for use by anyone until a chosen hero appears."

"Something like the sword in the stone?"

"Not exactly, because the sword is one of the four holy heroes' weapons. But in concept, yes—the weapon is there for whoever can claim it."

I was starting to understand what she was getting at. Anyone with the ability to wield the weapon had the opportunity to try and do so.

Then, if they were chosen as a hero, they would become physically more powerful, and the politicians would rally behind them too. Any adventurer in their right mind would love the idea.

"Additionally, there are more of these heroes than there are holy heroes. Whenever conflict breaks out, there is a chance that they will appear."

"Oh . . ."

"When the waves came, the majority of the seven star heroes were appointed."

"That just proves how dangerous the waves really are, doesn't it?"

"Yes."

She was saying that the upper class was considering the global problems that everyone faced.

"So? Does one of the seven star heroes use a scythe?"

"Unfortunately not."

"Oh . . ."

"As you may have surmised, those three individuals have only introduced more mysteries into the mix."

So it sounded like, as far as this world was concerned, only heroes could use weapons in the way that L'Arc had been able to use his scythe.

But he'd acted as though it was just an everyday kind of thing.

"That reminds me. L'Arc said that 'I needed to die for the sake of our world.' It sounds to me like they might be from another world too."

"What could it mean?"

"I have one idea. What if their world is on the other side of those rifts that appear during the waves? Could they be trying to invade this world for some reason?"

"I supposed that would make sense."

"And you know what else? Glass's weapons had gemstones set in them, just like our weapons do. Isn't that strange?"

"You mean her fans? Weapons like that do not exist in our world."

"What sort of weapons do the other heroes use?"

"Allow me to explain."

The queen stood up and began to explain the particulars of the seven star heroes' weapons.

"The first is the staff."

A staff? If it was a legendary weapon, then I guess it was intended for a magic-user.

Or maybe it was an ornate magical rod—the sort used by a certain magical young girl on TV.

"Mr. Iwatani?"

"Oh, sorry. Go on."

"The others are the hammer, projectile weapons, gauntlets, claws, axe, and the whip."

"Um . . ."

"The 'projectile weapons' one sounds a little vague," Itsuki said, raising his hand.

"Is it?"

"Do you know what sort of weapon it actually is?"

"Yes. In the legends it is a throwing knife, a small sword, a kunai, a small axe, etc. The weapon can turn into any small, throwable weapon."

That sounded like it might come in handy, but it sounded like it could only turn into small things.

Projectile weapons would overlap with Itsuki's specialty: bows.

If they were ranged weapons, then there was a chance they couldn't be used for close-quarters, hand-to-hand combat. Considering that I was the shield hero and I couldn't attack at all, that much limitation seemed likely.

"What's the difference between the gauntlet and the claws? Aren't those kind of the same thing?"

"Yeah, I was just thinking that too."

Ren and Motoyasu asked the question.

It sounded like nitpicking, but I could understand the confusion.

"I honestly don't understand it very well myself."

That was fair. We couldn't expect the queen to know the answer to every question that we could think of.

Regardless, it was a strange selection of weapons, no matter how you looked at it.

I guess the four holy heroes had already gotten the main fantasy-type weapons. There were only so many weapons they could choose from.

The last one, in particular, stood out to me.

"The whip . . ."

That was an odd choice for a weapon.

Where would they set the gemstone? In the handle?

I realize that, as the Shield Hero, offense wasn't really my specialty, but a whip sounded like a weak weapon.

Well actually, I guess I had played a game once where one of the strongest pieces of equipment was a whip.

"According to legend, the whip could transform into a chain at any time. I've also heard that the weapon could turn into a flail."

"That's not much improvement on the whip."

I just meant that it was a blunt weapon either way.

The seven star heroes' weapon categories seemed very

broad. I was stuck with only a shield, so I was a little jealous of the variety.

"Well, a spear and a pike are basically the same weapon. There must be some overlap."

"Yeah, I had a throwing knife once before," said Ren.

A small sword would definitely fit under the sword category. So in certain situations, it looked like the seven star heroes could use the same weapons as the four holy heroes.

And yet there had been no mention of anything like a shield.

"According to legend, the whip has a special ability that the other weapons do not possess. I've heard that it is capable of controlling the power of monsters."

"You mean like those special monster growth shields Naofumi was talking about?"

"Maybe it's a more specialized ability. I bet it's more powerful than the abilities I have."

I suddenly couldn't stop picturing the queen cracking a whip at a group of monsters.

I wonder if that was how it would work? The queen was sitting right in front of me . . . but maybe that was how she controlled Trash?

I couldn't care less. What was I thinking about that for?

"The hammer and the axe also seem like similar weapons."

They might be similar, but they certainly weren't the same thing.

"You think so?"

So the queen didn't agree. I guess if you had always known about the seven star heroes' weapons, it wouldn't strike you as odd.

I wanted to think about the gauntlets and the claws first of all. What if one of my teammates could equip one of those weapons? What would happen then?

That made me think of Filo, which made me realize something.

That's right—gauntlets would require the user to have hands, but you could technically use claws on feet if you needed to.

If Filo became a hero, I could hardly imagine how annoying she'd be. But when I thought about it more, it kind of made sense.

As for the hammer and the axe, they were similar in the sense that they were large and heavy and were swung overhead. But they weren't the same—they had different effects.

"I've never met one of these seven star heroes."

"They have been fighting in a place far removed from where you four heroes have been. Furthermore, a number of the weapons have yet to be assigned to a hero."

"Really?"

"Yes, really."

"Why don't we just let them deal with the waves?"

If we left everything up to the seven star heroes, then the queen of the filolials would come and kill us! Idiots!

"The world is too large for the seven star heroes to protect all of it."

Of course it was. Did they really just want to sit back and pray that someone else would take care of our problems for us?

"Anyway, I think we got distracted for a little bit there. What about the weapons that L'Arc and Glass were carrying? Have you ever heard of anything that might fit their description?"

"No. Never."

If that were so, then there was only one simple explanation that came to mind. There must have also been legendary weapons in whatever world they came from.

But there was a big problem with that theory.

"Here's what I don't get. When I asked L'Arc about his weapon, he acted as though it were the most normal thing in the world."

"So what?"

"Well, their weapons seem to be similar to our legendary weapons, right? But if he thought that they were normal, does that mean that legendary weapons are normal back in their world?"

The queen and the other three heroes all fell silent at the thought.

What if everyone on the other side of the rifts had weapons

like our legendary weapons? If that were true, we would never stand a chance against them if they came to attack our world in earnest.

After all the leveling and powering up I'd done, I had only just managed to hold my own against them in battle. If everyone from their world was as powerful as Glass, then we didn't have a hope of winning.

"I see what you mean. If the enemy we face is truly that powerful, then we have to put an end to this as soon as possible."

"I agree."

"Then perhaps it would be best if you heroes underwent some formal battle training."

The other three heroes didn't look too excited by the prospect of formal training.

Of course they would hate that. They just wanted to hang out and have fun and have the citizenry praise them for their deeds. They didn't want to do anything as dry and boring as *training*.

"The next wave will be upon us before long. We must do all that we can to prepare for its arrival. Mr. Iwatani, I trust that you will assist the other heroes in their preparations?"

". . ."

I wasn't confident that I'd be able to make much progress with them, but at the very least we could get some practice sessions in.

If I just kept telling them the same things over and over, maybe they would eventually be able to wrap their little minds around it all. Maybe.

Regardless, my life would be harder if they died, so it was in my own self-interest to see that they were as strong as possible going into the next wave.

"In the meantime, I will gather as many knights and powerful adventurers as I can. Hopefully they will be able to assist in your efforts."

"Thank you. You were a big help in the last battle against Glass and the others. If you hadn't stepped in when you did, who knows what might have happened."

In the middle of the battle, when Glass and the others were staring us down and planning their next move, the queen threw an exploding barrel of rucolu fruit at them. Rucolu were like very concentrated blobs of alcohol, and it really threw their game off, giving us the advantage we needed to survive.

"It was an excellent idea, but it wasn't mine. It was one of Mr. Kawasumi's party member's ideas. Her name was Rishia. If it weren't for Rishia, who knows where we'd all be now? We owe her a debt of gratitude."

"Really?"

Itsuki nodded to himself. He seemed concerned.

"Rishia? Hm."

"Mr. Kawasumi, please give her my thanks. We were only able to survive the wave because of her efforts."

"Very well. I'll tell her."

Itsuki's party members were forced to adhere to a hierarchy, and Rishia fit in right at the very bottom.

But she'd proven herself in the last battle. The bottom of the party meant that she was mostly treated like a slave. I hoped that this would help get her out of that situation.

"Excellent. Now then, until we are able to return to Melromarc, you are all free to do as you wish. Thank you for meeting with me today."

We had a lot of problems, but at least we had been able to organize our thoughts a little.

As for the other heroes, they weren't going to get much stronger unless they learned to level up their maturity first.

We would deal with their experience and leveling later. We had all probably leveled up sufficiently during our time on the islands.

"Mr. Iwatani? I have something I'd like to discuss. Do you mind staying for a little while?"

"Huh? Sure, what is it?"

The queen caught me on the way out of the room, just after the other heroes had filed out.

Was it something that she didn't want to discuss in front of them?

"What is it?"

"I didn't want to discuss this with the other heroes present. Honestly, I was planning on sending the other three heroes to another country to deal with the waves there."

"Aren't they too weak to entrust an important mission like that to them?"

"Indeed. That is why I was hoping to gain the assistance of the seven star heroes we were just talking about."

"Well, I guess that would depend on how powerful these other heroes actually are."

If they weren't any more powerful than the other three heroes, then they wouldn't be much help.

"But if I were to send you instead of them, you would have very little time to recuperate."

"True."

She was right. I could have gone by myself, but that was likely going to push me over the edge. My stats were still low from the last time I used blood sacrifice, and it cursed me. I didn't like the idea of entrusting the other heroes with anything remotely important, but there probably wasn't a better option.

"If the holy heroes are truly weaker than the seven star heroes, they will lose the respect of the people. Regardless, I cannot allow Melromarc to look like it sent fake heroes to assist another country."

"Of course not."

"And as for the seven star heroes, I have seen them before.

And after what I witnessed during the last wave battle, I think it is safe to say that they are definitely more powerful than the other three holy heroes."

"You're sure about that?"

"Yes."

I didn't really care about Melromarc's political problems, but I would end up in trouble myself if the other three heroes died in battle. That made me nervous about sending them off on their own.

I could have gone myself, I guess. But it wouldn't be easy.

But I was very curious about what was on the other side of those dimensional rifts.

"When is the next one coming?"

"It will arrive in a week. It will occur over here."

She unrolled a map of the world that had the locations of the dragon hourglasses indicated on it.

Judging from the history of my own world, it looked like the sort of map that people made of the world when they thought it was flat.

The far edges of the map were obscured with ornate pictures—a way to indicate they didn't have any information past the depicted areas.

"It will depend on the storm conditions, but if we were to travel by boat, I don't think it would take very long to get there."

"If we could teleport there then there won't be a problem."

"Yes, but when I think about the training that will be done in Melromarc . . . Besides, things need to take place in different places at once; it will split up everyone that we need."

What was the matter?

Originally the waves probably could have been dealt with by sending one of the heroes to each of the places where the waves occurred. That should have been enough to handle it, but then again, we were facing different enemies now.

"I do have some other optimistic news about the waves. It turns out that if you don't take any action during the waves at all, the dimensional rifts will eventually close all on their own."

"Really?"

"Yes. A great number of monsters will still come out of the rifts, and those monsters will have to be dealt with. But eventually the rifts will close on their own, so the waves can be ignored for a time."

What did that mean?

"That's an awful lot to put on my shoulders. The only plan that I can think of is to teleport while everyone is asleep and have Filo run us to the country where the wave is taking place. Then when morning comes we return to Melromarc to work on training."

It was sounding like a pretty tough schedule.

All of this was happening because the other three heroes wouldn't listen to me when I told them how to power-up. Just thinking about it made me irritated.

"I suppose we have no other choice."

The queen agreed with me.

I guess she was right. It would be really tough, but if we wanted to survive—if we wanted the world to survive—then we had no choice but to fight the waves.

Fitoria's words of warning were turning into a real headache for me.

"Thank you, Mr. Iwatani. Why don't you get some rest until the storm passes?"

"I will. Call for me if you need me. Later."

I finished my talk with the queen and left the room.

Chapter Two: An Unhappy Girl

I turned the corner and started to head back to my room, but I ran into someone on the way.

"Oh, um . . . Feeeeeeh . . ."

She was carrying a large number of bags, apparently on her way home from shopping. She was wearing a squirrel kigurumi and a Santa hat.

I recognized her. It was Rishia, Itsuki's party member.

"Hey, you alright?"

I spoke to her without even thinking about it. She was walking slowly and planting her feet carefully, looking like she might collapse at any moment.

"Feh?"

I reached out and grabbed one of the bags that looked like it was about to fall, then I placed it back on the stack of shopping bags, careful to keep the balance steady.

"You're the Shield Hero, aren't you?"

"They sent you out on errands for them?"

"N . . . No! I was just out shopping for the team, but I . . . huff . . . huff . . ."

She looked exhausted. She was carrying an awful lot of shopping bags, after all.

She was a just a young girl, and the way she was walking around in the squirrel kigurumi made it look like she was being punished or bullied.

"Want some help? You look like you're going to drop something."

A while back all the heroes had introduced their party members to everyone else, so I'd met her once or twice before.

So it wasn't like I didn't know her. Besides, she'd been a big help during the battle with L'Arc.

We had survived, in part, thanks to her. The least I could do was help carry her shopping bags.

"Feh . . . Bu . . . but . . ."

"You can take a break and blame it on me if you want."

"I could never!"

"Then let me help you."

"Oh, okay."

I could have taken the bags and helped her carry them all back, but I didn't know how Itsuki would react if I showed up with her. He should have just asked some of the soldiers for help. Why did he have to make this girl do everything?

I helped her carry the bags and felt a little conspicuous as I walked next to her.

"Feh . . ."

I was surprised she had stuck with them for as long as she had. From what I had seen so far, it looked like a pretty hostile environment.

They were just using her as their errand runner. They didn't even bother to introduce her when we'd all met.

Itsuki had structured his little party of friends with himself at the top. That meant there had to be someone on the bottom, and that someone was Rishia.

I'd been treated like crap since I first arrived in this world too, so I felt like I could empathize with her. I wanted to know more about her.

"Let's have a chat on our way back to Itsuki's room. Do you mind if I ask you some questions?"

"Me? Well, I don't know if I'll be able to answer them or not, but okay."

"Then I'll start with a personal one. Why did you join his party?"

There's no way that she felt comfortable in an environment like that. Who could be comfortable with a guy like Itsuki, with a guy that would stop at nothing to see his idea of justice realized? I wasn't about to ask her to join my party or anything, but at the very least she would be happier traveling with Ren.

"Of course it's like this, I just joined the party."

"That's not what I mean. I mean, if they treat you so badly, why don't you leave?"

"Because Master Itsuki saved me."

"He did?"

"Yes."

"Do you mind if I ask what happened?"

"Feh?! Why would you want to hear stories about someone like me? Let's talk about something else!"

"What kind of a person do you take me for?! Just tell me already!"

"Oh, okay . . ."

So Rishia started to explain the events and circumstances that led to her joining up with Itsuki.

To sum it up, Rishia came from a ruined noble family.

They had very little money and were forced to live frugally.

A neighboring town was ruled by a rich, rotten nobleman. To protect themselves, Rishia's village was forced to spend an increasing amount of their income on bulking up the town's defenses.

Doing so used up all the remaining money they had. They were insulted by their fellow villagers and accosted by the neighboring town. She cried herself to sleep at night.

One day, a terrible plan was hatched. Unable to contribute additional funds to the village's defenses, it was decided that Rishia would be offered up to the barbaric noblemen in the neighboring land. In the end, she was taken by force.

It was a situation that Itsuki simply couldn't ignore.

The rest went just as you would expect. Itsuki stormed in and, wrangling all the power of the Bow Hero, defeated the evil noblemen and saved Rishia from their clutches.

Rishia felt very much indebted to him, so she turned her back on her family and village to join his party.

It was a classic love story.

But what was with all the "feh" stuff? I felt like I'd heard it somewhere before.

Where was it? Oh! I just remembered.

"Wasn't that town having trouble because the bad governor had increased the taxes so heavily?"

"Yes. The noblemen that Master Itsuki defeated were enacting policies like that."

Yup, that was it. She was talking about the town that I'd passed through when I first heard about Itsuki's secret activities.

That would mean that Rishia had been traveling with him since then.

But I'd seen Itsuki in the tavern of that town, and she hadn't been with him.

A little after that though, I'd seen a young, pretty girl profusely thanking Itsuki in the street. That must have been her.

"Weren't you talking out in the street? You were speaking very loudly."

"How did you know that? I remember that scene as if it were yesterday."

"You said 'it's a secret!' didn't you?"

"How did you know that?"

"I'll test your memory. When you were talking in the street, do you remember a giant pink filolial walking by? That was Filo!"

"Fehhh?"

Rishia nodded to herself.

"Fehhhhhh! I remember! She was pulling a carriage!"

"You have an awesome memory. I can't believe you could remember that."

Maybe she just thought she was remembering it, because I'd painted the scene for her.

"You were there?!"

"Alright, alright. Calm down already. I just happened to be passing through."

She freaked out over the littlest things. Her eyes were always darting this way and that, ready to panic over anything that happened.

She looked really on edge, but it was a little hard to tell what she was thinking underneath the kigurumi.

"Oh, okay. I, well . . . I feel like I need to pay my debt to him."

From what I could tell, everything that Itsuki did was only in the service of his own ego. But to Rishia it must have looked as though he was behaving exactly as a hero would be expected to. The way she spoke about him made it clear that she really did feel indebted to him.

At the very least, she was able to sit through Itsuki's other party members' boasting and not go insane—that had to mean something.

"I see . . . Sounds like you're in a pretty tough spot."

"Yes. I don't know how well things are going."

"From what I've seen, it looks like you are suited to battling from the back line."

"I've never been very talented or skilled with weapons. If I'm good at anything, I guess it would be magic. But Master Itsuki said that he needed front line fighters, so when it came time to class up, I changed my stats to increase my skill in melee."

"Why would he . . . ?"

He'd ignored her strengths and forced her to focus on her weaknesses?

Granted, Itsuki used a bow in battle, so he would need more frontline fighters. But if he didn't choose the right people for the job, then he was only going to make everyone's lives harder. If she'd been in my party, I'd have asked her to focus on what she was already good at.

"Well, good luck with everything. If you keep it up, nobody will say that you're untalented. You'll impress them all yet, you'll see."

"Thank you!"

She was skittish, but deep down she seemed to have a pretty strong heart. She was going to be fine.

I'd fallen pretty low myself before. But eventually, I found a way to make it work, and look where I am now.

If Rishia kept making an effort, I was sure she'd prove herself essential to Itsuki's team.

"Sorry about all the questions. Did I wear you out?"

"Not at all. I'm fine!"

"Well, that's good . . ."

Just as the conversation was trailing off, we turned a corner, and Itsuki's room came into view.

"Later."

"Feh. Thank you."

I handed the bags I'd been carrying back to Rishia, turned, and went back the way I'd came. I was heading for my room.

"Welcome back, Mr. Naofumi."

"Thanks, Raphtalia."

When I got back to the room I found Raphtalia waiting for me.

"How was the meeting with the other heroes?"

"Not so hot. They're set on believing that I cheated to get as powerful as I am. They won't believe anything that I tell them."

"How will you get them to come around?"

"Who knows? I've tried all I can, but they don't seem to want to listen."

I'm the protagonist of my very own game! That's what they

thought. They didn't want to believe that someone they thought was weaker than them could somehow level up to overpower them. That would break their fantasy rules! The protagonist never loses!

Besides, they came into this world with tons of knowledge about it from the games they'd played. How is that not cheating? It all sounded like sour grapes to me.

In the end, we were all probably thinking of this world as if it were a game.

The weapon power-up system and the leveling were definitely reinforcing that idea.

But that's just the sort of world that we were in. For modern Japanese people like us, of course it was like a game.

In the end, it didn't matter whether it was a game or not; we needed to survive it.

Those three were like children. They would do whatever it took to win. They would cheat and steal to win, but they would always point their fingers and accuse everyone else of being unfair.

If I didn't get a grip on their psychology, I was never going to be able to rein them in.

Honestly, as long as they were strong enough to battle through the waves without dying, I didn't care what they did after that.

If we were all battling together, then I would probably survive this whole ordeal.

Why? I told them how to power-up and demonstrated it right in front of them. So why? Why wouldn't they believe me?

Because more than they wanted to win, they wanted to be special.

I would probably have thought the same thing, had I been transported to a world similar to a game I was already familiar with.

"The other heroes are too weak to be trusted, so it looks like we are going to be sent to another country to battle in the next wave that appears there."

"I guess we will be pretty busy."

"I guess so . . ."

"I'm baaaack!"

Filo came skipping into the room.

Had she gotten sick of swimming already?

"What's wrong, master?"

"I guess I'll tell you about it. Remember how Fitoria said that we needed to get along with the other heroes? Well, in order to get them to power-up a little more, it looks like we're going to have to put in some serious work."

I didn't think that Filo was going to understand what I had to say, but I made an effort to explain what we'd discussed during the meeting anyway.

"So when we are training with the other heroes, you have to be honest with them about how everything works."

"Huh?"

Of course she didn't understand. That's Filo for you.

"Anyway, it looks like we're going to have to go to another country and fight in the wave battle there."

It happened just when I said it: Filo's cowlick started to twitch back and forth. Filo looked a little confused.

"Huh? Oh . . . um . . . You mean you'll go for me?"

"What was that?"

"Oh, Fitoria was watching our conversation. She can see what we are doing through my hair thing!"

"She's spying on us?"

I guess she needed to keep an eye on how the situation was developing. I should have known better than to think she would have just let us go with a verbal agreement.

Fitoria was the legendary queen of the filolials.

She had a deep understanding of the waves and seemed to know a lot about everything.

She was the one that had told me the heroes could not tolerate infighting. She was the one who had given Filo her cowlick.

"And she was saying that if the weak heroes are going to battle against a wave, she could offer them some back up."

"So we don't have to go? She'll do it for us?"

Filo nodded.

"She says it's not a problem, as long as we are trying to get along with the other heroes and grow more powerful."

"That's a big help. To tell the truth, the other heroes won't listen to anything I say. It's been a real struggle. We were going to have to take on responsibility for everything."

"Yeah, that's why she says she'll help!"

That cowlick was proving itself convenient, even if it had interfered with Filo's class up ceremony.

"Hey Fitoria. Do you know anything about L'Arc and the others?"

"She's um . . . she's thinking! Ok, she says that sometimes people like that come out of the waves, but she doesn't know what they are."

That's right. She'd mentioned that she had forgotten a lot about the past. So I couldn't expect her to know everything.

But did that mean she had fought against them herself?

"So she's fought against Glass and the others before?"

"No. She says it was someone else."

But that meant that this had happened before. It meant that people lived on the other side of the dimensional rifts. What did it all mean?

"Maybe it's like the other heroes? Heroes aside from the four holy heroes?"

"I thought so too, but it doesn't sound like that's the case."

"Fitoria says that she doesn't really understand it either. She just says that things like this happen sometimes during the waves."

"Oh yeah?"

But what *were* the waves?

"An idea? Hm . . . She says that there might be a clue in the story of the four holy warriors."

"That's great. I'll tell the queen about it and see what she says."

Personally, I didn't know very much about what the legends of the heroes said. All I knew was what I had read in the *Records of the Four Holy Weapons*. But maybe the queen, or a scholarly advisor of hers, would be able to find a clue.

Fitoria would be a historical witness if they needed one. If she was bringing it up, then there had to be something to it.

"But . . . she says that she wants you to take care of the waves that occur in the country that the four heroes are currently in."

"Fine. That's still a load off of my shoulders. I can handle that much."

The biggest problem would be facing off against Glass again before we understood the nature of her existence. At least we had some time to figure it out.

I wasn't very confident we'd find a solution though.

"You know though, honestly, I think we'd all be better off if you were the one to fight Glass."

"She says that she'll beat them back if she ever runs into them!"

Filo's cowlick stopped twitching, indicating that our conversation was over for the time being.

"Anyway, I'll tell the queen about all of that. At the very least, she just took a major job off of our plates, which will be a big help."

"How wonderful. I'm glad that Ms. Fitoria wants to help us."

"I wish she would just take care of everything."

"Mr. Naofumi, I don't think that . . ."

"I know, I know."

If a legendary filolial could calm the waves on her own, she'd be unbelievably powerful.

My mood felt a little lighter after that talk, like a load had been lifted from my shoulders. Still, I didn't know any more about the nature of the waves.

I sat by the window and started to think as I watched the sun set over the ocean.

We would have to get the other heroes to understand the power-up system. Then we'd have to figure out some way to get around the defense rating and defense ignoring attacks that Glass and the others had at their disposal.

Once the other heroes were powered up, they would rely on my defenses to coordinate their attacks.

After that, I wanted to stop by the weapon shop in Melromarc to see the old guy there and stock up for the next wave.

The weapons that Raphtalia and Filo were using, the

Karma Rabbit Sword and the Karma Dog Claws, were new. They didn't have a blood clean coating applied to them, which meant that they would eventually get dirtied and blunt. I would have to keep sharpening them.

If there were stronger, more durable weapons that we could replace them with, that would probably be a better option for us in the long run. I bet the queen would be willing to provide us with whatever materials we need to craft new weapons. Or if we had enough time, we could go find the materials ourselves, leveling up on the monsters we encountered along the way.

Finally, I'd have to make sure my shield was as powerful as possible. I still felt like there were plenty of areas in need of improvement.

Besides, I still wanted to see what sort of shields I could unlock with the materials I'd gotten from the Inter-Dimensional Whale.

Chapter Three: Framed Again

Night fell. I had dinner and a bath and then went out on the terrace to cool off.

I looked out at the ocean and relished the cool night air. Had the storms finally subsided?

I caught sight of Filo out in the water. She'd wanted to go swimming after dinner. She was borderline obsessed with swimming lately. I decided to pretend I didn't see her.

"Huh?"

At the far end of the terrace I saw Motoyasu walking with . . . Rishia? They seemed to be walking back to the hotel.

She wasn't wearing the squirrel kigurumi.

Was he hitting on her? That would make sense. He had indicated that she was on his list of pretty girls.

I guess the guy really wanted to build a harem for himself. What did he think Itsuki would have to say about his ambitions?

I decided I had better warn him to keep his distance.

"Hey! Motoyasu! Better stop hitting on everyone you see!"

"Hey! Naofumi! It's up to you now!"

Motoyasu looked pale when he walked over to me and slapped my shoulder. Then he shoved me in Rishia's direction.

"What's your problem?"

"Nothing! She's yours!"

What was going on? He was a real womanizer, so why would he want me to have her? I looked over at Rishia and was shocked by what I saw.

Her eyes were red and puffy, as if she'd been crying for a while. I took a seat next to her.

"Hey, what's the matter?"

"Alright, I'm out of here!"

"Wait! You didn't . . ."

Could it be that he was so rotten he'd done something awful to her?

She didn't want to be with him or something, so he said something like, "It will be fine. It only hurts the first time . . ." And then raped her?

I wouldn't be surprised if Motoyasu had done something like that. He seemed like the sort of person that would push and push until he got his way with a girl.

She was crying so hard that she was shaking.

That was too awful. I couldn't let him get away with it.

"I did not!"

"Prove it!"

"No . . . It's not the Spear Hero's fault . . ."

Rishia collected herself and whispered.

I guess I let myself get carried away. Motoyasu probably wasn't *that* terrible. Right?

"Then what happened?"

"Something's up, but I'm not so good at dealing with this sort of thing. So I'm leaving it up to you!" Motoyasu said as he left. He was smiling, but he also looked sick, like he might throw up. He ran off on shaky legs.

I'd never seen him look like that before. And I'd never heard him say that he wasn't good at dealing with something.

What had happened? Had she done something to him?

"What happened?"

"Please don't worry about it."

"I can't do that. I was afraid that he had raped you or something."

"No . . . I just . . . I couldn't hold myself back anymore."

"Hold yourself back from Motoyasu?"

"N . . . No!"

She looked angry, like she might burst into tears again. At least she had the energy to be angry.

"The Spear Hero tried to cheer me up, but I . . . Actually, I probably shouldn't be talking about it."

"Well, you've already started. Is it about what we discussed earlier?"

I don't know why I wanted to help her. Maybe it was because I felt like we were in the same situation, and I couldn't help but empathize.

"No, please. Don't worry about it."

She jumped to her feet, made an apologetic face, and ran off.

"What was that all about?"

I was left alone, having no idea what had happened, but feeling terrible about it.

The next morning I lay in bed reading, but my mind was still occupied with worries about Rishia.

We'd already done plenty of leveling up here, so there was really no need to do any serious leveling while we were confined to the islands.

So I had some time to myself with nothing important to do, but I couldn't stop thinking about the previous night.

"I really want to know what happened."

Normally, I would probably feel fine just ignoring it, but this time I couldn't help but dwell on it.

I felt the way that I had when Bitch had framed me, or when I'd been attacked and forced to defend Melty.

Basically I had a bad feeling about it, a feeling that something bad was about to happen.

"What do you mean?"

"Oh nothing. I'm going to go look into something, so you can just relax here."

"Hm . . ."

Raphtalia wanted to know what was going on, but I left the room without explaining.

I didn't know what I would say anyway. What *was* happening?

I was nervous about it, but I decided to stop by Itsuki's room and listen in on them to see if I could figure it out.

I could hear exuberant voices coming from the other side of the door. Was I overthinking this?

"Ah . . ."

I spotted Rishia. She was gazing at the room enviously from far away.

Then she noticed me and ran off.

What was going on?

I figured that all I could do was try to get Motoyasu to fess up and tell me what he knew.

So I went to his room and knocked on the door.

"Coming!"

A woman, one of his party members, came to the door.

His party consisted of Bitch and two other women. The woman at the door was one of them, so I'll call her woman #1.

She was smiling from ear to ear. She wore a look on her face like I was the last person she expected to find knocking on their door.

"You?! What are you here for? What do you want?!"

She looked at me for a second before realizing who I was. Then she accosted me.

I really couldn't stand talking to these people.

"Is Motoyasu here?"

"Why should I tell YOU that?"

"Hey! Motoyasu!"

"Don't you ignore me!"

"Yeah! Don't ignore her!"

Woman #2 came up to the doorway to join her friend. As for Bitch, she had apparently decided to ignore me, despite sitting right where I could see her. I really wanted to assume that meant that she was traumatized, but I shouldn't let my fantasies get ahead of me.

These two didn't mean anything to me.

Bitch had been ordered, by her mother the queen, to assist Motoyasu in his fight against the waves so that she might prove herself useful in some capacity.

When the queen had been away on diplomatic missions to other countries, Bitch had spent her time doing whatever she pleased, and the queen returned to find much of the crown's money had been spent.

She had red hair that she often pulled it back into a ponytail. She had the sort of face that was pretty enough but grew more irritating the more you had to look at it.

As you'd expect of Motoyasu, she was on his list of pretty girls along with Raphtalia and Filo.

She was Melty's older sister, and she had the worst personality of anyone I'd ever met. She was an amoral monster that got her kicks from setting traps for people and watching them suffer.

Her equipment looked a little shabbier than it had before. I wonder if the queen had completely cut her off financially?

"What do you want, Naofumi? None of these girls like having you around."

Motoyasu stepped into view, surrounded by his harem of girls.

Seeing him standing there with his confident swagger really got on my nerves. If I didn't want to get information out of him, I would have just told him off and left.

"I don't really care what your girls want. I have a question for you."

"What is it?"

"It's about last night. You said you were leaving it up to me, but I don't know what I'm supposed to do."

"Fine, I'll tell you, but you have to take responsibility for everything else."

"How convenient for you. But fine, I'm curious enough. I'll agree to that."

He must have known something. His face looked suddenly pale, and he stepped out of the room, leaving his harem to watch over the place while we spoke.

We both walked out to the terrace, which was mostly deserted. He looked at me again, and sure enough, his face was very pale.

That wasn't like him at all. I didn't know he was capable of actually worrying about things.

Usually, he would just call me a criminal, blame everything on me, stand up for Bitch, and make my life a living hell.

Oh, and of course he would hit on Raphtalia and Filo the whole time.

He seemed to have a thing for Filo in particular.

"You're talking about Rishia, aren't you?"

"Yeah."

Had he made her cry like that? Or had she been crying before he met her?

She had been very tightlipped with me, and I hadn't been able to get an explanation out of her.

But Motoyasu had a way with women, and I thought that he had probably gotten her to tell him about it.

"So actually . . ."

And Motoyasu started explaining the whole thing to me.

When he did, I realized that my intuition had been right. I felt anger bubbling up from deep inside my guts.

"At first I wanted to know why she was crying, and I might have been a little overzealous when I asked her what was wrong, but . . . Sorry, you know, I . . . I'm no good with girls when they are like that. Can you step in for me?"

"Itsuki!!!"

I kicked his door with all my might and barreled into the room.

The door crashed open and everyone in the room stared at me in the doorway.

"Wh . . . What is it?!"

"You're the Shield Hero! What do you want with us?!"

The leader of Itsuki's underlings, Armor, glared at me.

Armor apparently had a real name, but he was always wearing a suit of flashy armor, so I'd taken to calling him that.

Armor had a crappy attitude. He was the sort of guy who always acted like he'd been put in charge.

He wanted power and respect, and I think he was mostly just hanging with Itsuki to make sure that he got what he wanted.

I didn't know how powerful he was. I didn't see him doing anything very impressive, or really helping anyone at all, during the last wave.

L'Arc might have been the enemy, but I shared his assessment of Armor: he looked like a criminal of some kind.

"What do I want? I want to know how you live with yourselves!"

I was shouting and I felt like the whole room had become chaotic.

I must have really looked unstable, because Armor and the rest of the group looked suddenly intimidated.

Itsuki was the first to come to his senses. He was very angry now. He shouted back at me.

"What are you talking about?!"

"Still playing dumb?"

Damn, I was getting so angry that I felt like I could switch to the Shield of Wrath right then and there. Hate billowed up inside me like smoke.

If Ren showed up, I'd probably go crazy. The Shield of Wrath contained the core of a dragon that Ren had killed, so the shield itself responded dramatically to Ren's presence.

"You're trying to seed doubt about our master, aren't you Shield Hero?!"

Armor took a step in my direction, so I reached out, grabbed his arm, and tried to use a judo hold on him.

"In violation of the legendary weapon rules, you have touched a weapon besides the weapon with which you specialize."

There was a crackle and hiss, and pain shot up through my arm. It wasn't that bad though.

I was surprised that the legendary weapon rules applied to things like judo holds. I'd been able to hit things in the past though. What was the difference?

"Ouch!"

"I came here to speak with Itsuki. Don't get in my way, underling!"

I shoved Armor back and glared at Itsuki.

I hadn't felt this angry in a long time. Raphtalia had done so much to help keep my rage under control.

But I didn't want to keep it under control right then.

"You . . . You're always going on about justice and honesty, but you don't understand anything at all!"

"What are you . . ."

I was really shouting at this point, and apparently Rishia had come to the door to see what all the fuss was about. When Itsuki saw her there he finally understood what I was upset about.

"You mean to tell me that you are upset over THAT?"

"Now you're talking sense."

"She's in the wrong here."

"Are you out of your mind?!"

Here's what I heard from Motoyasu:

Here's why Rishia was so upset.

Yesterday, Rishia finished her shopping and was heading back to the party's room.

This happened right after I'd parted ways with her.

"Rishia? Was it you?"

"Hm? What do you mean?"

Right after she got back to the room, Itsuki approached her looking very upset. But she didn't know what he was upset about.

"There's no point in pretending you don't know. I know that you're the one who broke my accessory."

She looked around and saw that Itsuki's favorite bangle was broken into little pieces.

"Me? No! I, I don't know anything about it. What happened?"

"I can't believe you would lie to me. We have proof that you did it."

Itsuki turned to his other party members.

"That's right. I saw it. I saw Rishia break Master Itsuki's prized bangle and then hide it."

"Yeah."

"I saw it too."

"What?! I did no such thing! I . . . I really don't know what you're talking about!"

Rishia emphatically denied the charge. But Itsuki wouldn't believe her.

"Look at all the witnesses that claim they saw you. I guess there's no avoiding it. Shame, had you repented I would have forgiven you. Rishia, you are no longer a member of this party."

"But! But I really didn't do it!"

Just then, Rishia saw Armor smile.

But she didn't have time to try and figure out what had happened; she simply wanted to keep her place in the party. So she fell to her knees in front of Itsuki and begged him to reconsider.

"Please! Please! I want to be by your side, Master Itsuki!"

Itsuki wavered, perhaps feeling guilty. His eyes filled with tears.

"You mustn't forgive her now, Master Itsuki!"

Armor and the other party members shouted to him.

"I'm sorry. We must part ways."

"Master Itsuki?! I'm telling the truth! Please believe me! Please reconsider! I'll do anything!"

She was crying at his feet, but Itsuki turned his back on her.

"How long will you beg for his emotions?! You're a liar! Why should we allow someone like you to get close to our master?!"

Itsuki's remaining party members chased her out of the room.

She still tried to get back to Itsuki, but her efforts proved futile.

And that is pretty much everything that Rishia told Motoyasu.

"You're not going to forgive Rishia after all she did for us during the battle with L'Arc?"

"That's not it at all!"

Itsuki snapped, suddenly fierce.

It sounded to me like I'd stumbled on the truth.

The queen had praised Rishia for her help, and that was something that he simply couldn't stand. He couldn't let that happen because his party and he had spent so long condescending to her.

So he was jealous that the weakest member of his party was getting praise from the queen, and the only way he could deal with it was to frame her and get rid of her.

From what I'd heard, Rishia hadn't done anything wrong. Someone else had broken the bangle, and they were clearly trying to frame Rishia for it.

I hate cowards that frame people for crimes they didn't commit!

That was why I was so upset with Itsuki, because it was a personal issue for me.

"So you didn't get what you wanted by begging, so you'd get another hero to come beg me on your behalf? Do you really think I'm going to let you back into my party?"

"Rishia didn't tell me anything. Our womanizing friend, Motoyasu, used his 'charm' to pry the story out of her!"

Speaking of which, Motoyasu had come to this world because he'd been killed in an emotional fit back in his own world.

He was probably nervous around girls that seemed to have an unhealthy obsession with guys.

I guess it was like a *yandere* character from a *gyaryge*.

There were *gyaruge* like that back in my world too. It was infamous for the bad ending.

If Motoyasu had experienced something similar in his past, then hearing about Rishia and her relationship with Itsuki would have prompted memories of his own personal traumas.

But that wasn't the issue here!

"What I've already said about it is the truth and needs no elaboration. Rishia lied about her actions. She forgot about her debt to me and was only using me for her own ambitions. Removing her from my party is only natural."

"And you don't think that any of your other party members are just lying about it?"

"Seriously? You would accuse my trusted teammates of lying to me? I don't think that is likely. Rishia has been with us for the shortest amount of time. Therefore, I have reason to trust their word over hers."

The idiot. He wasn't even trying to make sense!

Obviously, I'd taken the time to look into the issue before I came breaking into his room.

I knew that I couldn't just run in there without proof and use my emotions to change his mind. Luckily, reason hadn't completely abandoned me at that point.

Rishia was not the real culprit. Furthermore, I'd already figured out who the real criminal was.

It was actually pretty simple. I just asked a shadow.

Shadows were secret agents under the command of the queen.

They were a lot like ninjas. They snuck around in secret, gathering information on people.

I knew that they had been watching all of the heroes since we'd arrived in Cal Mira. So I assumed, correctly, that they might have insight into what had really happened to Itsuki's bangle.

Rishia didn't break the bangle. One of Itsuki's other party members did.

Apparently the shadow had even anticipated this turn of events and had therefore met with Itsuki and explained the situation to him. But Itsuki chose to believe his party over the shadow.

When I heard that Itsuki had already been informed of the truth, there was nothing left for me to do but barge in and demand answers.

"But there is a witness! And it's a disinterested third party who watched with objectivity! Think about it! Are you really going to believe that your party members watched her break the bangle without stopping her?"

"So you've already investigated . . . Well, I suppose there's no getting around it. It was all for her, you see? They weren't just giving her the opportunity to confess. By setting her up, they were really giving Rishia a way to avoid conflict."

"What are you talking about?"

I didn't know about this "setting up" business . . . but it all sounded very coercive.

"It was a way to get Rishia to leave the party. My teammates here, by taking these actions on their own, were giving Rishia a way to avoid battle. Don't you see? They did it out of concern for her."

". . . ?"

What was he saying? I couldn't make heads or tails of it.

They did all of this on purpose? They made it all up to get her to leave the group?

"Rishia doesn't belong on the battlefield. Everyone talked about it, and we decided that it would be better for her to live out her life, happily, back in her village."

"Yes, exactly. We did all of this for Rishia."

Other party members were jumping in and agreeing with Itsuki's story. They were trying to make it look like this was all done out of concern for her.

I guess they thought it made it okay to falsely accuse her of a crime?

Did they think about what life in her village would be like after that? Did they think of how people would treat her?

Was that really their best idea?

Rishia understood perfectly well that she wasn't the most powerful fighter around.

If they wanted to protect her from the danger of battle, why didn't they just sit her down and talk about it sincerely?

Granted, Rishia was very passionate about wanting to help

them, so she probably wouldn't have immediately agreed to leave. But if Itsuki had sat her down and sincerely explained his feelings, wouldn't she have choked back her tears and nodded?

Whatever. I knew one thing for sure.

Itsuki wanted to get Rishia out of his party. But Rishia was insistent about helping, and he didn't know what to do.

So his party members decided to commit a crime and frame her for it?

Did that make any sense? No. The truth was that he was upset that she'd proven herself useful in the last battle.

So they all framed her—out of jealousy.

They did it out of concern for her? Ha! Give me a break!

It seemed more likely to me that he knew he wasn't in any risk from the plan, so he thought it up and asked his party members to carry it out.

He could have made a sincere request of her, but instead he tricked her and ended up hurting her in the process. And all because he was jealous of her success in the last battle!

When was he going to understand that we weren't playing a game?

Besides, had this been a game, a party member probably would have just left the party if he'd asked her too.

But that's right. Itsuki had been used to playing *console games*. If those were single player, then he would be accustomed to his party members being NPCs.

I was really at the end of my rope with this guy. Exhausted, I turned to Rishia.

She looked like she was on the verge of tears. She was shaking as she looked at Itsuki, clearly using what energy she had to stay composed.

As for myself, well, this was really the last straw. There's no way I could respect Itsuki at all after this.

Motoyasu was an idiot who believed everything Bitch said, sure. But he wasn't the sort of person that would cast off one of his teammates and leave them to rot.

As for Itsuki, if he were facing an enemy he couldn't defeat, would he run away and leave his party to die?

"The truth is that Rishia never really quite fit in with the rest of the party. I don't want to force her into unnecessarily dangerous situations, so I think it would be better for her to live in a peaceful place. I think she would be happier that way."

"Did you stop to think about how Rishia might feel about it?!"

"That's easy to say, but a battle for the fate of the world isn't the sort of thing that we can risk on someone's emotions."

"Then why didn't you just tell her that in the beginning?"

"I will say it now. She simply isn't powerful enough to be of use in battle. I thought that if we gave her time to level and power-up, things might change. But nothing changed. Therefore, I think it's best that she goes back to her village."

That was what I expected him to say.

Basically, he was just trying to make himself look better.

"Then why didn't you tell her that honestly? Were you afraid of being the bad guy?"

"Not at all! Why are you so simple-minded?"

"If you think being thoughtful means framing someone for a crime so that you can get what you want, then yeah, I'm fine with being simple-minded."

"She won't be able to keep up as the battles get harder. We had to be tough to protect her!"

"But you're the one that ignored her real potential and forced her to be a fighter! Why won't you let other people control their own lives?"

Hasn't she said that she was better with magic than a sword?

He must have known that, but he told her to focus on melee when she went through the class up ceremony. He should have known that she'd end up useless!

And then when he realized she couldn't keep up, he decided to do away with her. *That's* the Itsuki I know.

What a jerk!

If he'd just been honest with her, she would have understood!

In the end, he came up with this elaborate scheme just so he wouldn't have to look like a mean person.

And that's basically what he had done to me too.

They'd had a specific goal in mind and they had schemed to get what they wanted. And Itsuki had been in on it the whole time.

"Then this is a good opportunity to be clear about it. My party is not going to be able to continue working with you, Rishia. To be frank, you are too weak to keep up."

Which meant that he would only say what he really meant if his back was up against a wall—which it only was because I'd stormed in.

On top of it all, he must have felt like he was being blamed for his behavior, so he reasoned that it was because of Rishia, and therefore Rishia must be in the wrong.

How hypocritical and self-righteous can he be?

Compared to him, I preferred the company of slave traders and con men. At least they knew that they were evil.

They didn't pretend to be something that they weren't, and their intentions were clear. That alone made them way better than someone like Itsuki.

"..."

Rishia tried to reply to Itsuki but couldn't find the words. She turned and ran out of the room.

"Rishia?!"

"She's just trying to get your sympathy. Now please get out of my room!"

"You . . . You want to make innocent people suffer—again!"

"When did I ever do that?!"

"Oh, I guess you've forgotten? About Bitch? About your little disguised hero antics?"

"I don't believe I have anything to do with the Bitch incident."

Nothing to do with it, eh? He was standing with her, blaming me for everything. But I'd yet to hear an apology for it.

He really thought that he was the center of the universe. He didn't care a lick about the thoughts and feelings of others.

I didn't have enough energy to be angry anymore. I was just tired. The boiling rage I'd felt was starting to cool off.

I thought that this made me feel the way that Bitch had made me feel when she betrayed me. But I was wrong. This was different.

"Oh well. I thought you had a sense of justice. I thought that you had some issues but that you could at least be a decent hero. And now this. I suppose I'm surprised. Surprised and disappointed in you."

I shot him a nasty look.

I'd heard that the opposite of affection wasn't hate—it was indifference.

So that meant that the opposite of hate was also indifference.

I couldn't bring myself to care about Itsuki anymore. I couldn't get mad at someone I didn't care about.

"We don't have the sort of relationship that permits you to

say things like that! Please keep your distance from me in the future!"

Itsuki was furious. He was shouting at me.

I was starting to understand. Itsuki thought very highly of himself, so there was nothing worse for him than knowing his estimation had fallen in someone's eyes. He must have found it traumatic.

"I don't care. Why should I spend time with a self-righteous brat like you? Just keep doing your best to keep your nasty, true nature hidden from everyone."

"I told you to get out of here!"

Itsuki looked like he was about to reach for his bow, but I just glared at him with cold indifference.

"Go ahead . . . do it. Take that beloved bow of yours and shoot me. You coward!"

"You asked for it!"

Itsuki pulled the sting back on his bow and fired an arrow.

His bow was magical. The arrows just appeared when he pulled the string back.

I just took one step after another towards him.

His arrows hit me, but clattered to the floor with an ineffectual clang.

"What?!"

"You monster!"

Itsuki's party members couldn't believe how ineffective the

arrows were against my defense. They were already calling me a monster!

"You know that evil attacks don't work against me, right?"

I continued walking towards Itsuki, and he kept backing away to keep his distance. Soon he was in a corner, shooting arrow after arrow at me.

"Eagle piercing shot!"

I couldn't believe he was going to use a skill inside a small room like that.

I squinted at the arrow and steadied myself, then reached out and snatched the eagle-shaped arrow out of the air by its throat.

"You . . . You stopped my eagle piercing shot?"

"I'm sure it's a defense ignoring attack, but it doesn't matter. It's not even worth it to defend myself against something so weak."

I tensed, looked down at the magic eagle, and then I squeezed its throat and killed it.

It wasn't an actual monster, so I was able to kill it with my own strength.

I dropped it and approached Itsuki until we were face-to-face.

"You say Rishia is weak? Ha! And you think *you*'re strong?"

". . . !?"

His face flushed red with anger.

I didn't care. I know that Fitoria had warned me about it, but I no longer wanted anything to do with Itsuki.

I turned and left the room.

"I hope you enjoyed that! You won't be able to boss us around for much longer!"

I didn't care. Maybe he'd finally understand how substantial the difference in our strength was. Maybe it would inspire him to get stronger.

I chased after Rishia.

I'd seen her running off in the direction of the harbor, but when I got there she was nowhere to be seen. She wouldn't . . .

Just as I was considering it, I saw Filo pulling Rishia out of the water.

There was a crowd of people standing around them.

"Hey, do you like swimming? It didn't look like you were having very much fun though! And weren't you sinking?"

"Let me go! Please, I . . . I . . ."

"Filo, you did good. I'll get you a treat later."

"I don't know what you mean, but yay!"

"Tell me what happened."

"This nice girl just fell into the ocean. But she started to sink, so I jumped in and pulled her out."

"She jumped . . ."

She was sad enough to attempt suicide. It was horrible just thinking about it.

I suddenly understood why Motoyasu had been so freaked out.

Someone you liked might say terrible things to you, but why would you try to kill yourself over it?

"Good work, Filo."

"Heh, heh, heh."

I rubbed Filo's head.

If Filo hadn't been there, that might have been the end for Rishia. The harbor was very deep in places.

The spots where the large ships docked were especially deep. If you tried to drown there, you could do it.

We had just managed to avoid a real disaster.

"Ok, Rishia . . ."

Filo was still holding Rishia, who seemed to be very distraught. I took her hand and talked to her.

"Let's just say that you succeeded, and that you've died here. Now what do you want to do with the life that was saved?"

"Let me die. Master Itsuki rejected me. I have no reason left to live. I'm not worth anything to anyone."

"No one said that. *You're* the one who decides what you are worth."

"Then let me die."

"You can do what you want, but I won't forgive you!"

I couldn't stand the thought of her being treated this way.

"Are you just going to accept that they've pinned a crime on you? Don't you want to prove them wrong?"

"But I . . ."

"Don't you want to make Itsuki say, 'Please come back. We need you'?"

"I know that I'm weak. I know it!"

"Who says you'll always be weak? Only Itsuki. But he's wrong."

They'd told me that I was the weakest hero too. They'd looked down on me.

That's why . . . that's why you can't just accept the things that people say about you.

"Can I . . . Can I be stronger? Will he respect me someday?"

"I promise you that. We'll show Itsuki just how strong you can be!"

We'd make him regret kicking her out of his team. The fool!

If we made Rishia stronger than any of his other teammates, then eventually Itsuki would have to believe the things I told him about the power-up system.

"Rishia, I'll help you. I'll help you until you are strong enough to help yourself. We can do it!"

That was how I really felt.

We'd been through the same things. We'd been framed, called weak, and condescended to. I saw myself in Rishia, and I was going to make sure that Itsuki understood how wrong he had been.

"Come with me!"

I reached out a hand to her. She hesitated, then took it.

"But I love Master Itsuki."

"Fine. Love who you want. I don't care what you think of me. I care what you think of yourself."

It's not like I was inviting her into my party because she was a girl.

I just couldn't forgive Itsuki's actions. He'd forced her to level like he wanted her to, then tossed her to the curb when she didn't suit his needs.

And I felt like I'd been through the same things she had.

That's why I knew what I was talking about.

"You'll be strong. We'll do whatever it takes."

"Okay. Thank you."

She was still sobbing when she accepted my party invitation.

So Rishia ended up joining my party, but . . .

When we were on our way back to the room, we ran into Raphtalia.

"I heard you screaming. You sounded very angry! What happened?"

"Itsuki pissed me off."

"But . . . Oh, isn't that Rishia behind you?

So she knew about Rishia. Good. That would make explaining it easier on me.

"Oh, um . . . yes."

"What happened to you?"

"I'll explain when we get back to the room."

"What about Rishia?"

"She's in our party now."

"R . . . Really? Okay."

Raphtalia nodded. It looked like she had already run through the possible scenarios in her mind.

We went back to the room, and I told her what had happened.

Raphtalia reacted like I expected she would. She was half annoyed, half angry.

"Itsuki . . ."

"Please, don't speak ill of Master Itsuki."

"After all he did to you, you still want to defend him?"

Raphtalia looked like she couldn't believe her ears.

I felt the same way.

"If Filo hadn't stepped in, she would have drowned."

"Did I do goooooood?"

"Yeah, you did great. I already told you that though."

"Heh, heh."

Apparently Filo hadn't gotten enough praise yet, so I reached over and ruffled her hair.

Her cowlick was kind of annoying.

"Master Itsuki isn't bad. It's my fault for being weak."

Rishia looked like she was about to burst into tears again. Raphtalia reached out and took her hand.

"You really care for him, don't you?"

"Yes."

"He'll come around someday. Until then, you and I just need to be patient."

"You feel the same way then, don't you? Very well."

Huh? What were they talking about? I didn't really understand, but the room felt a little claustrophobic all of a sudden.

What did she mean by "you and I"? Whatever, at least they weren't being antagonistic with one another.

"Okay, first things first. Rishia, no stalking Itsuki, okay?"

"Oh . . . Okay."

She was already well on her way to being a stalker, so I felt like I needed to nip that in the bud.

 What she really needed now was distance and space to think.

"I'll do my best."

"Itsuki is pretty pissed off right now, so it's best to keep your distance."

I didn't want to see him either. His whole self-satisfied attitude really got under my skin.

"So what role should Rishia take on in our party? What do you think she's best at?"

"Oh no!"

"Calm down. We're not going to force you to do anything you don't want to."

All I was saying was now that she was a member of our party, we needed to figure out what role she was going to play.

But she'd been in Itsuki's party this whole time.

Which meant there was a good chance she thought I was a sexual predator or something like that.

"What are you good at? From what I've heard you've been a melee fighter?"

"Well, I was doing my best, but . . ."

"Everyone has things they are good at and things they are bad at. We'll just have to practice different things to help you find your niche. My party really doesn't have enough members, so there's sure to be something perfect for you."

Both Filo and Raphtalia were already excellent melee fighters, so I think we were going to be just fine on that front.

With melee taken care of, it probably made the most sense to have her focus on magic use, since we didn't have any dedicated magic-users.

"What sort of magic can you use?"

"I don't have a specialty. But that also means I can use all different kinds."

"That sounds pretty useful."

Filo, Raphtalia, and I were all limited to one particular type of magic. I could use support and restorative magic, Filo could use wind magic, and Raphtalia could use illusion magic.

But Rishia was saying that she wasn't limited the way that we were.

Unfortunately, that probably meant that she wasn't going to be very advanced with any particular type.

Regardless, it would be a big help.

If she could use any king of magic, then we would be able to adjust our battle plan on the fly, responding to whatever came up.

Strength wasn't only about your level and your stats, after all.

If we thought our strategy through, we should be able to perform above what might be expected of someone at our level.

So this was a good opportunity for us to sit down and decide on the most strategic way to divide up the necessary roles in the party.

I was in charge of defense and healing, which made me the supporting player.

Raphtalia was an attacker that could offer support in a pinch: our version of a shortstop.

When she was attacking, she would follow up on Filo's offense. In a pinch, she could use her illusion magic to give us an advantage.

Filo was a flat-out attacker.

She was strong and fast. She could use haikuikku to take out and decimate a range of monsters quickly.

So I needed to find a useful job for Rishia to perform and then adjust our strategy to accommodate her.

"Don't worry, Rishia. Mr. Naofumi comes off as pretty rough and mean, but he's actually not nearly as bad as you might think."

"Maybe you and Rishia should have a long chat about it someday."

What was that supposed to mean? Not as bad as you might think?

Oh well. It wasn't who I really was, but I can imagine that people might be intimidated after hearing about my merchant life and association with slave traders.

"Oh, well . . . I . . ."

Rishia's eyes flit over to me, and then she looked away again before nodding.

I guess she agreed with Raphtalia?

"Hey, what are you trying to say about me?"

"Nothing . . ."

"I don't think it's nothing. Tell me."

"That's the kind of person he is."

"I see."

What did she see? I can't understand the way that women think.

They were a mystery. They were way easier to understand in *gyaruge*.

"That reminds me of something."

I looked Rishia over from head to foot.

She didn't have very good equipment.

The squirrel kigurumi, I think it was called a Risuka Kigurumi? They probably forced her to wear that because she had been in the party for the least amount of time.

"Rishia, what level are you at?"

"Hm? 68."

That was higher than I'd expected. I didn't check on her stats directly, but if she were at level 68, then she would probably prove useful.

Rishia was going to be a jack-of-all-trades type of magic-user. Should I have her focus on healing and support magic?

If she were a magic-user though, I would have to worry about her defense rating. I had to realize that there were going to be times when I wouldn't be able to completely protect her in battle.

If she were at level 68, then she would be a little behind Raphtalia and Filo, but she would still be able to participate in battles.

The only thing that really worried me was that Itsuki had gone out of his way to drop her. Could she really have been that weak? Granted, Itsuki wasn't the smartest guy around.

"Um, Shield Hero? You used to have a Pekkul Kigurumi, didn't you?"

"Huh? Yeah, I've got a couple of them. Oh, and don't call me that. It's too stuffy. Call me by my name."

I'd gotten in a fight with Melty over this in the past, so I'd come to realize that calling each other by our names was important.

"Feh? Okay, um, Naofumi."

"Good. Now what about the kigurumi?"

"I was wondering if you might let me wear it."

"What?"

"Well, I had to beg them all to let me wear the Risuka Kigurumi, but eventually . . ."

"You mean they didn't force you to wear that?"

"No, they didn't."

Oh, give me a break! And she was nodding along like she was saying the most obvious thing in the world.

She was so pathetic. She played right into their bullying and smiled about it the whole time!

"It's an excellent piece of equipment. But when they kicked me out of the party I had to give it back."

"Well . . ."

"It had a lot of special effects that made everything easier."

"I guess so."

The Risuka Kigurumi probably had magic-enhancing

effects, which would have worked well with Rishia's innate tendencies.

I pulled out the Pekkul Kigurumi and passed it to Rishia.

It did have a lot of equip effects and in many ways was better than Raphtalia's armor.

"Mr. Naofumi, are you really going to make her wear that?"

"I'm not *making* her wear it. She requested it."

If we'd just given her some cheap equipment we had lying around, it wouldn't be much of an improvement over what she was already wearing.

And besides, we had three of them. We'd gotten them from the Karma Pengu bosses on Cal Mira.

The other karma series bosses we defeated hadn't dropped any kigurumis though.

"Do you like it?"

"Yes, it's very convenient. Even when I'm sad or depressed, no one can really tell when I'm wearing it."

Well, that was a depressing thing to say. How badly had they bullied her?

"Are you sure you want to wear it?"

"Yes!"

Yes?! Give me a break. She sounded pathetic.

This put me in a touchy spot. I wanted her to be herself, but if she didn't truly want to get better, then she wasn't going to.

And here she was asking to wear a kigurumi so that she could cry and it would go unnoticed?

"You can wear it for a little while, but eventually I'm going to have to ask you to move on."

Sigh

Raphtalia looked concerned.

Were they going to be friends? Could Raphtalia stand it?

Personality-wise I'm sure we'd be able to get along, but it was too early to make a judgment call anyway.

"Let's work together and get stronger, okay?"

"Yes!"

At least she could answer with some vigor. It seemed to me like she might get along with Ren's party.

Slowly, but excitedly, Rishia unveiled how she looked in the Pekkul Kigurumi.

"How's it look? Pen-Pen!"

"Um . . . yup."

She seemed a little too excited about it. She reminded me of myself, before I was summoned to this world.

But now I'd met another person, besides Filo, who actually enjoyed wearing those things.

She didn't seem to know how to make friends with humans, but she could probably make friends with monsters.

"Thanks for inviting me into your party."

"No problem. Thanks for joining."

"Yay! We can dress the saaaaame!"

"Pleasure to be traveling with you, Rishia."

And so my friends welcomed her to the party.

Chapter Four: Custom Order

The offshore storms finally calmed down. The heroes and royal soldiers all prepared to leave the islands.

The activation event was going to continue for a few more days, but we had leveled all that we could, and we'd accumulated more drop items than we knew what to do with. So there was no reason to stay.

But I didn't want to end up stuck on a ship with Itsuki and his friends, so I had the schedule changed to make sure we weren't going to be traveling together.

Besides, I was just going to use a teleport skill to get back to the castle once we got in range.

I'd told the queen my plan, and she decided to travel with us.

The other heroes were also going to return to the castle.

And we were all going to start training to prepare for the next wave.

Before all that started though, I decided to check out the shield I'd unlocked from the last wave's boss monster.

Whale Shield conditions met!
Whale Skin Shield conditions met!

Whale Meat Shield conditions met!
Whalebone Shield conditions met!
Whale Eye Shield conditions met!
Whale Magic Core Shield conditions met!
. . . and others.

When you broke down an animal and got a shield from each of its parts, you ended up with a long list of things like this.

When I figured out how to use the power-up system, I realized that most of the information concerning the individual shields wasn't important. Lately, I just checked them for their equip effects and stat boosts, then ignored the rest.

Out of all the new shields, the only interesting things were:

Whale Shield 0/50 C: abilities locked: equip bonus: skill "dritte shield,": mastery level 0

Whale Magic Core Shield 0/45 C: abilities locked: equip bonus: skill "bubble shield," naval combat 2: mastery level 0

Whale Horn Shield 0/60 C: abilities locked: equip bonus: undersea battle ability 3: mastery level 0

Dritte? I looked up what that was, and apparently it was a skill that could be linked with air strike shield to form the third skill in a chain.

I tried using bubble shield, but all it did was make sound like it was leaking air—nothing more than that happened.

I wondered if it was meant for use underwater. Maybe you could make a stream of air bubbles with it?

So I went ahead and tried it underwater. It was actually a skill that made a bubble that allowed you to breath under the surface.

But you couldn't use it forever. If you used it once, you would have to go to the surface before it would become available again.

It would be useful if we had to fight underwater again. But I was hoping it wouldn't come to that. We'd just finished an undersea battle a few days ago.

The other heroes had also tested out the new weapons they'd unlocked during their time on the islands. I hoped that their parties understood that the real training hadn't started yet.

The queen and I left on the earliest ship and teleported to the castle as soon as we were within range. So we were the first ones to arrive.

"Oh no!"

Once we stepped out of the portal, Filo shouted.

"What is it?"

"The carriage . . ."

"The other soldiers will be bringing it back with them on the ship. Do not worry," said the queen.

"Oh gooood!"

"We never ended up using it on the islands though."

Filo had been taking exceptional care of the carriage. She worked on it every day. But the carriage was made of metal, so I'd been worried about it rusting in the sea breeze.

Why did she insist on bringing that carriage everywhere, even to places where we couldn't use it?

Besides, if we were going to be getting around by teleportation from now on, the carriage was only going to be a burden.

Come to think of it, that's probably why I never saw the other heroes using carriages at all.

"Very well then, I will see to it that skilled warriors are sent."

"Thanks."

The queen had already agreed to send soldiers to assist Fitoria in the wave that she had agreed to handle on our behalf.

Thanks to Fitoria, we would finally have some spare time to collect our thoughts and come up with a plan.

The next wave would fall on Melromarc in about two and a half weeks. We needed to find a way to make the other heroes more powerful before that happened.

The other heroes would be teleporting into the castle pretty soon. I wanted to figure out what to do with Rishia before I had to deal with them.

"Why don't we begin by looking over the materials I had prepared for you before your departure for Cal Mira?" the queen asked.

She was talking about materials she had previously agreed to stockpile for me.

"Good idea. That's a good a place as any to start."

We made our way to the stuffy, dusty castle warehouse. Had this been an old RPG, it was the sort of place where you would find really excellent equipment.

I looked over each of the articles in the room.

I'd visited the room once, before the wave in Cal Mira, but I hadn't had time to look over everything in detail.

Yup, sure enough, there was a lot of equipment set aside for us. All of the castle knights stored their equipment here too.

It looked like there was plenty of generic equipment, but finding something really good might prove difficult.

"When I had these things collected, I still didn't have a clear understanding of what you wanted, Mr. Iwatani. So I apologize, but aside from the things you specifically requested, the rest is a bit generic."

"No problem."

I found a magic silver sword in the clutter, but it turned out that the Karma Rabbit Sword had a higher attack stat.

I'd have to do something about that sword though. I decided to visit the weapon shop and see if the old guy there could do anything for us.

"Thank you for your understanding. I did, however, gather all the materials you requested."

We moved on to another warehouse that was filled with different materials.

The queen appeared at my side and passed me a sheet of parchment that seemed to have an inventory written on it.

"This is an inventory of the assembled materials. If there is anything else you would like us to prepare for you, I will call for the blacksmith."

"Thank you for all your help."

Materials . . .

"Can I take some of this stuff?"

"Of course."

I walked around the room absorbing various things into my shield and unlocking new shields. Many of the new shields indicated that their growth trees still needed to be unlocked, but I did end up with quite a lot of new things to work with.

I couldn't unlock all of the new options before the next wave came though.

"Oh, and you don't need to call for the blacksmith. I have someone in mind that I'd like to work with, so I'll go visit him myself."

"Very well, if that is what you wish."

Honestly, aside from the old guy at the weapon shop, I couldn't think of anyone else that worked with equipment. He'd done so much to help us already that I felt I owed him the business.

And besides, I trusted his work.

It was probably high time I paid him a visit anyway. We needed to get Raphtalia and Filo's new equipment worked on.

"Rishia, we're going to our favorite weapon shop. You should come with us."

"Oh, okay."

"But . . . um . . . Are you really going to wear that kigurumi all the time?"

"Hm?"

She tilted her head as if I'd confused her. She probably thought I had some kind of fetish.

If I weren't careful with my words, she'd probably freak out on me. I decided not to bother with it for now.

"It's been about a week since we last saw the old guy, isn't that right, Mr. Naofumi?"

"Yeah, I guess so. And just like we promised him last time, we're going to get our equipment from him. I can't wait to see what sort of awesome stuff he will whip up for us."

Most of the materials we had accumulated during our time in the islands would be arriving with the ships. But we had managed to bring a lot with us too, so I'd like to see what the old guy thought he could make from them.

Considering how many ores and different materials the queen had set aside for us, it wasn't like we had to risk running out of anything. I hoped he would come up with something good. If he did, it would be a big help in the coming battles.

And besides, I was hoping he could come up with some armor that had better stats and effects than that kigurumi.

"Hey there, kid!"

"Can't you come up with another thing to say when I come in here?"

"Oh stop that. You know I say it with affection."

I felt like he was telling the truth. I felt like he meant it.

"How was the activation event in Cal Mira? I heard there was a wave or something."

"We leveled up quite a bit. We probably gained over 30 levels in a day or two."

"Wow!"

The old guy seemed really surprised. Had I said something strange?

Raphtalia didn't seem to understand why he was so surprised either.

"You kids must have really pushed yourselves."

"Not at all. Monster hunting in the islands was easy,

especially with the activation event happening. What's so strange about that?"

"Well, I heard that it would help you level up, but I don't think I've ever heard of anyone leveling that much so soon after the class up ceremony. I've only heard of one guy that leveled anywhere near that. He hunted monsters all day long for the entire duration of the event, and he only gained 25 levels."

And we'd leveled 30 or so in a couple days? I wasn't sure what to make of that, but it seemed impressive.

"Well, we did level pretty efficiently, but I don't know how to explain it. Maybe it has something to do with the legendary weapons?"

"Maybe. The girls here probably don't know either, since they've only ever battled as your party members."

"True."

So it probably did have something to do with the legendary weapons.

There was no way for us to look into it now, because we didn't know anyone else that had leveled as much as we had.

I suppose the only thing we could do was ask the queen if she had any idea. I'd have to remember to bring it up with her.

"So? What brings you in here today? Is it about what we discussed last time?"

"Sure is. We got our hands on a lot of new materials on the islands, and the queen set aside a lot of materials for us here in

Melromarc. I was hoping you'd be able to make us something impressive from them."

I passed him the inventory parchment the queen had given me.

I had no idea what he was going to need, but I was sure that we would have enough of whatever it was.

"I'd like for you to make something out of the stuff you think would best suit us in battle."

"Got it. But I have to say this list has some pretty rare stuff on it. I think I can make some really good things for you. How much money are we talking?"

"The crown is going to cover the bill."

"Sounds like things are really looking up for you these days."

He was right, at least concerning our equipment, materials, money, and social standing. All in all, things were going pretty well.

But we still had to battle the waves. Which meant we didn't have all the time in the world to sit around chatting.

I still had a couple of topics I wanted to touch on.

"By the way . . ."

I looked over to Raphtalia.

Then I set the two new pieces of equipment, the Karma Rabbit Sword and the Karma Dog Claws, on the counter. I also showed the old guy the kigurumi and the materials we'd picked up on the islands.

"Can you do anything with this stuff?"

"You sure do have a lot of things to work with, kid. By the way, is that girl with you? The one in the sleeping bag?"

"Feh?"

"Yeah, that's Rishia. She looks weird, but there's a human underneath that thing."

"Mr. Naofumi, I don't think you should say things like that."

"Why not? She doesn't want to take that thing off, so I have to explain it."

She said she liked it because it hid her face, but I was starting to suspect she just had some kind of fetish.

"Well, that might be, but you really have brought me some strange weapons this time, haven't you? Anyway, it looks like it might be just what she needs."

The old guy regarded the Karma Rabbit Sword carefully before he answered.

The thing has a couple of issues that I would like to have addressed, but I couldn't argue with its attack stat.

Raphtalia had become very strong recently. If she were to swing a magic silver sword with all her might, she would probably break it.

I wanted to hear what the old guy thought about it so I could decide whether it was worth working on or if we should just toss it out. We could melt it down for materials, too.

"The problem is that it doesn't have a blood clean coating on it. Is there any way that you could apply one?"

"Normally, it's a process that you have to include in the production of the item. I can do it, but it might affect the overall quality of the piece. Do you want me to try?"

"Yeah."

"Well, of course, I could do that, but it might be more interesting to try and make something new out of it."

Was he saying he wanted to stick it onto my barbarian armor or something?

Come to think of it, that might be pretty interesting too.

"Thanks for all the projects, kid."

"No problem. While you're at it though, what kind of a weapon do you think would be best for Rishia here?"

"Hm? Do you think you could take off the kigurumi and show me your hands?"

"Rishia."

"I . . . I like to use swords."

"I'd really rather put you behind us as support."

"I can do either!"

"I appreciate your enthusiasm, but why don't you let him take a look?"

"Okay."

Rishia slowly slipped out of the kigurumi, then bowed awkwardly to the old guy before holding out her hands.

"Well, isn't she pretty? Lucky you, eh kid?"

"Lucky? I'm not like Motoyasu, so I don't think anything of it."

"Well, he's as dull as ever, isn't he? You've really got your work cut out for you."

"I know."

The old guy and Raphtalia nodded to one another as if they were in on a secret together.

"She looks like she might do well with a rapier. If you want to put her behind you as support, she should probably have something with magic protection.

"Could you choose one for us?"

"Wait a second. There's no reason she couldn't use a bow or a spear. She doesn't seem like she has a lot of upper body strength though, so I'm not sure those are the best choices."

"Feh . . . I don't want to use a bow!"

"You don't want to be like Itsuki?"

"It's not that. I'm afraid I might accidentally shoot one of you in the back!"

"Oh, right."

I guess I hadn't thought about accidentally being shot by one of my own teammates.

But as far as I knew, Itsuki had never shot anyone on accident. I guess that meant he was pretty skilled. Maybe.

"Anyway, what's your schedule looking like? How much time do I have to work on this stuff?"

"The next wave will be here in a little over two weeks. Anything you can do before then would be great."

"Got it, but . . ."

He held up the Pekkul Kigurumi.

"What do you want to do about this? Should I take it apart? Who made this thing anyway?"

"I know, I know. The thing has great equip effects, but it sure does look stupid, doesn't it? We got it as a drop item from a monster. It's kind of hard to explain. Legendary weapons can make these things from the materials monsters leave behind."

That was a fair question. We could say that a monster dropped it, but then he would just want to know what a monster was doing with something like that.

This was the sort of thing that reminded me of what a strange world I'd been summoned to. Of course it was strange, so how could I have been expected to know something like that?

Actually, what was strange was that the other heroes *had* known about it.

Think about it. How could monsters like rabbits and porcupines drop items that were bigger than they were?

"You do make some weird stuff. I can see that it really does have great equip effects."

"Can you somehow move the effects onto another piece of equipment?"

"That's tough. I can try a couple of things, but I wouldn't hold my breath. I will probably need to make some fine adjustments, so when I get into that job I'll ask you about the specifics."

"Great. If you can use the barbarian armor to power this other stuff up, I'll leave it here."

"That works. I'll try and make something for the girl here, but that will be one of the last things that I do."

He pointed to Raphtalia. I wondered what he was going to make.

"What is it?"

"Don't worry about it."

I had a weird feeling about this. Call it a premonition.

I couldn't shake the feeling that this new equipment was going to end up looking really odd.

"It's so exciting! I hope we get something good!"

The kigurumi fan behind me was getting really excited.

I was getting that weird feeling again. If someone as dour and quiet as Rishia was getting excited, it struck me as a major red flag. If we ended up with something ridiculous, I'd have Rishia wear it.

"Alright then, we'll be on our way. Thanks for all your help. If you need anything in the meantime, just show this paper to the castle guards and tell them I sent you—they'll let you in."

"Got it, kid. Just wait till you see what I put together for you."

"Thanks. See you."

We left the weapon shop.

We had just returned to the castle when I saw someone I recognized climbing down from a carriage.

"Ah, Shield Hero. I beg your pardon for all the trouble the last time we met."

It was Nice Guy, the nobleman who'd gone out of his way to help us when we'd been running from the law with a bounty on our heads.

I think the queen had said that he was sick and convalescing out in the countryside.

Standing next to him was a well-dressed child. The child had dog-like ears.

"Raphtalia!"

"Keel!"

That's right. His name was Keel, and he was from Raphtalia's village.

We'd found him in the basement of that evil nobleman's mansion. It was the same nobleman that had tortured Raphtalia.

"Were you safe after all of that, Raphtalia? Did anything bad happen to you?"

"I've been fine. Nothing bad! And no one is chasing us anymore."

"That's good!"

Keel looked at me.

"You're not pushing her too hard, are you?"

". . ."

"Why don't you answer him?!"

"I was just thinking it over. Maybe I have been pushing you too hard."

"Mr. Naofumi, you're the one that is overdoing it! Keel, don't you worry about me. I've never been seriously injured or anything!"

"You did end up getting cursed once."

"Mr. Naofumi! Be quiet!"

"Isn't he your childhood friend? It's rude to lie to your friends."

"Ahahaha! The Shield Hero is always surrounded my such interesting people!"

Nice Guy was laughing.

Did I say something funny?

"So what are you doing here?"

"Well, I'm finally back on my feet, so I decided to come pay you a visit."

"I'm glad you're feeling better."

Were we supposed to take Keel off his hands, since he was Raphtalia's friend?

Raphtalia noticed that I was looking a Keel, and guessing what I was thinking, she fell into deep thought.

"What should we do Raphtalia?"

"What do you mean?"

"About this kid, are we just supposed to leave him with this nobleman forever?"

I looked over at Nice Guy. He smiled and rubbed Keel's head.

"I don't have a problem with it. It's up to him."

Well, that was nice of him. But I'm sure Raphtalia had something to say about it. Keel probably had an idea of what he wanted, too.

"Raphtalia! You're fighting against the waves, aren't you?!"

"Yes. I'm fighting them with the Shield Hero: Mr. Naofumi. Just a couple of days ago we were fighting a wave in a place called Cal Mira.

"Wow! That's so cool! I want to be strong enough to fight the waves too!"

I liked the kid's spirit.

"But . . ."

Raphtalia looked upset.

"Raphtalia?"

"I . . ."

"You don't like that idea?"

Raphtalia responded by giving me a troubled look.

"Big sis, what's wrong?"

Filo and Keel both cocked their heads in confusion.

I understood what she was feeling.

She was probably thinking that she didn't want Keel to be put in harm's way again. Just when he was safe, he was about to jump back in the line of danger.

Raphtalia looked at me like she was asking me for something. I understood.

"If you join in on our training exercises, I'm sure you'll get stronger. You just have to make an effort."

"Mr. Naofumi . . ."

"There's nothing bad that can come of being stronger than you are."

Raphtalia's village had been decimated when the first wave came. Hordes of monsters poured over the town, and slave traders hunted down all the survivors.

Had the survivors been stronger, they might have gotten out of it with less casualties and tragedy.

"Raphtalia, you don't want me to fight, do you?"

". . ."

Raphtalia looked at him but said nothing. She was thinking.

"It's not that I don't want you to fight. But it's harder than you think. Are you sure you're prepared for it?"

"Of course I am! I . . . I want to be strong enough to help protect other people!"

"Sounds like we have our answer, doesn't it? If you try and control someone that has already made up their minds, you'll only make them miserable. We can help him get strong enough to protect himself."

Raphtalia said nothing, but she nodded.

That settled it. I decided to invite him into my party.

We didn't have enough people anyway. If there were people we could trust, it made sense to team up with them and help them get stronger.

He was Raphtalia's childhood friend. There was no way he would betray our trust.

"Alright then, Mr. Naofumi. Can we take care of Keel for now?"

"Yeah. Of course."

"He's from the same village that Ms. Raphtalia is from. Isn't that right?"

Rishia stepped forward and introduced herself to Keel.

"Whoa! What's with this person's outfit? It's weird!"

"Feh?"

I guess he'd just noticed her standing there.

"Very well then, Shield Hero, I'll leave this . . . boy in your care."

Nice Guy smiled at Keel and then left to go meet with the queen.

"Let's all get acquainted."

"I'm Fiiiilo! We met before!"

Before I could even finish talking, Filo jumped forward and introduced herself.

Why couldn't she ever wait?

"My name is Rishia Ivyred. Very nice to meet you."

"You're the only one left, Mr. Naofumi. Please introduce yourself to Keel."

"Sure. My name is Naofumi Iwatani. I'm the Shield Hero. Battle might be tough, but step forward and don't be afraid. I'll protect you."

When I finished talking, Keel decisively nodded and stepped forward.

"My name is Keel. I'm very happy to meet you all!"

Keel was nearly as tall as Raphtalia.

They were from the same village. That meant that he probably looked younger than he really was.

I suddenly realized that he was the first male party member I'd ever had. I hoped that we would get along.

Raphtalia, Filo, and Rishia sometimes had conversations that I didn't really feel like I could participate in.

"Alright then, let's get started. Rishia, Keel, what do you think?"

"About what?"

"What do you mean?"

"Just how strong do you two want to be?"

Raphtalia looked me over as though she was trying to find a dark undertone to my question.

Her instincts were sharp. These two probably would be freaked out by what I had to say.

"I want to be the strongest there is! Obviously!"

"Feh?! Yes, exactly!"

They both seemed to really mean it too. Good.

Then there was only one thing to do. I said it plainly as can be: "Then both of you need to become my slaves."

Chapter Five: Battle Advisors

"Fehhhh!"

"Wh . . . What the hell? You were lying about being the Shield Hero, weren't you?!"

Rishia's gasp was still echoing throughout the castle courtyard. Keel was glaring angrily at Raphtalia and I. Then Rishia took off running as if she were a startled rabbit.

They certainly were spurred to action at the strangest times.

"Don't let them escape with their lives!" I shouted.

"Why would you say that?"

"I knew it!"

"Keel! Calm down! I know that Mr. Naofumi can seem a little rough around the edges, but trust me. There's a reason for all this!"

"What kind of reason could there be?"

Hm? I suppose I was causing more confusion than necessary.

"Okay!"

Filo turned into her filolial form and chased after Rishia.

Keel was stunned. That's right. He'd never seen her transform before.

"That was a joke! Filo! Just bring her back normally! Don't claw her!"

"Or peck at her! Rishia wouldn't survive your attacks!"

Whoops. I should control myself better. I had almost gotten Rishia killed.

Filo wrapped her wings around Rishia and pulled her back to me.

But Rishia was writhing wildly.

"Let me go! I'm going back to my village! I'm going back to my mom and dad! Master Itsukiiiiii!"

"It was just a joke."

"About turning me into your slave?"

"No, that part was true."

"But why?"

"How do you get stronger? You raise your level by defeating monsters, right? The heroes have a special ability called maturation adjustment that can make your growth more efficient. That's one of the reasons that Raphtalia is so powerful."

"R . . . Really? Raphtalia, are you really that powerful?"

"Well, yes."

Raphtalia quickly shuffled around to stand behind Keel.

She moved so quickly that Keel didn't have a chance to react. By the time he noticed she'd moved, she was already behind him.

"Wow!"

"The only characters my shield can help grow faster are slaves and monsters."

In addition to the maturation adjustment skill, I also had a skill called ability adjustment. That would help them master new abilities faster.

If I could get those two to accept the conditions, then they would level up a lot faster than they would have otherwise.

"Whether you want to do it or not is up to you. But if you don't become a slave, you won't level up nearly as quickly."

"But . . ."

"Think about it. What do you need to do to get stronger? Be greedy about it. Think about what you can do to get what you want. I'm only offering you the option."

". . ."

Both Rishia and Keel fell into deep thought. It was their lives, so they needed to make up their minds for themselves.

But I could give them a little push.

"Well, Rishia is already at level 68. If you've already leveled that much, then it might not be as effective for you. Still, it would make you stronger than it would if you didn't become a slave."

It was the sort of skill that worked best the earlier you started to use it. It snowballed over time.

It really was like a game.

Characters that had high levels at the beginning either died or betrayed you. Either that or they basically never leveled up more.

That described L'Arc pretty well. But no—I couldn't let myself fall into that trap. This wasn't a game.

"Or we could reset your level. But the next wave will be here soon and I want you to be powerful enough to fight in it. So if we were going to do a reset, we should probably wait until after the wave.

The rest of us were in the 70s, so if we were to reset her levels and continue leveling from that point on, the gap between us would only get worse.

"Oh . . . Alright."

"But if you become my slave then don't run! I mean it's not like I'm going to keep you in chains or . . . Hey, are you listening?!"

The second I started talking about slaves, Rishia snapped her head left and right, looking for a way to escape. She was driving me nuts.

"Are you listening? I'm telling you that you won't be forced to do anything you don't want to do!"

"Fehhh!"

"Rishia, please listen to me. I'm telling you how to get stronger. What do you want to do?"

Her eyes were wandering around the courtyard, but she was thinking about the offer.

Fair enough. Not many people I know would be first in line to volunteer for slavery.

But Raphtalia had.

"I will technically hold the reins. But I promise that I won't force you do to anything against your will."

"He really is a good person. Although he can be a little selfish from time to time, he won't ever hurt you. You can trust me."

"Raphtalia . . ."

"Master, you never tie me up or nothing!"

Raphtalia and Filo had both chimed in, but to Rishia and Keel it probably just sounded like they were brainwashed.

"I'm not going to force you. You don't have to do it if you don't want to. I'm just telling you the best way to move forward. Keel, I'll tell you the same thing. All I'm doing is giving you the option. It's up to you whether or not you want to take it."

"Yeah. I want to be stronger! If it would make me stronger, I'd sell my soul to the devil. If it would help me bring them back."

"You think I'm the devil?"

"He just pretends to be mean! He's actually very nice!"

Keel didn't answer Raphtalia or me.

Did that mean he thought I was the devil?!

Rishia held her hand over her heart. She was wearing the kigurumi, so I couldn't really make out her expression, but she spoke as though she had made up her mind.

"I've decided. Please, make me your slave!"

"Are you sure?"

I hadn't expected her to decide so quickly. Judging from what I knew about her personality, I'd expected some vague foot shuffling for a while.

But it looked like once she'd made up her mind, she threw herself into it completely. I liked that.

"Yes! I want to be strong!"

"Alright then. Let's go see the queen and get this matter settled."

And so we left the courtyard and went to go visit the queen.

"Ugh . . . Uh . . ."

The slave sealing ceremony went off without a hitch.

Both Rishia and Keel ended up with powerful slave seals on their chests.

Keel had already been a slave though, so first we had to have the original seal removed. I'm sure he didn't like being freed only to immediately become a slave again.

The queen had applied the same sort of seal that she had used on Bitch. It was the sort that was invisible unless it was activated by something.

A list of actions I could prohibit appeared before me in the air.

I unchecked all of the options. Or I tried to. I couldn't uncheck them all!

Apparently I had to leave at least one thing checked or the spell wouldn't work. So I picked a minor condition and finished the process.

It was a simple thing. They were not permitted to lie to me.

I didn't want to think about it, but there was always the possibility that one of them might try to betray me.

What if Rishia was actually a spy sent by Itsuki?

Granted, the very fact that she had agreed to be my slave made that pretty unlikely.

Huff. Huff.

"Are you okay?"

"Yes. I'm fine."

"I'm good. That was nothing!"

"Yeah? Good."

I felt a little guilty, but there was no use dwelling on it. I opened up Rishia and Keel's status screens.

I decided to check Keel's stats first.

He was at a pretty low level. I couldn't be sure how he would mature. But from the looks of it his agility rating was very high. He was a demi-human with dog-like features, after all. Maybe it was wise to assume that speed was his specialty.

I looked as Rishia's stats next.

"...!"

"What is it?"

"It's nothing. Don't worry about it."

I had gasped without thinking.

I didn't know how to explain it. Compared to Raphtalia, Filo, and I, her stats were unbelievably low.

She was at level 68, but her stats were barely any higher than Keel's. Now I understood why Itsuki wanted to get her out of his party.

But I wasn't going to abandon her like that. Figuring out how to make a weak person stronger was my specialty.

Maybe those were the kind of stats that normal people had in this world?

If there was anything of interest about her, it's that all her stats looked to be roughly equal. There was nothing in particular you could point to as a weakness.

But the stats themselves were all very low. It was exactly what you would expect from a jack-of-all-trades.

Was she really level 68? If she was, then I really had my work cut out for me.

"Mr. Iwatani."

The queen was talking to me. A knight I didn't recognize was standing by her side.

"What?"

"I am in the process of calling for an experienced combat advisor. But when it comes to sword fighting, this person is easily one of the best in the kingdom. If you would find her of use . . ."

"Why don't you call for ALL of the best?"

"Mr. Naofumi, you don't need to be so crass."

"Sounds good to me."

What would be the best use of our time though? I'd have to make the most of what time we had.

"Hey Keel, you're the lowest level member here. Filo's going to take you out leveling."

We needed to bring him up to fighting level if he was going to get any use out of the training.

To do that we'd have to power level—at least that's what it was called in the online games I used to play. A weaker character would go level with a high-level, fast character, and then they would level up very quickly. At the very least, we had to get him ready to class up.

"I'm supposed to help him?"

"Yeah. Take him out leveling. Just make sure you're back before dark."

"Okay!"

With a puff of smoke, she transformed into her filolial form, then picked up Keel and placed him onto her back.

"Huh? But . . . Raphtalia?!"

Before he could finish his sentence Filo used her wings to hold him in place and took off running.

"AAAHHHHHHHH!"

"Oh! Keel!"

"Don't worry about them. Filo's strong—they'll be fine."

It was important that they started with the fundamentals. That was the only way to make the most of the following training. And besides, focusing on the fundamentals would probably be good for higher-level characters, too.

"Rishia, once the next wave has come and gone, you'll be doing the same thing as Keel. So look forward to it."

"Fehhh!"

She never calmed down, did she?

Oh well. I guess there was no getting around it. Even Raphtalia got a little freaked out when she had to ride Filo.

They needed to think of it as a trial on the path to strength. There was just no getting around it.

"The Shield Hero's companions are boisterous, aren't they?"

The knight standing with the queen removed her helmet. She looked like the typical strong, female knight character than you ran into in RPGs. She was very beautiful also, like Raphtalia.

She had long strawberry-blonde hair. She must have kept it tied up when she wore her helmet. Had she dressed like a man, she could have passed for a prince.

"Please introduce yourself," said the queen.

The knight took a step forward, saluted, and spoke loudly and clearly.

"My name is Eclair Seaetto. I am honored to assist in the Shield Hero's training exercises."

"Seaetto? I don't think we've met before, but . . ."

I felt like I'd heard that name somewhere.

"Mr. Naofumi. Seaetto is the name of the territory my village was in."

"That's right. Nice Guy had mentioned that."

Did that mean this woman was part of the nobility that had ruled over Raphtalia's region?

But I'd heard that the nobility there had been killed.

"This woman is the daughter of the nobleman who once governed the land that Raphtalia's village was a part of."

Heh. I liked her choice of knights.

I'd heard that the noble family that had ruled there was exceptionally talented. Raphtalia had mentioned that losing them in the wave had been another major tragedy for her people.

"Okay. What has she been doing this whole time?"

"When my father died in the first wave, a portion of our knights and soldiers tried to take advantage of the ensuing chaos by hunting down survivors and selling them off as slaves. I have been hunting those cowards down and ensuring their imprisonment."

Well, well. I never expected to find someone so upstanding in such a rotten country. I appreciated that she had taken that upon herself, both as the Shield Hero and as Raphtalia's friend.

"It is just as she has said. They have been imprisoned in

the castle dungeons. She finished her work while you were in the islands. So I have selected her to assist in the training of the other heroes.

I guess the church and Trash had still been in power before we left, so if she had tried to hunt down the slavers at that point they might have had her killed off.

There was only one problem. Was she any good?

That was the most important thing. There was no reason to receive instruction from anyone who wasn't at least as strong as Raphtalia.

"Is she any good?"

"Very. She was the winner of the last national fencing tourney."

"Are there others as good as she?"

"Not ones that haven't been imprisoned, killed, or demoted."

So there was no one else in the kingdom that was good enough to train us further.

She seemed like an upstanding person, but . . .

"You can hate me if you like. I realize I was unable to defend your lands after my father's death."

"I would never. That was not your fault. Please, don't bow to me."

The introductions just kept on going.

This Eclair woman was talking to Raphtalia as if she had nothing to worry about.

"If that is how you feel. I am happy that I can do anything in the service of our people. Thank you for the opportunity to help, Ms. Raphtalia."

"Please, just call me Raphtalia."

"Understood. Now then, Raphtalia, I do not know how worthy I am to be teaching you anything at all, but I will do my best to show you the things I know."

So this Eclair person was going to be teaching Raphtalia what she knew about sword fighting.

"I should probably participate in the training too, huh?"

"I do not know if I have anything to teach you, Master Shield Hero, but I will certainly do all that I can to assist."

She was so proper! I could tell she was one of those overly serious types.

"Thank you for your time. I will be returning to my duties now. Please let me know if there is anything you need from me."

The queen turned and left us alone with Eclair.

"So what should we do? Do you want to start training right away?"

I felt like they were going to make us run laps, or whatever counted for combat training in Melromarc.

"We must begin by evaluating your current skill level."

"You're not going to make us run laps, are you?"

"I am confident that you are far beyond that level of

training. I would like to start with actual battle operations."

I wondered if I should tell her that I wasn't a track star or anything like that.

The only work we'd really done was that I taught Raphtalia how to hold her sword and we did some pull ups. And I only did that when we'd had free time.

And as for myself, all I'd really done was sit around making medicines and accessories.

Oh! I had made dinner a few times, too.

That made me nervous. We hadn't really done any physical training at all. All the exercise we had gotten had just been from fighting monsters.

"Honestly, we haven't done much. All the skill that we do have really just comes from my shield's abilities. Raphtalia is the only one that has actually done some work."

"Mr. Naofumi, don't be so crude."

"Really? Well then, shall we start with a run around the interior courtyard?"

I didn't really want to run, but Eclair was probably right.

We should go for a run. At the very least it would loosen us up a bit.

Eclair took the lead, and we ran a few laps around the castle training grounds.

We ran at a pretty good clip, but the stat boosts I had from my shield kept me from tiring.

I was sort of annoyed by it the whole time. Running behind Eclair.

She was kind of slow.

"Do you mind if we speed up a little bit?"

"I'm sorry if my pace was holding you back. Please, run at whatever speed you like. I'll adjust my pace to match yours."

"Hear that, Raphtalia?"

So we picked up our pace a little. It still wasn't giving Raphtalia or I any trouble.

"Fehhh . . ."

But Rishia had run out of stamina and had started walking. It was probably because of that kigurumi she was wearing.

Then just when we had been running for a while . . .

"Just a moment please, Master Shield Hero."

Eclair called for us to stop. It sounded like she was getting tired out.

Rishia had run out of steam a while back, but I was doing just fine, so I'd picked her up and continued running.

"I think you are plenty fit for the training to continue. Shall we move on?"

"Really?"

"Your advanced level is no doubt an advantage, but from what I've seen you are more than ready to move on."

Had the levels we'd gained in Cal Mira really helped us that much?

I didn't get tired no matter how much I ran. And I could carry Rishia easily—she was so light!

I felt like I could have easily kept running with heavier baggage. Actually, I hadn't even really been running, just walking quickly.

The game-like system of powering up had really changed the meaning of physical training.

Of course, I was glad that it was easy, but I still felt that if we made light of the training fundamentals, we would end up regretting it.

I wanted to raise my reaction time, and I wanted to get some good physical workouts in to help me move better in battle.

If I could improve my speed and strength, that would give me a better chance of dodging L'Arc and Glass's attacks.

But Eclair was huffing and puffing, clearly out of breath. Maybe she was still recovering?

"Then let us move on to battle tactics properly."

Eclair took Raphtalia aside and started showing her the minutiae of sword handling, from how to hold the sword and regard your opponent to how to set her footing.

Thinking back on it, the only instruction she had ever really gotten was a perfunctory lesson at the weapon shop. Everything since that time she'd had to teach herself. She'd managed to handle herself with magic and luck, but she had once had a difficult time taking down a particularly powerful bandit we ran into. She was sure to benefit from instruction by a real swordsman.

"Now then, may I ask Ms. Rishia to act as Raphtalia's opponent?"

"That makes me a little nervous, but go ahead and do as she says."

Rishia's stats were so low that I was worried on her behalf. But I'm sure she would be fine.

Raphtalia was given a wooden training sword. She set her feet to stand against Rishia.

Rishia was still wearing that kigurumi. It made for a ridiculous-looking scene.

"Here I go!"

"Um . . . Okay!"

Raphtalia dropped her weight low and struck at Rishia just as Eclair had instructed her to.

"Fehhh!"

That's all she'd done, but suddenly Rishia was flying through the air.

Oh jeez. I'd known she was weak and all, but she couldn't even block an attack? I was hoping she'd be able to handle some melee work, but that wasn't looking like an option.

What were we going to do about her?

"Huh? What?!"

Raphtalia was stunned. She kept looking from the wooden sword in her hand to Rishia and back again.

"Do us a favor and hold back a little."

"I did! But she still went flying."

Oh boy. I couldn't let her get hurt, so I ran over and caught her out of the air before she crashed into the ground.

"Fehhh . . ."

"Hm. It may be harder to train Raphtalia and Ms. Rishia together than I had expected, Master Shield Hero."

I was ready to throw in the towel and keep her out of melee entirely. She was so talentless there was really no hope.

But another part of me didn't want to admit defeat so easily.

What was talent anyway? What she lacked in talent she could make up for with effort.

"Maybe so."

How were we going to train her? Maybe I was the only person that she could handle facing off against, considering the fact that I was basically incapable of attacking or doing damage.

But there was still a problem. I wouldn't get anything out of it!

"What would you like to do, Master Shield Hero?"

"I'll focus on defending myself against your attacks."

"Understood. Shall I come at you full-force?"

"I don't know how strong you are, but if you think you can get through my defenses, give it your best shot."

"Understood."

Eclair readied her sword and turned to face me.

"Hya!"

Huh? She was really fast! There was nothing unessential in her movements. She thrust at me, her body shooting forward like a coiled spring. I was only able to respond just in time.

The point of her blade clattered against my shield.

"You were able to parry my thrust, just what I would expect from a true hero. Let us see how you do with this!"

She shot forward again, delivering thrust after thrust very quickly.

It was hard to keep up. It was like she was attacking with more than one sword at once.

Still, I was able to block the thrusts. But it was exhausting. I wasn't sure I felt like it was a good skill to use in training. What if my shield had a counter attack skill? That could have caused real problems, so I stuck to mostly trying to dodge the thrusts.

Still, there were times when her attacks connected through an ingenious move on her behalf. She hit my shoulder and arm once or twice.

So these are the kind of attacks a skilled swordsman could deliver?

I was pretty sure that my stats were higher than hers, but I still hadn't been able to completely cover myself from her attacks.

"You really are good with that thing."

If Raphtalia could learn to use a sword like Eclair, she'd probably be a lot stronger than she was now.

During the last battle, Raphtalia hadn't been able to defeat a powered-up Glass. But if she learned to fight like this, then she could probably do the job of the all the other heroes combined. We might even stand a chance.

"As for you, Master Shield Hero, it seems to me that you are already advanced beyond the point where my instruction will be of any use."

"It's only because of how high my stats have become. Don't worry about it. Though that reminds me . . ."

"Yes?"

"Is there any way to imbue those sword attacks with additional effects? I mean, can you have magical sword attacks or anything like that?"

"It is possible to apply such effects. Try to block this one."

The female knight laid her hand on the tip of her blade and chanted a spell. When she finished, she readied herself and thrust at me again.

When she did, the blade was immediately engulfed in glowing energy that expanded to form the shape of a wide lance.

She was fast!

I readied my shield, and the lance energy blade glanced off of it, shooting over my head.

From what I could tell, it didn't seem powerful enough to hurt me, even if the attack had connected. That was only because of my special defense rating though. I bet it would really do a number against a monster, or against Glass.

"I see. That was pretty impressive."

"It is called the 'applied sword technique.'"

"Another question. Could you use that to make your attacks turn into defense rating attacks or into attacks that ignore the enemy's defenses all together?"

Eclair rubbed her chin and thought for a minute.

"Not in the school I've been trained in. But I have heard rumors to that effect."

That's right. Normal humans in this world didn't have access to the same sort of skills that the heroes did.

But I could tell from the way she was fighting that they DID have access to attacks that could be just as effective.

It was probably similar to what Raphtalia had done with her magic and the magic sword.

I think she'd called it "illusion sword."

It was an attack that turned her invisible long enough to sneak around behind the enemy for a thrust at their backside.

Aside from that, Raphtalia had probably done something similar without intending to. I'd seen her sword glow in the same way that Eclair's just had.

So Raphtalia would be able to make attacks like that when she was done training with Eclair— awesome.

"Do you mean to say that you've seen an attack like that before?"

"Yeah. One of the enemies that we fought in the last wave used it. As you can tell, I am the Shield Hero. Which means that I'm very weak against attacks that can break through my defenses. So I'm trying to find a way to get around those defense rating and defense ignoring attacks."

"I see. I do not know if I will be of much use to you in that regard. I do not believe that I have much to teach you at all, Master Shield Hero."

Eclair nodded slowly to herself, looking a little wistful.

"Don't worry about it. I'm a weird case. I can't even attack on my own. But I hope that you'll help teach the other heroes a thing or two."

"Your judgment is impeccable. I agree with you."

She was so proper!

I didn't like to be so polite. It made me feel like she didn't know who she was actually talking to.

Anyway, at least I'd gotten to see her real skill level.

If Raphtalia could learn from her, we'd be in better shape than we were now.

"Fehhh . . ."

As for Rishia, we couldn't start with anything advanced. She could barely run around the courtyard.

For her level, she was very weak. She was probably too weak to even participate in the training exercises.

She did have the drive to work at it, but did she have the necessary stamina?

"Okay, well, until the other combat advisors arrive, I'll be working with Rishia on the basics."

"Understood! I will also assist Madam Rishia with the fundamentals of sword use!"

"Fehh . . ."

"Stop with that weak sigh. You're trying to toughen up, aren't you?"

"Feh . . . Yes!"

She did seem committed at least.

We spent the rest of the day training on the castle training grounds.

Just before evening fell, Filo came trotting back with Keel.

"We're baaaack!"

"How was it?"

"After all the running, it looked like the sun was going to set. So we had to come back! I guess we didn't get to fight very many monsters!"

Keel was limp and exhausted where he lay on her back. I checked his stats.

Level 14. That seemed like good progress to me.

"I feel sick."

"Keep it up. You're getting stronger."

"Did Raphtalia have this hard of a time?"

Raphtalia had gotten really sick after riding in the carriage for a day. She was out for a while after that.

So in that regard, yes, she'd had a hard time. But to be fair, she'd never gone out fighting monsters on Filo's back.

"She never tried leveling from Filo's back."

"What? Then why do I have to do it?"

I had sent them out as an experiment, but it looks like Filo's version of boot camp was pretty tough.

I couldn't wait to see how quickly Keel leveled up.

"Ugh. I'm hungry."

Keel's stomach was growling loudly.

Demi-humans' bodies matured with their level, not their ages.

"Keel, how was it?"

Raphtalia finished her training with Eclair and came running over to see him.

"Filo, you can't push him too hard."

"Huh?"

Filo had no concept of what people's limits were, regarding anything.

"Anyway, why don't we all have dinner? Tomorrow is going to be another busy day."

"Good point. According to Eclair, we'll be studying magic in addition to sword skills, so I think it will be another full day. The other soldiers say they have things to teach us before we go to sleep, too."

"Fehh . . . I'm better at studying than training anyway."

"Right. Got it."

We finished the dinner that had been prepared for us. Keel and Filo ate like pigs.

And that was the end of our first day of training.

Compared to the leveling that we'd done on the islands, this felt more like we were living together as a team. It was like summer camp.

Personally, I never really hung out with people outside of school, so I'd only seen things like that in anime and manga.

"Hey, that reminds me. Haven't the other heroes shown up yet? What's taking them so long?"

I asked the queen, and she answered.

Apparently, they had all gone their separate ways immediately after arriving and were all doing their own things.

From what the queen said, it sounded like they were all still in Melromarc. But no one had heard from them directly.

Hadn't they promised to participate in the training?

I guess it didn't matter if they skipped out on the first day, considering we hadn't really established a system yet. But we needed to start training seriously the next day.

I wondered if we were really going to be able to get them to join in.

Chapter Six: Hengen Muso Style

The next morning.

"Shield Hero, the queen would like to meet with you."

I was still asleep in the castle chamber when someone knocked on the door and delivered the message.

"Erm . . ."

I stumbled over to the door, opened it, and thanked the soldier standing there.

"Good morning."

"Morning. What does the queen want this early in the morning?"

Raphtalia was already awake, and she had changed into clothes that would allow her to move easily during the training exercises.

Rishia had fallen out of bed and was still asleep on the floor where she had fallen.

I guess that was one advantage of sleeping in the kigurumi. It was a bit like pajamas after all.

Keel was lying on top of Rishia and snoring loudly. I guess he had fallen out of bed too.

"What are you doing, Raphtalia?

"I agreed to meet Eclair for early morning drills."

"Did you? What about Rishia?"

"Rishia too. Rishia! Wake up please! You too, Keel."

"Fehhh . . ."

"Uh, Raphtalia, I'm still sleepy!"

Raphtalia walked over and shook Rishia's shoulder until she suddenly woke up.

Something about the way she was collapsed there looked unsavory.

"Better start getting ready. Our morning drills will be starting soon."

"Fehh . . . Good morning!"

"Morning. Look, I have to go meet with the queen now. I'll meet up with you later, so just go ahead and get started without me."

I was afraid that there might be a problem on the horizon. Rishia might end up meeting Itsuki on the training grounds.

That could be a real pain if it didn't go well.

"Raphtalia, look after Rishia for me, okay?"

I waved my hand to call her over, then whispered in her ear.

"If Itsuki shows up, do your best to keep Rishia separate from him. I don't want things to get out of hand."

"Understood. Let's get going then, shall we?"

"Okay."

"I'm tired."

I left them all to their preparations and went to go see the queen.

"What do you need so early in the morning?"

I'd arrived in the throne room. The queen had been waiting for me.

"Thank you for coming. You will recall that yesterday I said I would be looking for other combat advisors to assist in the training exercises."

Had she been up all night working on it?

She looked like she hadn't gotten any rest.

"Yeah . . ."

"I sent correspondence to a number of individuals, and one of them has decided to participate."

"Oh yeah? Who?"

"This warrior is well advanced in age, having fought in a war for Melromarc long ago. I believe that if you train with this fighter you'll find it a great contribution to your efforts."

Who knew there were still such powerful fighters around?

I had never heard of anyone like that. I naturally imagined she was talking about some kind of mountain-dwelling ascetic.

Was this person going to come down from the mountains to teach me secret martial arts? I'd heard stories like that before.

It's true that I didn't want to depend on my levels and ignore fundamental battle skills.

"The fighting style you'll be taught is known as the 'Hengen Muso Style.'"

What kind of name was that? It sounded like some kind of old action manga.

I must have scrunched my face up in confusion, as the queen quickly offered an explanation.

"There is a famous legend about this combat style. They say that it was once able to solve a problem that, theoretically, was only able to be solved by a true hero."

"Oh yeah?"

"According to the legend, this style commands a power commensurate with that of the seven star heroes. This person is the very last practitioner."

"And what has this person been doing the whole time? Relaxing?"

"I do not know. There are many mysteries surrounding the style."

I guess this world had its fair share of esoteric martial arts. It really was like some old action manga.

"And you're sure about this?"

"Yes. I saw it in action once when I was very young."

I wasn't sure I could really buy into all this.

It all sounded like hearsay to me. I'd have to see a demonstration of these skills with my own eyes to believe it.

"Actually, it seems the warrior had been training on one of the outlying islands in Cal Mira, unable to return to the main island in time to offer us assistance during the last wave, and so asked when the next wave would arrive. I informed the warrior of our current efforts."

"Okay?"

"Had this person been there to help, the battle may have turned out differently."

She was really talking this guy up. Could he really be that good?

I looked around the throne room.

"Where are the other heroes?"

"Mr. Amaki has left to hunt monsters, Mr. Kawasumi is still asleep, and Mr. Kitamura has gone to take his morning bath."

They obviously weren't taking this seriously.

"Mr. Amaki said he would be back before noon."

"Am I the only one you called for?!"

"I am terribly sorry. I sent for the others but received no response."

Just thinking about them was giving me a headache. If I was going to be dragged out of bed so early, at least make it worth my while!

I guess Raphtalia and the others were getting up too. I would have had to wake up anyway.

"So when is this warrior going to show up?"

"The warrior was on a ship that arrived at the harbor last night. I expect the fighter to arrive at the castle just after noon."

That would mean he was either on the ship I'd been on or had been on the ship with the other heroes.

Could there really have been someone that impressive in

the crowd? I would have to wait and see if he was all that the queen said he was.

I was thinking it all over when the door to the throne room creaked open. A soldier came running in with a report.

"The combat advisor has arrived!"

"Well, that was fast."

"Yes, sir! It seems the combat advisor traveled through the night to get here!"

The soldier saluted and bowed.

"Where is this combat advisor?"

"Actually. ..."

Noticing that the queen and I had cocked our heads in confusion, the solider explained where the combat advisor had gone.

"Well, well! This girl is one in a million!"

"Fehhhhhh!"

I went to see the new combat advisor and hung my head when I found him.

He was waiting at the training grounds.

But why was there an old lady rubbing Rishia's soldiers?

I recognized her face. When I had been traveling around and peddling my wares, I'd given her medicine. She'd been very sick in a village that was in the midst of a deadly epidemic.

Shortly after that, a wave had come—we'd first run into

Glass during that wave—and she had fought with us in the town square. She'd definitely managed to hold her own against the wave of monsters.

I'd been calling her old lady—I meant it affectionately.

The old lady's son was decked out in some fancy-looking armor.

The old lady was wearing some Chinese-looking martial arts style uniform.

Was that supposed to mean that *she* was the Hengen Muso Style practitioner? The new combat advisor?

"Holy saint! It's been a while!"

"I'll just ask right up front. Are you the new combat advisor?"

"Yes, I am."

I probably sounded rude questioning her like that.

I had already figured it out, but I guess there was a part of me that hadn't really accepted it.

"After you saved my life, good saint, I dedicated that life to helping this world."

"Right, yes, I can tell. What are you doing to Rishia?"

"Don't you know? Within this girl a very unordinary power sleeps. I believe she has the potential to be the heir to my school of martial arts."

"Fehhh! Naofumi! Save meeeee!"

I ignored Rishia's shout. Could it really be true? Could

Rishia really have a talent for martial arts?"

"So if you're a combat advisor, what level are you at? I think you said before it was the same as your age?"

"Yes, but after that I recovered my commitment to my craft and was able to level further. I am now at level 95."

Level 95! That was really high!

"I had planned to reach out to you, holy saint, once I reached the leveling limit of 100. But if my services may be of use now, I will happily offer them."

The leveling limit was 100?

If we were in the upper 70s, then we were almost maxed out.

That must be why we needed to start focusing on technique.

"Oh, so the max level is 100?"

"Well, yes—normally. However, I've heard legends of another class up ceremony that may allow further leveling."

She could take care of training Rishia then. That would be a big help.

Because when you really think about it, I didn't know very much about how things worked in this world, so how was I supposed to help my party learn anything?

"What about the four holy heroes?"

"They don't share that limitation."

So it sounded like the legendary heroes could level past 100 if they wanted to.

But for everyone else, leveling past 100 would mean finding

out how to perform a legendary class up ceremony. And that knowledge had apparently been lost long ago.

"Where's Raphtalia?"

"She's just over there."

An exhausted Eclair pointed across the courtyard.

Raphtalia was sitting on the ground, looking pretty tired herself.

I wonder what happened. I suppose it was easy enough to guess.

"Are you okay?"

"Y . . . Yes, but that old woman really had her way with me. She said she needed to check to see if I was who she thought I was."

"She's supposed to be really powerful."

She was at a higher level than Raphtalia was. I didn't know what her stats were though.

"Every time I tried to move, she was on me in a flash, holding me back. Nothing I did could throw her off."

"That's really something."

Was she using judo holds or something? Not that I knew anything about that sort of thing.

Back in my own world I was just your everyday otaku. I guess I'd seen some martial arts in anime, but that was the extent of my knowledge about them.

Regardless, if she was able to restrain Raphtalia, then she

must have really known what she was doing.

"I'm sure you are already aware of this, holy saint, but status magic and its effects are simply tools to help lead their user to victory. But they cannot ensure victory. One's true strength, experience, and training all affect the outcome of battle."

"Sure."

It didn't matter how much power you had if you didn't have the skills or the training to know how to put it to use.

Actually, if you didn't know what you were doing, really high stats might end up getting you hurt.

With all the fighting I'd done since I got there, I had come to understand at least that much.

I'd run into plenty of people that, judging from their stats, should have been powerful warriors. But they just didn't know what they were doing. I guess the other three heroes were a good example of that kind of person.

There were many measures of strength that couldn't be summed up by a person's level. I'd just realized the leveling limitation for normal people. If we were almost at that limit, then we needed to think of other ways to improve our battle prospects.

"What sort of weapon do you fight with?"

"The Hengen Muso Style does not require the use of weapons."

"What?"

"Any item that the user comes across can be turned into a weapon—that is the true strength and advantage offered by the style. All enemies fall in its wake."

I had seen her fighting off monsters with a hoe. What sort of martial art didn't choose a weapon to specialize in?

"Now then, holy saint, shall I demonstrate the extent of my abilities in a sparring match with you?"

"I'll be your sparring partner, sure. But how are you going to come at me? You know I can't attack, right?"

"Then I will only use a tree branch as a weapon. You will be fine, holy saint, if you can withstand even one of my attacks. If you withstand the attack, then you can send me away from here."

The old lady broke a branch from a nearby tree and set her footing to fight me.

Just to be safe I decided to change to my highest defense rated shield, the Soul Eater Shield.

"Here I come."

In a flash she was right up against me.

She was so fast! She moved even more quickly than Eclair had the day before.

She didn't move as well as Glass did, but she was moving at least as well as L'Arc.

But it wasn't so fast that I couldn't respond in time.

Before the tip of her branch could connect with my shield,

I held it out further away from my body.

That was something I'd learned to do. It would lessen the power of her attack.

"Excellent. I would expect no less from you, holy saint. You know your way around a battle. But how will you fair against this?"

There was a loud clang, and even though she was only using a small branch, my shield shook and vibrated violently in my hand.

"?!"

The vibration shot up through my arm and over my body.

When it reached my torso, I felt as though I'd been kicked in the ribs.

"Ugh . . ."

Wh . . . What was that? Wait, I'd experienced something like that before. But it had hurt much worse this time.

"This is the first form of the Hengen Muso Style. It's called 'point.' It was originally developed for use against opponents in stiff armor with high defenses. It seemed to be an appropriate form to use with you, holy saint."

I concentrated on a healing spell.

"Zw . . . Zweite Heal."

It was hard to believe she'd generated that much power from a stick. It must have been an attack that was based on the opponent's defense rating.

That was the exact type of attack I feared.

Had he ever managed to use it properly, Itsuki's eagle piercing shot probably had a similar effect.

I'd been able to grab that skill of his out of the air, rendering it useless. I couldn't do anything to prevent the old lady's attack though.

"And yet I'm sure that you know there is simple way to counter this attack, don't you, holy saint?"

"Is there?"

"Yes, there is. I'd very much like to show you."

"Please do."

She'd convinced me. She was a powerful fighter.

If we'd been forced into a real battle, we could still probably defeat her, but as a battle advisor I couldn't have asked for more.

If she wanted to help us, there was no reason to turn her down. In fact, she was about to teach me how to handle the exact attack that had been bothering me the most.

If Raphtalia and the others could learn to fight like that, we'd have a definite advantage.

"So how do I stop an attack like that?"

"That attack works by sending energy at the enemy's interior. It uses the enemy's rigidity and strength against them."

"Hm . . ."

I imagined something like a ceramic jug. If you put a hard bead inside and shook it, it was probably something similar to the effect she was describing.

It was probably wrong in theory though.

If you shook the jug really hard, it might eventually break. But that only worked because the jug was completely hollow—I was not hollow. If the attack worked like the ceramic jug and the bead, that would really screw up my insides.

"The simplest way to repel this sort of attack is to purposefully create a softness and then to use that softness to reject the destructive force."

"I think I get it."

So basically, I had to release the energy before it could start to run wild.

If that jug was more like a piggy bank, then before the coins inside could be shaken around, you had to make a slot for the coins to escape from.

But I wasn't living in a manga. If I could really do something like that, then this really was a fantasy world.

Granted, I had been summoned to another world with a magical shield. I'd been making magical barriers out of thin air. It was probably time to get used to living in a fantasy world.

"I understand in theory, but I don't know how I would go about actually doing it."

It didn't seem like the sort of thing that you could just will into being.

This old lady really knew her stuff.

"Alright, you've convinced me. Please become our combat advisor."

"Thank you very much. Then I will focus my efforts on you and the girls here."

"Good. Just so you know, this woman here, Eclair, is also going to be working with us on swordsmanship. Please teach us all you can."

I pointed Eclair out, and she saluted the old lady.

"I never would have dreamed I might receive instruction from a master of the legendary Hengen Muso Style. Please include me in your teachings. It would be a great honor."

"Ha, ha, ha! My training is tough work. I hope you can keep up."

"I will certainly do my best."

"You're supposed to be the teacher here, aren't you?"

Why was Eclair acting like she was showing up for lessons too? She should be focusing on teaching Raphtalia to use her sword.

And Keel . . . Keel was clearly intimidated by all the strangers. His tail was curled between his legs.

He really was like a dog.

"You want to get stronger, don't you? I'll go through the whole thing with you, so buck up and let's get to it."

It was a good chance to teach him the basics.

We couldn't level past 100, but we could still get stronger if we learned how to fight.

I needed Raphtalia to get stronger than she was, and even Rishia seemed like she sincerely wanted to get stronger.

"Then the training is about to get tough!"

"Yes. Understood."

"Fehhh . . ."

"The other heroes have yet to arrive."

I took the opportunity to explain to the old lady just what sort of a situation we were facing.

I told her that while I wanted her to teach Rishia as much as she could, I also wanted to keep Rishia separated from the Bow Hero.

The old lady waited until I was finished talking before agreeing. She didn't ask any obnoxious questions about it.

"That reminds me, where's Filo? I wanted her to take Keel out leveling after we finished breakfast."

He'd probably throw up if he had to go for another ride on Filo's back.

When he heard me ask about Filo, Keel looked startled and ran behind Raphtalia, shaking in fear. I guess he really didn't like the idea.

"I think she might be with Melty."

"Good thinking. Okay, I'm going to go get Filo and have her take Keel out."

"No! Shield guy! Anything but that!"

Damn, Keel was getting too familiar for my liking.

"You won't get any stronger if you give up now."

"You mean I have to make myself sick or I won't get stronger . . . oh no . . ."

"Not exactly."

"Keel, you're not leveled up enough to make use of the training we're doing here. You have to go level up first."

Considering how much he'd leveled yesterday, it probably wouldn't take very long.

The only way for a lower-level character to get stronger was to start leveling.

Even if he didn't level enough in time to participate in the training, we could always just teach him the things that we'd learned later.

"When Filo gets back, you need to go out with her. But you can work with us here until then, okay?"

"Okay!"

Keel nodded.

We spent the rest of the time until breakfast was ready, learning the basics of the old lady and Eclair's techniques.

It started off with a lecture from the old lady.

"The Hengen Muso Style was first developed so that weak fighters could hold their own against enemies far superior to them in strength."

Apparently, the style relied on the user's manipulation of life energy, or something like that. It was the sort of concept you came across in older manga from time to time. Now we would have to learn how to use that energy ourselves.

"Energy, hm . . ."

Was it something different from SP? Probably.

"For example, the Shield Hero's abilities are enhanced because he is given energy from his legendary weapon."

"Does that mean that I can't practice it?"

"Of course not. It does mean that you are unlikely to have much success manipulating your own energy. However, if you learn the techniques of the Hengen Muso Style, then you will be able to apply those techniques to your skills."

"Huh? What's that supposed to mean?

"The shield hero may be able to increase the power of his special skills. Or at least there is a legend among practitioners of the Hengen Muso Style to that effect."

It sounded like there was another power-up system separate from the legendary weapon's skill system.

I guess that meant I might be able to make air strike shield even more powerful than it was already.

"I see."

So there was a reason for me to participate in the practice, but I wouldn't benefit from it as much as Raphtalia and the others.

"The most important aspect of this is that the techniques that make up the Hengen Muso Style can easily be applied to other martial arts."

"Is that the reason that you don't specialize in any particular weapon?"

"Yes. The trade-off is that you will have to study your weapon of choice separately. Once you have grasped the fundamentals, you can practice applying them to your preferred fighting style."

So what she was basically trying to say was that while there are some attacks that are specific to her style, if you want to use a weapon to carry out her techniques, you will have to find a way to apply the energy manipulation skills of her style to your chosen martial art.

Did that mean that other martial arts would necessarily have better and stronger attacks?

I tried to think of it in terms of magic and skills.

A skill would be equivalent to the Hengen Muso Style techniques, while magic would be like another martial art.

It would be like if Raphtalia was chanting a spell like First Hiding, and I was going to use air strike shield.

When we did that, we had the chance to perform a combo skill called hiding shield, which produced an invisible shield.

Or when Filo used Zweite Tornado and I used air strike shield.

Then we would have the chance to use a combo skill that literally blew the enemy away: tornado shield.

In both situations, air strike shield did something and was important.

But it could be used with different types of attacks to produce different combo skills.

I think that the system she was suggesting worked the same way.

I don't think her style was like a formal school or art but more like a flexible concept that could be applied to any fighting style.

So the beginner user would learn to use Hengen Muso Style techniques, then go on to specialize in a particular martial art as a mid-level user, and finally advanced users would learn how to combine the two to make their attacks even more effective.

"Those are the basics. Now, learning to actually perform these skills is another story."

"You mentioned that Rishia had a particular aptitude for it. What makes you say that?"

"Good question! That girl has an innate skill for energy manipulation!"

"Rishia does?"

"Fehhh!"

The old lady had reached out and touched Rishia's arm, which caused Rishia to scream.

"She learns very quickly. Surface! She will understand the system. Depths! She will master those techniques. That is my plan."

"Surface? Depths?"

"It is a way to express the different capacities we all have. On the surface, anyone can grasp the concepts. But to master them requires a depth of understanding and innate talent."

So without talent, there wasn't much point to it all? With an understanding of the surface concepts, anyone could be stronger than they were. But to really implement them would be more difficult.

"Do Raphtalia and I have a talent for it?"

"It is difficult for me to judge in your case, because you are a hero. Raphtalia, on the other hand, has the potential for discipleship."

It was hard to figure out what she wanted to say. I was starting to get a little irritated by it.

But what I knew for sure was that, after suffering from the attack she'd used against me, I had something to learn from her.

At the very least, if I could learn to defend against defense rating and defense ignoring attacks, I would stand a better chance of surviving my next encounter with L'Arc and Glass.

"Anyway, breakfast is almost ready. Hey, old lady, could I get you to explain all this to the other heroes too?"

"Naturally, that was my intention."

"Any idea what we are going to need to practice these techniques?"

"To truly understand and master them, some time spent alone training in the mountains is necessary. For a naturally talented individual, a month or so of asceticism should be sufficient.

A month? The next wave would he here in two weeks, so

that wasn't going to work. And that was for someone with a natural talent?"

"What about for a normal person? How long would they need to really learn it?"

"Ten years or so."

Well, that wasn't going to work! We couldn't afford to spend years just learning the basics.

We had other things we had to do. I guess we could go to the mountains and wait for the wave to come, but there was too much else to do.

We could continue the training after the wave had come and gone.

"Got it. Heroes have a pretty convenient means of travel available to them, so I guess we could think about a mountain hermitage. We'll keep that option on the table."

We left the training grounds and went to eat breakfast.

Chapter Seven: Impossible Training?

"Is that really what you're thinking?"

After we finished breakfast, the old lady began to tell us more about her fighting style. She had started acting as our combat advisor in earnest.

Just as we were about start the training for the day, the other three heroes all decided not to participate.

We were in the castle courtyard when they decided to leave. Raphtalia, Eclair, the queen, and I all called for them to stop.

Rishia had agreed to study in the castle library until the old lady called for her.

That was the plan we came up with to keep her from running into Itsuki.

Filo had already left to take Keel leveling. Keel shouted something to me as they ran out through the castle gate, but I couldn't make out what he was trying to say.

"We are already leveled up, and we already know how to hold our own in a battle. We don't have enough time to spend training with you."

Ren told us why they were leaving. Motoyasu stood next to him, spinning his spear in circles.

"Yeah. Is that really how you think we should spend our time? I'd rather try and find a better weapon."

I guess that meant he thought his weakness was his weapon's fault?

As for Ren, the way he'd phrased his refusal made it sound like he had something else in mind.

"There's a problem with your reasoning, too."

"Oh yeah? And what's that, Motoyasu?"

"Only boxers can use energy attacks. I'm a spear fighter, so it wouldn't do me any good anyway."

"What are you talking about? You mean monks, right? The class that can't use weapons?"

"You mean ascetics! It's not that they can't use weapons. It's that they don't specialize in any of them."

Okay, it was time to explain a few things to these morons.

Games often had job systems that divided up players by the weapons, equipment, and abilities they were able to use.

I guess they were trying to say that their jobs, by which they probably meant the legendary weapon they were assigned, weren't able to learn the skills that the old lady was teaching.

But what they were really doing was admitting that I was right.

They had all given different answers, but all of their answers admitted that the concept of energy that could be manipulated in battle existed.

That meant that these energy skills really were possible.

Like all the trouble we'd gone through trying to figure out

how to power-up a weapon, it was probably safe to assume that all of their explanations held a kernel of truth.

"We're heroes, aren't we? Don't you think the rules might be different for us?"

"No way. It's not like we can just do whatever we want. What would the point of these weapons be if we could?"

"Yeah. Maybe one of the seven star heroes could learn it. Like the Claw Hero, or the Gauntlet Hero."

I had to admit that they might have been right.

It's not like I could just decide to learn the skills that were available to Motoyasu as the Spear Hero. That wouldn't make sense.

That would be like Motoyasu yelling "shooting star sword!" Would you expect his spear to turn itself into a sword?

And yet the old lady had said that the skills she taught didn't rely on any particular weapon. She'd said they could be applied to any school of martial arts.

They needed to stop thinking of this world as though it operated by the same rules that the games they were familiar with did.

We had an opportunity to learn a new and powerful attack style here. Why not jump at the chance?

I didn't know ahead of time whether or not it would work, but I decided it was worth it to try.

"It appears that the other three heroes reason differently than the Shield Hero, does it not?"

Eclair regarded the three heroes with confusion.

"Who the hell are you?"

Ren was glaring at Eclair. He did not look pleased.

It was his fault though. Didn't he realize that he'd been defeated in one wave after the other?

He probably still thought that the only reason I was successful was because I was cheating.

"Me? I have nothing to do with this Hengen Muso Style. My name is Eclair Seaetto, and I have been summoned to provide instruction in the sword arts."

"Sword arts? Heh!"

"What's so funny?"

His little chuckle had hit a nerve. Eclair took a step toward him.

"Your little tricks aren't going to make w
eak people any stronger. They should focus on leveling."

"Hm . . . It seems that the Sword Hero has confidence in his swordplay. I wonder if I may bother you for a lesson?"

"Eclair, calm down."

"Forgive me, Shield Hero. But I also have confidence in my swordplay. If I have been condescended to, I must stand up for myself."

Oh jeez. I had a regular samurai on my team. She must have been the sort of person that couldn't tolerate having their skills brought into question.

"If you want a lesson, I'll give you one. You'll regret it though."

Ren adjusted his grip on the hilt of his sword while his teammates looked on, concerned.

Motoyasu and his team were watching too. Bitch looked thrilled.

Itsuki and his team looked on but yawned. I guess they weren't so swept up in it.

If they didn't want to be here, I wished they would just hurry up and leave. I didn't want Raphtalia and the others losing the motivation they had.

"The knight, Eclair of Melromarc, will have a sparring match with Mr. Amaki, the Sword Hero. Is that your desire?"

The queen stepped forward and announced. Even if she hadn't, they looked like they were about to start fighting anyway.

I hoped there were rules in place. No one could afford to sustain a heavy injury at this point.

"Very well. The duel shall end when one of you has the opportunity to deliver a final blow. The opportunity for the final blow is the deciding factor. So do not make the final attack and do not use more force than necessary."

"Fine."

"You truly are a merciful queen."

Ren drew his sword and adjusted his stance. Eclair did the same.

"Oh, can I add another rule?"

"What?"

"Eclair is unable to use the type of skills that heroes have access to, so those should be forbidden. Also, I don't know if Eclair can use magic or not, but let's keep magic out of the duel. This is only to test your skill with the sword, after all. Okay?"

That was the only way the duel could serve as a test of their swordsmanship.

It was also a good chance to see how good Ren was, without using any "tricks" or skills.

"Fine."

"But we can use other techniques, right?"

Ren nodded.

I guess that meant that he knew about the ways that other people, ones without access to skills, could fight.

"Fine."

"Very well then . . ." the queen said, raising her folding fan into the air.

"Begin!"

The moment she dropped the fan, Eclair and Ren rushed each other, their swords clanging.

"Hya!"

"Kya!"

After they were locked in place for a moment, they both jumped back a step before rushing forward again.

Ren was faster. He swiped at Eclair a few times a second.

But Eclair could read the movements of his broadsword easily, and she kept out of the way of his blade without trouble. When she found an opening, she thrust at it.

Ren jumped to the side, avoiding the point of her blade, but he had to jump around so dramatically that it was affecting his footing.

At first he kept his feet planted, like in kendo. But now he was jumping around to avoid her thrusts.

"You're better than I thought."

"This is all I've done with my life. Now, Sword Hero, come at me!"

"You asked for it! Time to get serious."

He rushed at her, swinging his sword heavily, then followed up with a quick V-shaped slice.

I don't know much about sword fighting, but I think it was some sort of reverse cut.

From where I was standing, it looked like children pretending to sword fight. One attack didn't seem to lead into the next.

Eclair used the broadside of her blade to parry his attacks, then brought the blade around horizontally, to swipe at his face.

"?!"

Ren was clearly surprised, though he was able to get out of the way without ruining his form.

But he left himself open. Eclair saw the opening and sliced down at him, moving the blade overhead.

Ren saw it coming and jumped backwards to avoid it.

"Ha!"

He recovered his footing and charged her.

Eclair rooted her feet to the ground and thrust forward. Ren had to pivot around the blade to avoid its point, and in doing so he exposed his backside. Noticing his mistake, he immediately jumped away.

What kind of a move was that? It didn't look very cool. Eclair watched him try to recover, apparently rendered speechless by what she was seeing.

From what I could tell, Ren was slowly being put on the defense.

"Ha! I'm impressed that you were able to avoid my attack!"

"What? Excuse me, but Sword Hero, did you dodge my last thrust like that on purpose? Is that how you handle a sword in the world you are from? I've never seen anything like it."

Eclair seemed to be genuinely disappointed in him.

I thought it looked pretty ridiculous too. Why would he show his back and then jump away? Anyone could have just attacked his back.

The two of them kept talking to each other as they traded attacks and blocks.

It looked like Eclair was slowly pushing him back.

She had mostly stopped cutting and parrying. Most of her movements now were thrusts.

Ren had to spend most of his time dodging, jumping to the left and right. It kind of looked like he was just doing whatever he could to keep his distance from her.

"Ha!"

Ren, suddenly decisive, jumped back and kept his distance.

What was that huge back step supposed to mean?

"Not so fast!"

Ren had jumped back to get some distance, but Eclair dashed forward and was right up against him in a heartbeat.

Her sword was ready, and she thrust at his chest. He was wide open.

"No way! Air strike bash!"

"Damn!"

Ren's sword suddenly flashed a bright light, and Eclair's sword was knocked from her hand.

"Well. You got me to use a skill. You must really know what you are doing."

"That means you lost, right?

I know it was just a training drill, but I stepped forward and made sure Ren knew he'd lost.

He could try and be cool if he wanted to, but the rules were the rules.

"I just let her win."

"Oh yeah? It looked to me like you knew you couldn't win on your swordsmanship alone, so you cheated."

Eclair said nothing. She looked irritated that Ren had stooped so low.

"The rule against skills was just something you randomly said."

"If that's true, then you would have been alright with Eclair using magic in the middle of your duel, right?"

Obviously he'd known he was going to lose the fight, so he decided to forfeit by breaking a rule. That was the less humiliating way to lose.

Then he said that he admitted she was a strong fighter because he'd had to use a skill.

Didn't he realize that was the least cool way he could have handled the situation?

"There are no rules in a real battle!"

"Oh, right. Yeah. Got it. Okay."

Even Motoyasu and Itsuki looked annoyed by Ren's behavior.

"You're at a really low level, so anytime I use just a fraction of my *real* power, this is what happens. You need to be stronger if you want to fight me for real."

"Sword Hero, is that all you wish to say?"

Eclair was trembling. She must have been really angry.

I understood how she felt. She'd spent her life working

on her swordsmanship. Of course she would be irritated if someone condescended to her on those terms.

"What?"

"At first I'd thought you were using a style from another world, but in the end, anyone could see you were being dominated. To be honest, I don't believe you have anything to teach me about swordsmanship at all."

"You only think that because you're so green. Go train for a while and come back."

"Really, Ren? I think you might be the green one here."

Ren looked very irritated by what I said. He glared at me.

"I once fought a top player in Brave Star Online. Granted, he was a top player in a different game, but I still beat him! And you call me green?"

"What are you talking about?"

"You said the same thing once, Naofumi. You managed one of the most powerful guilds in an online game once!"

He was right. I had told him about that.

It was when I was trying to convince them that I knew what I was talking about when we were planning a battle formation to take on a coming wave.

"Well, this is just like that. My skills with the sword are first-rate."

"All I said was that I have experience managing teams. Don't you think that's a little different from claiming practical battle experience?"

He seemed to be very proud that he'd once defeated a random player in an online game, but that type of victory was obviously no good for anyone when we were talking about battle skills in the real world.

I was a good example of that too.

Back in my world, I had managed one of the top guilds in a popular online game.

But now I was in another world all together. According to Ren's theory, I was in Brave Star Online. Even if I knew what the rules were, I could win a battle just by wanting to.

Granted, that didn't mean I was necessarily going to lose. But it was a different world. Some of the things I'd learned elsewhere might not be applicable.

So even if I had skills from another game, it didn't mean that I was going to be able to put them to use here.

And that's exactly what had happened. I'd been stuck with a shield instead of a weapon. That meant that the way I fought in this world had to be completely different from anything I'd already learned.

In a situation like that, who would expect me to just walk on up and win battles?

Even if you knew the controls, the rules were different. A top player in one game might not even be average in another game.

"It's the same thing to me."

"No, it's not. If there are any differences between what you've learned and the reality you're in now, then you'll lose. Trust me. I know all about it. Did I ever say what I knew from my guild was definitely going to be applicable here?"

"Meh."

"Meh? I don't think so. You seem to be pretty satisfied with your victory, but do you think you could win if you stuck to the rules?"

Ren crossed his arms and looked away.

Why was he so haughty? He could only win a battle when it was set up to guarantee him victory!

That confidence of his was full of holes. It would come crumbling down someday.

"What's the point in being proud of yourself for winning a game you're already better at anyway?"

"Yeah! I actually agree with Naofumi this time! You're proud of yourself for beating someone who was good at a *different* game?"

"I actually agree with him also. It looks like you think highly of yourself for winning when you've forced your opponent to play an RPG they are unfamiliar with."

Even Motoyasu and Itsuki agreed with me. Ren seemed irritated by their outbursts.

"You're only saying that because you don't understand what VR is really like!"

"You're right. I don't. But look at how upset you are about it. That makes me think that maybe in your world, this person you beat in Brave Star Online was a top player in a game that wasn't VR."

I felt like I was starting to understand what was going on here.

He was thrilled with himself because he'd won a battle against a famous player. That could only mean one thing.

When he saw Motoyasu and Itsuki's reaction, Ren seemed to understand that he was starting to look pretty bad. He pointed his sword at Eclair and shouted.

"Whatever! You're weak!"

"You . . . !"

Eclair was about to scream, but the queen stepped between them and shot Eclair a menacing look.

"Do not disgrace the Seaetto name. Calm down."

"Forgive me."

"Please understand that we have requested your assistance in our training efforts and that this training is of the upmost importance. You are the country's combat advisor, and in doing so you must help us prepare for the coming wave. I believe we discussed the necessity of teamwork during the meeting."

The queen was very forceful in telling Eclair to stand down.

But if we didn't find someone to make the other heroes understand their own weakness, then it was looking like they weren't going to participate in the training that we had planned.

"Of course. I understand."

Our immediate goal was to make the other heroes stronger. We had to do whatever we could to make an environment that would contribute to that goal.

The other heroes and their parties were standing around looking very satisfied with themselves. I hope they didn't think that they were going to get out of this.

We needed to start working together.

And so we decided to listen to the advice of the old lady about Hengen Muso Style and leave to go begin our ascetic training.

"If we have to be mountain hermits, where are we supposed to go?"

"There is a place in the mountains where you can train, in private, to work with energy. It is a few days' walk from here, or one day by horse or filolial. Now then, hero, it is time we departed."

We collected our belongings and left for the mountains.

The castle guards had prepared filolials to take us there. And so we made our way deeper and deeper into the mountains.

We made it to the training spot deep in the mountains. When night fell we would be using teleportation to move, so we didn't bother to set up a place to sleep.

There were wild dragons roaming about the nearby wilderness. We ran into them from time to time.

With all the heroes together they weren't too much for us to handle. I took the lead and held the monsters back, while the others dispatched them.

They were dragons, but they were nowhere near as large as the dragon zombie that we had fought a while back. These ones were only about two meters tall. That larger one we found was probably around three meters tall.

The other heroes were weak, sure, but they weren't so underpowered that they couldn't defeat a dragon here or there.

Finally, we reached the spot we'd been looking for. It was a shallow mountain pool complete with a waterfall.

It was late in the afternoon, and evening would be on us soon.

"This is the place for you to train with energy. Everyone, please take a deep breath and assume a meditation position."

Meditation? She clearly didn't understand the kind of people we were working with here.

Motoyasu clearly didn't care. He climbed up onto a large boulder and crossed his legs.

They'd been complaining the whole way, so I wasn't feeling very optimistic about our prospects.

"God, what a PAIN!"

I could hear Bitch whining off in the distance.

A shadow appeared and whispered something in her ear. She made an irritated face before walking over and sitting down next to Motoyasu.

The other parties all did the same thing. They complained a little bit before finally sitting down.

"Mr. Naofumi."

"Hm . . ."

Raphtalia did the same. She sat down, closed her eyes, and began to breathe deeply.

I followed her lead. I sat down and tried to concentrate.

We were supposed to focus, but what exactly were we supposed to feel when we were sitting down?

Besides, I wasn't really sure what "energy" even was.

I guessed that it was different from magic. Eclair had left trails through the air with her sword though, so I guess that this energy stuff was something like that?

I felt like it would be easier to understand how to manipulate energy if I could figure out what it was.

Only heroes had SP. Was it something else?

For heroes, soul-healing water would restore SP. But for normal people, soul-healing water just helped them concentrate or could bring people back to normal if they had been knocked unconscious.

That made me wonder if this "energy" they were talking about really referred to SP.

Although, come to think of it, I didn't really know what SP was either. Did it stand for "soul points"?

That actually gave me an idea.

I wondered if it felt anything like how it had felt when I first learned how to use magic.

The first time that happened, I had touched a fragment that the accessory dealer had given me. When I did, I was suddenly able to feel the magic power inside of me. Now, whenever I imbued an object with magic, it felt a bit like I was moving another arm that I'd never known I had before.

It felt similar whenever I used magic in battle.

I wonder. If I were to approach energy the same way, maybe I could learn to control it the same way as I learned to control SP.

I decided to try using my SP the same way that I had learned to use magic.

I sat there and spent about 30 minutes trying to manipulate it, but then . . .

"Good! That is enough meditation for today!"

The old lady clapped her hands loudly, signaling the end of the session.

"This all seems completely useless to me."

Motoyasu didn't waste any time getting to his complaints.

I guess you could either choose to see it as a waste of time or as an opportunity to reconnect with yourself.

Ren and Itsuki probably agreed with him, judging from how grumpy they looked.

"Now then, I suggest we move on to sparring work. Is

there a hero who would be so kind as to act as my partner?"

The old lady crossed her arms. The other heroes probably thought she was just a little old lady.

The three of them kept looking around, trying to see which one would have to agree to work with her.

Sigh . . . I assumed it would come down to me. I stepped forward.

"I will."

"Very well, holy saint. Let us begin."

"Sure."

I held my shield forward to defend myself.

The old lady held a stick in her right hand and held her left hand behind her back.

"Hmmm . . ."

She dropped her weight low and then, in an instant, appeared right in front of me.

I knew she would be coming though. She was fast, but I was ready to stop her attack because I'd expected it.

I caught her attack with my shield.

My real concern was that her attacks were defense rating attacks.

My shield reverberated in my hand. The vibrations moved up my arm and spread out to my chest.

She'd said that I needed to create a softness to let the energy out, right?

I focused my magic power in my chest and tried to guide whatever she had put into me back out of my body.

Ugh, it was harder than I'd thought it would be. I kept focusing though and was able to move the thing into my shoulders.

"Excellent work, holy saint. How about this?"

She came thrusting at me with the stick.

I could tell from the feeling I got when blocking her attacks that each thrust was a defense rating attack.

Ugh, I couldn't keep up.

"Argh!"

I suddenly felt as though I'd been kicked in the stomach. She'd knocked the wind out of me. I doubled over and held my stomach in pain.

I hadn't been able to stop her.

And I was sure she was holding back. Had she really tried to hurt me, I don't think I would have been able to stop her first attack.

"You've got the right idea, but your execution is incorrect."

"What do you mean?"

"You think you can do it with magic power, but you are wrong. You need something else as well. You must learn to manipulate your life force."

Didn't she realize that I was using magic power because I had no idea what she meant by life force?

The only way I was going to figure it out was by relying on the sensations I'd learned about my magic power, even if this "energy" she spoke of was something else.

The old lady went on to spar with each of the remaining heroes.

None of them were able to defend against her attacks. They all fell at her first strike.

Finally, after coming all the way out into the mountains and sparring with her, the other heroes finally understood how powerful she was.

And yet they just stood around complaining that they'd lost.

Why did they all have such a bad attitude?

They liked leveling up, didn't they? Why couldn't they apply that attitude to training?

"The holy saint Shield Hero fights differently than the other heroes here today. Today's goal is to destroy these boulders using only your energy. Like this."

The old lady touched her fingertip to a nearby boulder.

It reacted like a piece of soft tofu. Her finger slipped right in, and a massive crack appeared in the stone around it.

"This is performed without using any of the special powers available to you heroes. You can clearly see what I've done, so I would like you all to do the same."

What she'd done was amazing, but how were we supposed

to do the same thing? Was she planning to continue asking the impossible of us?

The other heroes all walked over to boulders and started touching their fingertips to the stones. They complained about it the whole time.

"What about me?"

"As the holy saint is incapable of attacks, I suggest you use this time to meditate on your life force. You must learn to feel it."

"Oh, okay."

I was the only one that had to return to meditation.

I looked over at Raphtalia, who was working a boulder with her fingertip. For a second, I was jealous. I wanted to try alongside her.

Apparently, I was the odd man out.

I sat down to meditate, only to find all sorts of ideas running through my mind.

What was energy? It wasn't magic or SP?

Well, if soul-healing water restores SP, then maybe I'd be able to feel something when I drank it. That something might be energy.

I decided to ask the old lady.

"Hey."

"What is it?"

I got up from my meditating and tossed her a bottle of soul-healing water.

"Tell me something. Does this energy that you keep talking about respond to that? If I drink it, will it help me feel this energy?"

"This is soul-healing water, isn't it? The holy saint certainly does possess some rare items. Unfortunately, no. This is not related."

"Oh . . ."

I guess it was safe to assume that "energy" didn't have anything to do with SP then.

"However, soul-healing and magic water may have the effect of circulating your energy."

Maybe I was getting closer after all. I just didn't really understand what it was yet.

But I couldn't ignore the possibility that one of the other heroes might have known about it.

I had to think. There must be shortcut through all this training. If there was, I needed to find it.

"It's only been a single short day. For such a short amount of time you heroes seem to be on the way to grasping the fundamentals."

The old lady whispered to herself as she watched the other heroes and their parties practicing on the rocks.

I didn't know what she meant. I didn't feel like I was any closer to understanding anything.

All I'd learned was that if I stirred up my magic power,

it had somewhat similar effects to what would happen had I learned to use energy. That was it.

Chapter Eight: Life-Force Water

We ended up training until nightfall.

When the sun went down, we teleported back to the castle and were finally free to do what we wanted.

"Man, I'm really tired."

"I know. That was more taxing than I'd expected it would be."

I was far more tired after the training in the mountains than I had been after the previous day's work with Eclair.

The thought of going through all that again with Rishia and the old lady was depressing.

"Raphtalia, are you going to spar with Eclair?"

"Yes. She says that she has a lot of things to show me."

There was no time to relax. But there was no getting around it—there was only so much time until the next wave, and we had to do what we could.

"I think I'll make up some nutritional drinks. I'll go swing by the apothecary in town. Raphtalia, you go ahead and start your training with Eclair."

"Understood. The castle wizards offered to teach us what they can about magic once dinner is over. If anything comes up, let us know."

It really was starting to feel like we were rushing to get everything in before the wave came.

There was training, sparring, and studying to do. We need to level, and to raise money too, but there just wasn't enough time.

I wonder if that was why Melty's level had been so low?

Thinking back on it now, Melty was very powerful, considering how low her level had been.

I decided to save those thoughts for my walk. I had to use the limited time I had to stop by the weapon shop and the apothecary.

Unfortunately, the old guy at the weapon shop hadn't finished any of the projects he was working on for us.

Granted, it had only been a day, so it wasn't surprising. I moved on to the apothecary.

"What is it?"

Just like last time, the grumpy-looking-but-actually-kind man at the counter greeted me gruffly.

"I was hoping you could show me how to make an effective nutritional drink to combat exhaustion."

"Oh yeah?" he said, sounding uninterested before calmly telling me about the most effective medicinal herbs. Then I had an idea.

If anyone knew about items and the way they affected

people, it was this guy. So maybe he knew something about herbs that affected the "energy" that the old lady kept talking about.

"Do you know anything about a weird medicine that acts kind of like soul-healing water or magic water?"

"What exactly are you looking for?"

"I'm trying to experiment with this . . . thing that doesn't show up in your status menu. I've got reason to believe that it is somewhat excited by soul-healing or magic water. Any idea what I mean?"

That's it. It wasn't exactly a shortcut, but maybe there was a tool out there that would help me figure it out. Like that fragment the accessory dealer had shown me that got me in touch with my magic power.

Come to think of it, I'd gotten completely accustomed to magic use in a relatively short amount of time. That wasn't something I'd been able to do when I first arrived in this world.

"Hm . . . Well, it was a long time ago, but I think that my teacher's teacher had a recipe that sounds like it might fit the bill. Wait a minute."

The man vanished into the back storeroom for a few minutes and returned carrying an old book.

The pages were tattered and worn. It seemed like there were holes here and there in the fragile pages.

"Here it is."

"Life-force water?"

It wasn't a life-restoring medicine; it was a medicine that gave the user more vital energy.

It wasn't very good at helping its user heal their wounds directly. It was used to help the body heal *itself* better. Apparently, it was difficult to combine with other medicines and so never gained much distribution in the marketplace.

Maybe it was like soul-healing water. If anyone who wasn't a hero drank it, it was just a medicine that would help them concentrate.

"To make it, you need soul-healing water and magic water. They need to be filtered and then run through a centrifuge. Then you must collect the resultant liquid."

That was not the sort of process that I had been expecting to hear. To centrifuge the liquid, you needed to have a magic stone, the sort of thing that we had needed to have Filo's clothes made.

"The medicine can be made from the by-products resulting from the production of very strong soul-healing water and magic water. Both of those medicines are quite rare in and of themselves, so you can imagine how few people use this life-force water."

I nodded at his explanation.

So it was like collecting the *sakekasu* from sake production. You could only get that by squeezing the sake liquid from the mash.

It wasn't something that put you at a loss to produce. It was just very rare because the original materials were rare.

Come to think of it though, I didn't know what sort of materials you needed to try and make a vial of strong soul-healing or magic water.

When I say "strong" medicine, I don't necessarily mean super concentrated; I mean super effective. If you made medicine too concentrated there was a chance that it could act as a poison on the user. That was probably why this recipe never found any wide use.

And if it only helped wounds to heal, there would be little incentive to make it in a world where healing magic was commonplace. The simplest potions available were very effective at healing wounds anyway.

Maybe you'd need a stronger potion if your arm had been blown off, but the book also clearly stated that the medicine was unlikely to cure such a grievous injury.

Basically it was a medicine that was very difficult to make with dubious efficacy.

But it might have been just what I was looking for.

"If you already have soul-healing and magic water, can you make it? I think the magic shop down the street has a magic stone that could to the centrifuging for us. She'll let you borrow it."

"Huh? Yeah, I could probably make it in an afternoon. But you don't really want it, do you?"

"I do, and I have the materials."

My shield had given me advanced compounding abilities that had enabled me to make the soul-healing and magic water. I passed them to the man behind the counter.

"Your payment will be the leftover soul-healing and magic water. Will you do it for me?"

The process itself shouldn't have been very difficult. All he had to do was filter the liquids and give them a spin.

I would use the extra materials I had to give it a shot myself back at the castle. But I couldn't make very much of it, which would make experimenting difficult.

"Sure, but that payment won't cover it all."

The guy knew how to run a business.

I found out later that he was actually an old friend of the accessory dealer I'd met on my travels, the one that taught me how to make accessories.

The dealer recognized the taste of one of my medicines and immediately realized where I had learned to craft it.

"So that's how I made this life-force water stuff."

It was evening of the following day. We spent the day training, though I, once again, didn't feel as though I had got much out of it. So when we returned to the castle I stopped by the apothecary to pick up the medicine, then I took it out to where Raphtalia and the others were training in the courtyard.

Just like the previous day, Raphtalia and the others trained with the heroes during the day, only to continue training Rishia and studying magic in the evening.

There were a couple of breaks throughout the day, but all in all it was a very tough schedule.

Still, the evening training was pretty simple. Rishia mostly just sparred with me or the old lady.

Filo and Keel were out leveling on their own.

Keel had already reached level 25, so I was feeling pretty good about that.

But he was having severe growing pains and could barely move by the end of the day. He collapsed on Filo's back while she transported him back to the castle and then fell asleep in his room.

"I've never heard of this kind of medicine!"

The old lad looked fascinated by the bottle I'd given her.

"Yeah, well, I still haven't really figured out exactly what this 'energy' you talk about is. But I think there's a chance that this medicine might replenish whatever it is. Maybe."

"Hrm . . . Well, there are no shortcuts through training, but I can't really deny giving it a try. Rishia has great potential, but she can't go with us to the mountains to practice energy manipulation. Why don't we try it?"

"Fehhh . . ."

Rishia let out a weak little whine. She must have been afraid to act as our guinea pig.

"It's fine. I already tested it to see if it was poisonous. It's not."

Granted, I did have a poison-resistance ability, but I hadn't felt anything odd when I sampled the medicine.

I let the shield absorb a portion of it, along with the soul-healing and magic waters, and while they did unlock an ability related to compounding, it didn't look like it was going to be particularly useful.

I'll go ahead and tell you what shield they unlocked

The magic water unlocked the Ether Shield. The soul-healing water unlocked the Spirit Shield. And the life-force water unlocked the Aura Shield.

Aside from the Aura Shield, they both came with equip effects that restore magic or SP (strong). Those effects apparently naturally refilled those energy sources when they ran low.

But something about that got me thinking.

I guess that could be said about all the shields that I had unlocked up until that point, but when I decided to believe in what the other heroes had said about the way to power-up the shields, new options made themselves available, and those options made the extent of possible power-ups clear.

I had to wonder if believing in the energy that the old lady talked about would create a new power-up option, or some other kind of change, in the Aura Shield.

"I didn't know there were items like that."

Eclair looked at the bottle of medicine I'd brought and nodded to herself.

"I just found out about it myself. How's the training going?"

"Well, Raphtalia gets the hang of things very quickly. Her progress is astounding. I think she will wield a power in the coming battles unlike anything you have seen so far. I cannot wait to see it."

"That's great, but back to the medicine. Rishia is supposed to have an innate talent for this kind of thing, so I was hoping I could get her to try it out."

I could have drunk it myself, but I wasn't confident that I would be able to notice the subtle changes it might cause.

The old lady was pretty confident in Rishia's ability to master energy manipulation. So if I was looking for some sort of effect I'd probably have better luck if I let Rishia try it out first.

"I see. Very well then, disciple Rishia! Please take a portion of the holy saint's medicine, then spar with him."

"Okay . . ."

She was nearly twitching she was so nervous.

She took the medicine from me with a shaky hand, then raised the shaking bottle to her lips before closing her eyes, chasing away her fear and drinking the medicine.

"Oh, um . . . It's not bitter at all! It's actually kind of sweet."

"Well, it is made from soul-healing and magic water, after all."

Magic water tasted like soda, soul-healing water had a chemical taste to it, and life-force water tasted like a sports drink. They all had a pretty artificial taste though. I'd heard you could mix them with fruit juice and it wouldn't affect the efficacy of the medicine.

"Well? Disciple Rishia, do you feel any different?"

The old lady was very excited.

"Yeah, do you feel anything?"

"I'd expect no less of a holy saint. That medicine really does seem to have filled her with energy."

"What? Huh?"

Rishia kept looking at me, then the old lady. She wasn't relaxed at all.

"So? Do you feel different?"

"Um . . . well . . ."

I guess she couldn't really tell. I shouldn't have gotten my hopes up. We were fine without it anyway.

I started to give up, when . . .

"I feel, um . . . warm? And my mind feels clear!"

Rishia explained as if it were the most normal thing in the world.

Really? I hadn't felt anything like that when I tasted it.

"But now I feel like I'm slowly cooling down."

"Disciple! Focus on keeping that warmth within your body!"

"Fehhh!"

Rishia was startled by the old lady's sudden outburst. She hesitantly placed her hands over her stomach.

Was THAT how she was going to keep the energy in?

"Holy saint, it seems she is having trouble keeping the energy still. If she is going to learn how the energy feels, she must spar with it now."

"Got it."

I readied my shield for our sparring match.

Rishia's stats were really low though. So before we started fighting, I cast Zweite Aura on her.

That should have raised her stats enough to help her move and focus. It was a special spell that only heroes could use, and it raised all of the target's stats.

"Zweite Aura!"

The spell reached Rishia, and once it took effect, she looked even more confused.

"I feel even warmer now! Here I go!"

"What the?! Holy saint!"

The old lady called out just as Rishia started running at me.

"What? The match has already started!"

"It seems that the spell you have just cast has stimulated her energy!"

What?! Then I realized something. Another word for "energy" is "aura!"

Right—that's why the life-force water had unlocked the Aura Shield!

I hadn't thought anything of it at the time, bur Rishia's reaction confirmed the connection.

"What?"

Rishia was dashing straight at me, and I could tell she was moving much faster than she had before.

The stat boost that she'd gotten from Zweite Aura couldn't possibly have been high enough to explain the difference.

Rishia herself looked surprised. She looked like she couldn't control it, like she couldn't stop herself from barreling ahead.

"Fehhh! My body won't stop!"

I wished she would stop crying about it.

She came at me with a stick, but I got a hold of her wrist before she could hit me with it and slipped behind her.

Careful not to hurt her in the hold, I forced her down.

But I was in for a shock. She was stronger than she had been before!

Her elbow crashed into my ribs.

And it really hurt! What did it mean? My defense was so much higher than her attack ability that she shouldn't have been able to hurt me at all!

But my side was throbbing where she'd hit me.

"Stop fighting back!"

"Fehhh . . . I . . . I can't!"

Was she being overpowered somehow? It looked like whatever she was feeling was too intense to manage.

For another five minutes, Rishia seemed to be at the mercy of her rampaging body.

Finally, whatever it was wore off, and she sat down on the ground and stared at her hands.

"I . . . I can't believe I have so much power."

"So? Do you think you learned to feel it?"

"Fehh . . ."

I guess not yet. Oh well. If it were that easy, then everyone would know how to use it.

"I have to say, when Ms. Rishia ran to attack the Shield Hero, her speed was really something to behold."

"You're right. It really was."

Eclair and Raphtalia both agreed.

I agreed too. If a bottle of life-force water and a stat-boosting spell could have such a dramatic effect, then we must have been dealing with something powerful.

"There's more. She got in some effective attacks against me without even trying. When she hit me with her elbow, it really hurt."

"Fehh! I'm so sorry!"

"I'm not mad, so don't worry about it. I hope you learn how to control that energy, whatever it is."

There was a limit to how much life-force water we could make, and it wouldn't do us any good to use it awakening a power that we couldn't even control. I checked her stats and there didn't seem to be any change.

Was it just some sort of technical power-up?

"Ok, Raphtalia. You try it next."

"Alright."

If the training progressed faster by combining it with the medicine, then that was enough reason to use it.

I went ahead and cast support magic on Raphtalia, just as I had done with Rishia. Then we began to spar.

But unlike Rishia, Raphtalia didn't seem to be as dramatically affected by the water as I had hoped.

Maybe she had come a little faster? Just a tiny bit? It was very hard to tell regardless, which meant that it probably wasn't worth it.

"If we can use that medicine in her training, then perhaps disciple Rishia will be able to grasp the fundamentals of energy manipulations faster than I had expected."

"Yes! I will do my best to meet your expectations!"

She certainly was calculating. Oh well. If she ended up stronger than she was, that was all I cared about.

I had to admit though, by taking the medicine and then training, it kind of looked like steroid abuse to me. If the life-force water turned out to be addictive, I'd have to cut her off.

"Naofumi! I'm . . . I'm going to try my best!"

Rishia was optimistic about devoting herself to her training. Seeing her like that made me feel like I needed to do my best as well.

The next day I brought the medicine to the other heroes and had them drink it.

It hadn't had much of an effect on Raphtalia or I, so I wasn't sure if it would do anything to the other heroes.

I had them all try drinking it, but as expected, it didn't seem to do very much.

Apparently none of them were having much luck sticking their fingers into rocks either.

The next day, the other heroes began to sabotage the training.

Chapter Nine: What it Means to Train

On the fourth day of training, Ren didn't show up.

I went looking for him, and when I found him he made his irritation clear, saying that if we had enough time to waste on impossible things, we should spend it looking for stronger weapons. It sounded like an excuse to me.

That same day, at around noontime, Motoyasu and Bitch used a portal to escape from the training session.

It wasn't long before I notice that Itsuki had snuck off too.

The queen had already sent orders out to the borders, so they couldn't leave the country. And the guilds had been notified to send them back to the castle. So all they did was go back to their rooms.

In all that had happened, a week had passed, leaving us with only one more week until the wave came.

Then one day I saw the other heroes running through a gate that led to the outer fringes of the castle town. I yelled for them to stop and got them to agree to, at the very least, assist the rest of us.

They agreed to go back to the castle training grounds to help Eclair, the old lady, Raphtalia, Filo, Keel, and Rishia in their practice.

But right from the start it was clear that there was a problem. I didn't want them to ruin the training for everyone else, so I had to ask them to leave the field.

"Why are you bothering us?!"

"That's what I'd like to ask you. Why don't you take this seriously?

"Because there's no point to any of it!"

"If you're going to accept our help, don't you think you need to do what's asked of you? All we can do right now is practice and train!"

Did they think that fighting monsters and leveling up was all they had to do?

Did Itsuki just want to go on quests and pretend to be a secret champion of justice?

"Look, if you want weapons just ask the castle blacksmith to make them for you. As for your levels, they're high enough."

They only wanted new weapons because they wanted to entertain the notion that their weakness was because of those weapons. I felt like I was going to lose my mind if they kept talking about levels.

No matter how much I set things up for them and taught them how to power-up, they didn't listen. Any time they ran into something they didn't like they complained about it. They never thought of how we could work together.

At one point they gave up on trying to break the boulders

like the old lady had said. Instead they went out into the woods and hunted dragons. They called it training, but all they were really doing was playing with skills they already knew how to use—things that they thought made them look cool.

When I tried to stop them, they looked really pissed too.

To tell the truth though, my role in all this hadn't changed since the beginning. I was a shielder, and that wasn't going to change.

But that was fine. The problem was that they didn't plan their attacks with me, so we didn't cooperate as a team. They were only capable of thinking of their own parties.

I thought that maybe they would try and justify it as a means to accrue a stockpile of good materials, but we already had stockpiles of the materials they were getting.

"The blacksmiths in this country aren't very good," Ren said, clearly relying on whatever he had learned in the game he had played.

By extension, it meant that he was speaking ill of the old guy at the weapon shop, which kind of irked me.

It didn't really matter what he said now, but I felt like I wanted him to admit it.

"You know that, because of the game that you played? Have you ever actually used one of the Melromarc blacksmiths?"

". . ."

I'd been right, but it didn't make me feel any better.

Lately he had taken this stance every time we spoke. He didn't even listen to what I was saying.

It was like our relationship got a little bit worse every time we met.

Motoyasu and Itsuki nodded along with my line of questioning, but Ren wasn't ready to admit to his delusions.

"I don't have the materials that are needed to make the weapons I want yet!"

And in the end, all three of them used the same excuse. They didn't want to let the blacksmiths from Melromarc make their weapons.

I had already given all my projects to the old guy at the weapon shop, so I wasn't using the castle blacksmiths either. But by all accounts they were supposed to be very skilled craftsmen.

"What are you so dissatisfied with?"

"Dissatisfied? Fine, I'll tell you! I can't stand the idea of training with a cheater!"

Motoyasu jabbed his finger at me and shouted.

"You like watching us try and do impossible things? You like seeing us look stupid? You coward!"

Ren and Motoyasu nodded their agreement with Itsuki's complaint. They were all glaring at me now.

"I think you hold a grudge against us for not believing you when you were framed, so now you're trying to punish us. You just want to watch us suffer!"

They were really starting to get on my nerves.

Ren's party members were looking around like they could hardly believe what they were hearing, but Motoyasu, Bitch, and the others, including Itsuki and his pompous crew, were staring at me like I was criminal. They pointed at me accusingly.

They'd all used their game knowledge and techniques to level up and gain their power, but when another person outperformed them they called him a cheater? Is that how it worked?

As far as they were concerned, they were special, but any other special person was a cheater. What a bunch of children!

And besides, even if I *were* cheating, what did it matter? As long as we defeated our enemies, what was the problem?

And hey—the enemies were at least as powerful as I was. Did that mean that they were cheating, too?

"I cannot stand behind a country that would support a cheating coward! I'm tired of this place! We're going to do whatever we want from now on!"

Ren yelled, scowling, and turned to leave. Motoyasu agreed with him.

"Naofumi, you've been serving yourself selfishly ever since we defeated the high priest. I can't continue to support that."

Self-serving? The hypocrisy was nearly unbearable!

What was it they couldn't support? They just didn't want to put forth the effort necessary to get stronger.

"To tell the truth, I also cannot stand behind Naofumi or this country's plan any longer."

"Exactly! Well said, Master Itsuki! Let us depart for a new land, where we can further the cause of justice without obstruction!"

Armor shouted his agreement with an obnoxious smile before following Itsuki away.

"I agree. Everyone, the day will come when you will need me. Until then, let us go our separate ways."

What was that all about? Did he think it made him sound cool? He just sounded like a sore loser to me.

Besides, they'd already admitted that I was more powerful than they were, so why did they think I was going to depend on them?

I couldn't picture that ever happening.

But I couldn't hold myself back any longer. I had to say something.

"Ren, you're so smug I can't stand it. You haven't thought about how to cooperate with anyone, not even your own party. If you keep acting like this, you're going to end up dead."

That much had been made perfectly clear in the time since he'd introduced his party to us. I'd watched the way he behaved in battles since then.

Judging from what I knew about games, Ren was the sort of player that would let weaker members of his party die.

"Motoyasu, are you just here to get a harem going? When you find yourself up against a powerful enemy, your harem won't do you any good."

Whenever he had a spare minute, he used it to chase after girls.

He was a hero, so there was a certain amount of strength he could rely on to keep people close. But when the time came to face an enemy stronger than he was, did he think the girls were going to stick with him?

"And you, Itsuki. What do you think justice is? Is it refusing to make an effort so that you can keep patting yourself on the back? Justice without power is worthless, but power without justice is simply violence. Be more objective about what you've decided justice is. You're no better than Motoyasu."

When he came face to face with an enemy he couldn't overpower, his place at the top of the party hierarchy wasn't going to last.

I could only imagine what his crazy party members would do then.

None of them bother to listen to what I had to say. They all took their parties with them and turned to leave the castle grounds.

"Now I see."

The queen came over. She covered her mouth with her folding fan and nodded.

"Mr. Kitamura, I'm sure you are aware of this, but my daughter, Bitch, has a large outstanding debt to the kingdom. Therefore, I cannot allow you to simply leave."

"Kyaaaaaaa!"

Bitch tried to run but tripped and fell. Motoyasu ran to her side.

"How dare you!"

Motoyasu leveled his spear at the queen.

Damn. Had we really reached the point of no return?

"To those of you traveling with Mr. Kawasumi, your families will be saddened by the news of your deaths. Are you prepared for that?"

"Coward."

Itsuki and his party grit their teeth and glared at the queen. Then Itsuki readied his bow and turned to face me.

"Do you think we will give in to your threats?"

The queen ignored them both and turned to address Ren.

"I have informed the Melromarc border guards that they are not to let the heroes pass. I have also informed the guilds that they are not to issue any jobs or quests to the heroes. Knowing that, do you still plan on leaving?"

She was telling them that they would have nowhere to go.

If they left now, only death was waiting for them. It was probably safe to assume that any other country that had a connection with Melromarc wouldn't admit them either.

If they wanted to be free to go and do what they wanted, they would have to find a place far, far removed from Melromarc, both geographically and diplomatically.

Ren wrapped his fingers around the hilt of his sword. He looked ready to explode.

The queen sighed deeply, relaxed, and then raised her face to speak.

"Very well. If you will agree to do two simple things for me, then I will revoke the orders I have issued and you will be free to travel as you wish."

It was a compromise, a concession, and an effort to calm their nerves—a delay.

It was so many things at once that I didn't know what to call it.

She was right that they were all too close to their limit, too dissatisfied to listen to what anyone had to say.

So how do you persuade people like that? All you can do is leave them alone and let them cool off.

The other three heroes all thought that they'd lost the last battle because their weapons weren't good enough and their levels weren't high enough.

So the best way to get what you wanted from them was to give them the breathing room they wanted. Give them a measure of freedom and then offer your assistance when they hit a wall. She wanted to give them freedom so that she'd eventually be able to rein them in. What else could she do?

I was at the end of my rope, too.

Day after day I taught them how to get stronger and provided them with the means to do it, and day after day they refused to listen. I couldn't stand it anymore.

They would have to learn the hard way. They'd have to get themselves in deep trouble before they would understand.

I'd rather avoid that. If they ended up dying or unable to fight, then all of this would be for nothing.

"What?"

Motoyasu barked. He helped Bitch to her feet.

"For the last few days reports of a mysterious monsters have come in from many different countries."

"Mysterious monsters?"

"Yes. I do not have dependable reports on the details, so I cannot tell you much more than that. They are monsters that no one has seen before."

And they were showing up all over the world?

What did it mean? And was that a problem that really required the intervention of the heroes?

How could they show up in so many different places?

"My two requests are as follows: one, the eradication of these monsters, and two, participation in the wave next week. If you agree to follow through on both of these conditions, then I will guarantee your freedom."

"What about Bitch?!"

"Mr. Kitamura, that is another matter. She has a heavy debt to repay. Still, I will permit her to travel with you."

"That's ridiculous!"

Motoyasu was very upset. But didn't he realize that the country couldn't just let a criminal go free without any repercussions?

"Bitch, please understand. You have committed serious crimes and also have incurred a massive amount of debt to the kingdom. Those issues cannot simply be wished away."

"Mama, why do you want me to suffer?!"

"You have no doubt heard that a lion will push its child into a bottomless ravine. If you wish to follow in my footsteps, you must find your own way out."

Bitch stopped her fake crying and glared at her mother.

She really hadn't repented of her actions at all. How could anyone sympathize with her? Only the most miserable group of heroes could.

"Heroes! Do we really want this mother of mine on the—"

"If you finish that sentence, I will revoke my offer. Is that what you really want?"

If I didn't step in here, things might get even worse.

"Even if you killed the queen, would that solve any of our problems? Would it help us survive the next wave?"

I stepped between them and glared at the heroes.

Then I raised my right hand and spoke softly, but with evident provocation.

"Aren't you trying to leave the country because you say you don't have time to waste on this training? And now you want to waste time on something awful like killing the queen?"

I already knew from our time in the islands that they couldn't defeat me in battle.

Granted, I wouldn't be able to damage them either, but I could certainly stand there, deflect their attacks, and hold them off. If they were focused on trying to get through my defenses, the castle soldiers could pick them off one by one.

But that's not what I wanted to happen, obviously.

All I was doing was putting the negotiation skills I'd learned through peddling to the test.

The most important things were to give the customer what they wanted and not take advantage of them.

The queen was going to give them what they wanted—freedom—in exchange for having certain conditions met.

But they weren't listening and they were about to threaten her. To keep that from happening, I had to step in with a threat.

They were so upset and on edge that if I didn't put the brakes on, they were going to explode and do something foolish.

To think it had only taken a week of training for them to get this upset. Just how impatient were these guys?

Bitch hadn't come around though. She was staring at me with hatred burning in her eyes.

I kept wondering if there wasn't a better way, if I'd made a mistake by stepping in. But there was no point in worrying about it. They wouldn't listen to anything I said anyway.

"Fine. We just need to agree to those two conditions, right?"

"Ha! Oh well. But this is the last time we help you!"

"Yes, exactly. When those jobs are finished, we'll be on our way."

Understanding that there was no clean way out of the fight they'd picked, the heroes put their weapons away.

The queen must have been nervous. She relaxed, and the tension drained from her shoulders.

"Very well then, I will distribute instructions for you all. Please go to the indicated countries. If you run into any trouble, don't hesitate to contact me."

A shadow appeared at the queen's side and handed a scroll to each of the heroes.

"Also, please make sure to return to the castle at the end of each day."

"Want to make sure we don't run away?"

"Whatever."

"Oh well."

The three of them all nodded nonchalantly and left.

"So? Do I need to do the same thing?"

"Yes. I would very much appreciate your cooperation, Mr. Iwatani."

"Okay."

The shadow passed me a scroll. I opened it and began to read.

It mentioned a village in the southwest. Was that where the bioplants had gotten out of control? The scroll indicated that the mysterious monsters had appeared there.

There was no indication of a reward. I guess if the whole country was trying to solve the problem then they couldn't guarantee one.

"What about our training?"

"Put it on hold for the time being. This matter must be addressed."

"Fine."

Honestly, Rishia had been improving a bit, but Raphtalia and I weren't progressing very quickly.

We'd only gained a rather vague understanding of our energy. At the very least, I had learned to feel a certain something down within the depths of my being.

When I was very tired I tried drinking the life-force water and was able to sense a little of the warmth that Rishia had talked about.

I'd learned to respond to the old lady's defense rating attacks somewhat. Though the real fruits of the training still seemed far away and out of reach.

"What about Eclair and the old lady?"

"I would like them to accompany you."

"Right. Then I'm going to start preparing to leave."

I swear. Ever since we'd gotten back from Cal Mira it had just been trial after trial, and we'd ended up with little to show for it.

I hoped we could finish this new mission without much trouble, but who knew what was waiting for us?

Then the next wave would come and we might have to face Glass again.

I wasn't sure if we'd be able to count on the other heroes when that battle came, but whatever did end up happening, we had to put an end to all this.

Anyway, before we left I decided to review what we'd gotten out of the training.

Surprisingly, after the class up ceremony we discovered that Raphtalia was able to use magic aside from her illusion magic. In the last week she'd been learning new spells at an unbelievable rate. She was like a sponge soaking up water.

But of course she wasn't able to learn any of the more advanced magic, considering she'd only had two or three days to work on it.

She'd said that, with the help of the royal wizards, she thought it wouldn't be too long before she was able to master the Trifa class of spells.

So there was that to look forward to.

Filo had been taking Keel leveling during the day and then playing with Melty in the evenings. Melty said that she helped Filo to study.

She'd said that Filo was surprisingly good at studying and that she might have a future as a scholar—totally ridiculous if you ask me.

She participated in the energy training from time to time. The old lady said that Filo could naturally manipulate energy.

She said that it was common for monsters to be able to do so.

I asked her how she did it. She said that she "just kinda squeezed herself until it was all ready." Not even Melty could figure out what she was talking about.

Thanks to the life-force water, Rishia had apparently learned to identify the energy inside of her. Or so she said.

She had made the most dramatic progress out of any of us that week.

Her slow, deliberate movements had become smoother and more immediate.

However, perhaps because of that hesitant, unsure personality of hers, she said she didn't feel like she really understood how to control it.

Keel had been leveling quickly, and as you might expect, he had grown quite a bit in that time. Having said that, it would be a while until he grew to Raphtalia's level.

He was at level 34. But he didn't know how to handle himself in battle, so I had him training with Eclair.

"Almost ready to leave?"

"Wait!"

We'd finished preparing the carriage for departure. I was waiting for Raphtalia and Filo to arrive.

We were looking for mysterious monsters. I had no idea what that could mean, or what to expect.

"Excuse me, sir."

"Huh?"

Someone called to me. I turned to see who it was.

Someone was standing there in deep, heavy robes. They looked to be a little shorter than I.

"You . . . you possess the shield of the holy weapons, do you not?"

The person pulled back their hood and I saw her face. I had grown accustomed to pretty girls like Raphtalia and Rishia, but this woman was one of the most beautiful people I'd ever seen. It was the sort of face you couldn't look away from.

It was almost bewitching, in the way Bitch and the queen could be.

I wondered how old she was. Maybe she was in her mid-20s, maybe a little younger.

The queen looked much younger than she really was, so it was hard for me to judge the true age of people.

Even Rishia looked like she was in middle school, though apparently she was actually 17.

Her hair was brown, although it was a lighter shade of brown than Raphtalia's.

She wore it up in a Chinese-style chignon.

Her breasts were very large—large enough that you could see the shape of her body through the heavy robes she wore.

I could see her hands. It was clear that her skin was tight and smooth. I assumed that she had long legs.

She had long, sharp eyes that lent a very eastern look to her. I'll just go ahead and say it: she had a fox-like air about her.

That kind of woman wasn't really my type. I sort of assumed they were out to use you, like Bitch.

"I don't know how holy it is, but I am the Shield Hero. What do you want?"

I had to think of something to say. I'd been standing there silently.

If she started sauntering over to me suggestively, I'd have to cut this short and get some distance.

But she didn't do that. She acted as though she didn't understand how beautiful she was when she, without being seductive at all, humbly clasped my hand and bowed to me. She seemed to be in trouble.

"Please, I beg you. You must destroy me."

"What?"

She hadn't explained herself, and I had no idea what she was talking about.

And besides, I was the Shield Hero. If I couldn't attack, how did she expect me to destroy her? All my forms of attack put me at risk.

"As I am now, I cannot complete my task. So . . . So I beg one who possesses a holy weapon to help me!"

As she was talking, the jewel in the center of my shield suddenly flashed.

What? What was going on?

"What do you . . ."

What was she getting at? I couldn't understand what she was trying to say.

But if the shield was responding to her, then I had to assume that there was something to what she was saying.

"I . . . I'm up there. Please stop me."

She pointed to the sky.

"If I don't know what you are talking about, how am I supposed to help you?"

"Mr. Naofumi!"

"Sorry we took so long!"

I turned to see Raphtalia and the others coming my way. I waved to them.

"You're so slow!"

"Please. If you don't, there will be much unnecessary death. I . . ."

"You have to tell me what's going on or I can't help you—"
I said, turning. But then I caught my breath.

The woman had vanished.

Had she run away because Raphtalia and the others had shown up?

That couldn't be, there hadn't been enough time. It was like she had teleported or something.

"Did you guys see that woman just now?"

"Huh?"

"Filo, you saw her, right?"

"Um . . . ?"

"Rishia?"

"No?"

They all looked at each other, confused.

Filo tottered over and sniffed the ground all around me.

"Um . . ."

What had just happened?

Whatever. I don't know what kind of magic she had used, but we didn't have enough time to entertain everyone that stopped by.

She was probably a monster, or a ghost, or something creepy like that.

There were undead type monsters in this world. Maybe she had just been one of those out in midday, trying to scare me.

I filed the mysterious woman that asked me to destroy her

away in the back of my mind for the time being. There were more important things that needed my attention.

"Alright then, let's get going."

And so we were on the road again to search for the mysterious monsters.

Chapter Ten: Kigurumi

Before we set to work on what we'd been tasked with, I decided to stop by the weapon shop to see what sort of progress the old guy was making.

I asked Eclair and the old lady to wait for me in the carriage. The old lady's son kept watch outside.

"Oh hey, kid."

"How are things looking?"

"Good, good. You know your bird friend came over to play the other day with a friend of hers."

That must have been Melty.

She was the princess! And she was first in line for the throne, considering how unfit to rule Bitch was.

Besides, if he'd ever seen the wanted posters they'd put up about us, he should have recognized the girl.

I was surprised that, after all she'd been through, Melty would sneak out playing with Filo. She must have been feeling a lot better.

"That's great. I don't care about it though."

"I know, I know. But it has to do with why you came. Look."

He vanished into the back room before reappearing with weapons.

The first was Raphtalia's sword.

It looked a lot like the Karma Rabbit Sword. Except, while that sword had been all black, the blade of this one was white.

"That thing had some fierce power in it, didn't it? I used the black rabbit materials you brought me to level this thing up, but it ended up turning white."

"Huh . . ."

"And I went ahead and applied a blood clean 'rinse' to it as well. It's not quite as good as the 'coating,' but it will definitely help keep the blade in good condition."

A blood clean rinse? I guess that was a weaker version of the coating.

"It feels better than it used to, Mr. Naofumi."

"It's sharper too. And there are better equip effects. I have to say, I think this job went pretty well."

"I'm very impressed, sir."

"I did most of the same stuff to the little bird-lass's claws, and those came out well too. Are these from a black dog?"

"Yeeeeah!"

Filo's claws had turned white, just like Raphtalia's sword.

I wonder what it meant? Had the curse been broken? I slowly regarded the two new weapons.

Usauni Sword: quality: high: imbued effects: agility up, magic up, swordsmanship up, blood clean rinse

Inult Claw: quality: high: imbued effects: agility up, magic up, claw skill up, blood clean rinse

The negative effects had been removed, leaving the weapons with only good effects. That looked pretty impressive to me.

In games, I remember always having a pretty hard time removing negative equip effects from equipment.

If this world was anything like the games I'd played, then these weapons must have been a lot of work.

I'd run into the issue when working on accessories in the past. Whenever I finished a piece and found that it had a negative equip effect, I was always upset that they seemed impossible to remove.

"Nice job."

"No sweat."

If they were easier to use than they had been, then that was something to look forward to. And come to think of it, they had official names too, which was different from what we got when the old guy had worked on improving my barbarian armor.

Usauni. Inult. Those were the names of the legendary monsters of Cal Mira.

The Pekkul Kigurumi was in that category too, but I have to say that the boss monsters of the islands certainly dropped strange pieces of equipment.

"Is that your sword?"

Keel was looking at the sword in her hands when he asked.

"Yes."

"Hey, who's that? I've never seen you around these parts. You one of the kid's new pals?"

"Yeah. I'm Keel! I grew up with Raphtalia. Nice to meet ya!"

"Sure is!"

Keel and the old guy greeted one another warmly.

"So what are you going to do about the new guy's weapon?"

"I don't know yet. What do you think? He's started to work on swordplay a little."

"This kid? Hm . . . I would think claws, or maybe jamadhars?"

"Should we go with that?"

"I can't say for sure."

"Well, why don't we come back to it later then. For now he can just stick with a sword."

"Sure."

"Listen kid, of course I'll sell you whatever you want. But I have to say that the sword he's already using is pretty damn good."

That's right, we'd grabbed a sword for him out of the castle storeroom.

It wasn't anything very expensive, but it was probably perfect for him at his current level.

"That's what I like about you, old man: your honesty."

"I just thought it would be a shame to waste a good weapon on someone that can't use it."

It was that kind of behavior—that honesty of his—that kept customers coming back to his shop.

I might be biased because of how much we had worked together, but he certainly seemed more talented than the castle blacksmiths. I wouldn't hesitate to say so.

"The only thing I'm having trouble with is that kigurumi you left with me."

He sighed, sounding disappointed. Then he rummaged in the back room before reappearing with what used to be the Pekkul Kigurumi.

"Hey now, why would you keep it as a kigurumi if you were going to improve it?"

He was carrying something that looked like a kigurumi, but it was all white.

"I was hoping to do something about it, too. But then when the bird girl and her friend came by the other night, I figured it all out. It was a lot of work, you know."

"I've got a bad feeling about this. Don't you dare unfold that thing."

"What is it?"

"Rishia!"

Rishia hadn't heard me. She unfolded the kigurumi to reveal . . .

"Hey, old man. What the hell were you thinking?"

"I know, I know. But I couldn't help it!"

The old guy hid his face behind his hands.

That's right, the old Pekkul Kigurumi was now a filolial kigurumi.

And no matter how you looked at it, it was obvious that it was based on Filo. It was shaped like Filo when she was in her filolial queen form.

So I decided to call it the Filo Kigurumi.

Filo Kigurumi: defense up, agility up (large), collision resistance (small), wind resistance (large), shadow resistance (small), HP recovery (weak), magic up (medium): automatic restoration ability, traction ability up, carrying capacity up, size adjustment, type change/ type change unavailable when monster equipped

The old guy and I both turned our eyes away from the kigurumi.

"Wow! Is it Filo?"

"It's a perfect copy."

"It looks just like you, Filo!"

"What a lovely kigurumi."

"Hey! I didn't tell you to put that on!"

Rishia had already started to change into it.

"What do you think? Kweh Kweh!"

Now there was a filolial queen version of Filo standing next to Filo in human form. Granted, the kigurumi was smaller than her actual filolial queen form.

It was a depressing sight.

I hesitated and then decided to look at Rishia's stats.

They were high! They were high because of the shield's adjustment effect!

They had risen to be one-third of Raphtalia's stats! Before now, her stats were like Keel's when he was in the single digit levels. I was amazed.

To think that a piece of equipment could have such an effect, the type change must have made the monster maturation adjustment effect apply as well.

Well, I couldn't argue with the effects, so I guess she could wear it for the time being.

"Yeah, it looks really stupid, but I guess it will have to do. Keel, you want one too?"

"What?!"

Keel looked at me. His eyes were filled with terror.

We still had the Pekkul Kigurumi that Rishia wasn't using.

The effects were pretty good, so I was just thinking that it might work for Keel.

"No way! I hate that thing!"

"Heeeey!"

"Keel, please choose your words carefully. You'll hurt Rishia's feelings."

Raphtalia chastised him. But Rishia didn't seem to be upset at all.

And there I was, expecting a weak "fehhh" from her.

Whatever. If Rishia liked it then she could wear it. No harm, no foul.

"That's the thing. It's horrible to look at, but the effects are pretty great. If you want to get stronger—beggars can't be choosers."

"Master! Reeeeealy?"

Filo was going to throw a fit. I didn't care.

"Well, that's what I've got for you now. I'll get to work on the lass's armor next."

"What about me?"

"If you leave your armor, I'll work on it. But I can't promise you that it will be ready in time."

"Right. Well, we're on our way out of town right now, so we'll have to do it later."

"Sure thing. I was thinking of making a little small sword for the kigurumi girl over there, but I haven't had the time."

"Oh, well, we still have some time before the wave. Think you can make it before then?"

"I can try."

I was still powering up my shield, so I would just have to depend on that. The armor could wait.

"Okay then, see you later. Thanks for everything."

"By the way, kid . . ."

"What?"

"I can make shields, too."

That was a good point. I could always have him make me shields that I didn't have the materials to unlock yet.

I could unlock shields by absorbing materials into it, but then I would lose the materials. If they were rare, then that might be a waste of good resources. If the old guy made me a shield, I could copy it using the weapon copy system.

I decided to see what he could do with the materials from the next wave boss.

"If I find anything good, I'll bring it over and you can try your hand at it. See you then."

"I'll be here, kid."

We left the weapon shop, climbed into the carriage, and went on our way.

Eclair was very impressed by Raphtalia's new sword. She let out a yelp when she saw it.

The carriage was pretty full—and noisy.

But I kind of liked it that way.

"So where are we off to, Shield Hero?" asked Keel.

"We're off to find this mysterious monster that is causing trouble all over the country. It shouldn't be very strong, so this should be good experience for you."

"Yeah!"

Keel tightened his grip on the sword hilt at his waist. He was ready for battle.

I looked him in the eyes and thumped my shield with my knuckles.

"I'm glad you're excited, but don't go rushing into trouble, okay?"

"I know that!"

"A long time ago, I said the same thing to Raphtalia, but she didn't listen. You're a lot like how she was then. That's why I'm telling you this."

"Really? Raphtalia?"

He looked over at her to confirm. She nodded.

"It's true. I nearly got myself killed. So please be careful, Keel."

"Oh . . . Okay."

I directed the carriage to the village in the southwest.

Chapter Eleven: ——'s Familiar

Filo was a fast runner, so it only took us a day and a half.

We arrived at the village to find it mostly overgrown.

"This was my fault."

"You don't think . . ."

We cut back the shrubs as we made our way through the overgrowth.

Keel was shocked when he found out that I was the reason the village was so overgrown.

I'd given the villagers an improved version of the bioplant seed. But had it sent them back to square one?

If so, then I couldn't complain about Motoyasu. Was this because of the mysterious monsters? Was it really my fault?"

I was thinking it over when we came across a group of adventurers. I could hear them talking.

"You know the monsters around here have great materials."

"Is that so?"

"Why don't you believe me? Anyway we should probably head somewhere with stronger monsters."

"But won't it take a while to level up that way? I don't think we have the time to waste."

"It will be alright. We'll help you, so just keep working until the next wave."

"Okay . . ."

So the other adventurers on the path were also leveling up for the wave.

The adventurers we'd met up until then hadn't seemed to know much about the waves.

That, I think, was the other heroes' fault for not using support troops.

Granted, the queen had mentioned that she would put out word to the adventurer guilds in Melromarc to try and recruit volunteers to help in the battles to come. Maybe these adventurers were part of that effort.

"Hm?"

Filo was looking around for the adventurers.

"What is it?"

"I, um . . . I think that was the scythe guy and the see-through person. Oh! And the sparkly girl, too!"

She had an odd way of putting things, but the only people I could think of that met that description were . . . L'Arc, Glass, and Therese?!

What were they doing in this world again?

But how did they . . . Whatever. If this was going to be a fight, then we needed to hurry and finish it.

"Are you sure?"

"Um . . . no. Maybe just someone similar?"

She seemed to have found something.

"What?"

I jumped down from the carriage and tried to look through the overgrowth.

Hey, I thought I caught sight of someone's backside.

It wasn't them. The hair color and clothes weren't right.

From what I could tell the person who looked like Glass from the back had red hair parted over her neck. And she was wearing armor, not a kimono.

"Was it them?"

"No—not at all."

Well, I hadn't seen their faces, but it certainly wasn't Glass.

"Really?

She chirped, cocking her head in confusion. She had me freaked out for a second there.

I guess she could have changed her hair color as a disguise, but I didn't feel that sense of pressure I had when Glass showed up. It couldn't have been her.

"Where are all the monsters?"

Filo whispered to herself while looking around.

"Huh."

I hoped they hadn't grown more powerful or virulent since I'd last been in the area.

What if the mysterious monsters we were looking for had actually come from the bioplant? Then we would be in real trouble.

"Isn't it weird how quiet it is?"

"Isn't it a good thing?"

Suddenly the bushes around us rustled, and someone who looked like a villager stepped out onto the path.

"Oh, Shield Hero!"

I thought about running away for a second.

If all this overgrowth was my fault, then it would be too awkward to face him.

"Thanks to you, Shield Hero, we've been working in peace."

"What?"

I looked around at the state of the jungle.

"But look at this place!"

"Yes, it's nearly ready for harvest."

"It looks like an overgrown jungle to me."

"We planted the seeds that you gave us and have been able to vastly expand our farming projects. We work on a scale like never before."

He pointed a finger skyward.

There were large, red, tomato-like fruits hanging from the trees.

"The main problem is that we can really only harvest a lot of the same fruit. We've become famous for it though."

"Well, that was fast."

Only two months or so had passed since I was last there. They must have really been working hard.

"So you haven't run into any problems with these plants?"

"Not at all."

"So . . . everything is good?"

The villager seemed to wince.

There used to be an alchemist in the area. He had originally made the bioplant.

He—or it could have been a she—probably would have loved to have seen the huge fruits that now surrounded us.

Honestly, it wasn't very picturesque, if you ask me.

"May I ask what brings you this way?"

"I've heard reports of mysterious monsters appearing in the area."

"Really! Well, it's excellent that you have come. We've been worried!"

"Mind telling me what's going on?"

The villager began to explain, but then . . .

Grumble.

"I'm huuuuungry!"

"Me too."

Filo's stomach grumbled loudly as she stood there staring at the red fruits.

I remembered how she had gobbled up a lot of those fruits the last time we came through.

"Go ahead."

The villagers pointed to one of the fruits and indicated that Filo and Keel could eat it if they wanted.

"Yay!"

They both joyfully started eating a fruit. We all followed suit.

It tasted like a mix between a tomato and an orange.

I guess it was alright. I wouldn't say that I loved it.

But Raphtalia and Eclair were both scarfing the fruit down and enjoying it. Was I different because I was from another world?

Lunch must have been over, because a bunch of villagers came over from the direction of the village. When they went by, they gave us some cooked dishes to eat.

"Thanks for everything."

"Not at all!"

"But be careful."

I tried to signal that those fruits could cause trouble like they had before.

"How did you make these, Shield Hero? They're amazing."

Eclair was stunned by how delicious the fruit was.

"It's like we're in a picture book."

Rishia gasped as she surveyed the bioplant. I actually *was* in a world that I'd found in a book though.

"How wonderful, holy saint."

The old lady seemed to be enjoying the fruits too. Anyway, we all finished eating and went to the village to find out what was going on.

"So what's all this about mysterious monsters?"

"Well, we haven't seen any yet today, but lately adventurers and some people from a nearby village have run into them and ended up hurt. Some have even died. Please, help us be rid of them."

The villager brought over what appeared to be a corpse of a monster that they had saved.

What was it? I turned my head to the side—I'd never seen it before.

It was like a one-eyed bat, but it had a shell of some kind on its back.

It was one of the strangest monsters I'd ever seen.

And it only had one eye! I know I was in another world, but I don't think I'd seen anything like that yet.

"Maybe it was some rich person's pet or something?"

The nobility was in the habit of keeping strange monsters around.

"What could it be?"

Raphtalia examined the body.

Eclair stood next to her, deep in thought.

"Have any of you ever seen one?"

"No, not in person."

"I've fought a lot of monsters in my day, but I don't think I've ever seen one like that. Certainly not in this country."

"In this country? You mean you've seen one somewhere else?"

"In Faubrey I once saw a one-eyed balloon type monster

called a winged float ball. But this is different."

She indicated its bat-like body.

"What is it?"

Rishia was looking at the body too. She was wearing the kigurumi, which sort of sucked all the tension and seriousness out of the room.

"Do you have any idea of what it could be?

"I, um . . . I feel like I've seen it before, but I can't remember where."

"You sure do know a lot. Take the time to think about where you've seen it."

Rishia rubbed her chin and thought about it.

"This isn't the only one, is it? There are more?"

"Yes, there seem to be many of them. But they appear suddenly and at random, which makes it very hard to fight them off."

"Do you mind if I let my shield absorb it? We might learn something about it."

"Not at all."

They agreed, so I absorbed the body into my shield.

———'s familiar (bat type) shield conditions met

What did that mean? It didn't say what the monster was! But it seemed to be a familiar, which meant that it belonged to a witch or something, right? Did that mean someone owned it, or made it? Or that it was a part of a larger creature?

"Apparently it's a familiar of some kind."

"A familiar? Does that mean that it has a master?"

"I guess so. Now we just need to find out who or what that is."

I was curious about what the other heroes had discovered on their missions, but we had to focus on what we'd been charged with first.

I was trying to figure out the next step when a scream pierced the quiet room.

"Monsters!"

I ran outside and looked to see who was screaming.

There was a cloud of the bat-like monsters, probably 30 of them, flying in our direction.

And then their eyes started to glow before shooting heat beams at the fleeing villagers.

"Kyaaaa!"

"Ahhhh!"

What?! The monsters seemed to be aiming for the weakest villagers!

The adventurers that happened to be in town had their hands full just trying to protect themselves.

I ran over to the injured villagers and used a skill.

"Air strike shield!"

The shield appeared in midair to block a heat beam.

"Everyone! Get on the offense!"

"Okay!"

"Okaaay!"

"Understood."

"Fehhh!"

"On it!"

All the people who were traveling with me ran to attack the monsters.

They were hard to attack because they were flying and very fast. It was very hard to get a hit in.

"Filo!"

"Whaat?"

"Use your wind magic! We have to get them down here to do any physical attacks."

Raphtalia was doing her best to fight the bats one by one. There were too many people that needed my protection, so I couldn't help her.

"Get everyone together in one place! That's the only way I'll be able to protect them!"

"You hear the Shield Hero! Everyone get together!"

"Okay!"

The terrified villagers all huddled together in one spot.

The monsters took notice and looked like they were about to attack. Perfect—that was the chance that we were waiting for.

"Air strike shield! Second shield! Dritte shield!"

Three shields appeared to protect the group.

"And then . . ."

I quickly added the group of villagers to my party as support troops.

"What's this?"

"Just accept it! That's the only way I can protect you."

The leader of the villagers nodded and accepted the invitation.

Yes!

"Shooting star shield!"

A protective force field about two meters in diameter appeared around the group, protecting them further.

The only problem with that skill was that it wouldn't let any non-party members pass through it.

Which meant that if I wanted to protect someone with it, they had to be part of my party, at the very least they needed to be registered as support troops.

And after all the leveling up I'd done, the force field would block pretty much everything except for very strong attacks.

I protected the villagers from the monster's heat beams as Filo prepared to cast her spell.

"Zweite Tornado!"

Filo's magic ripped through the air and the turbulence affected the way the mysterious monsters were able to fly.

"Hyaa!"

"Ryaaaa!"

"Take that!"

Taking advantage of the turbulence, Raphtalia, Eclair, and the old lady jumped to attack the monsters.

Rishia and Keel stood there unsure of what they should do.

But at least Keel made an effort. He ran for the weakened monsters and slashed at them with his sword.

"Fehhhh!"

"Stop whining! We need you! Pretend you're with Itsuki and help us fight these things!"

"Ok . . . Okay!"

She ran forward, swinging her sword.

She hadn't dropped her center of gravity though. She'd done better back at the training grounds.

"Ahh!"

But her attack landed. The mystery monster fell to the ground, splashed open.

She dived forward to deliver a final blow, but in her excitement she forgot to account for the shell. Her sword hit it directly.

She was like one of those students who can get good grades, but when it comes time to take a test, they freeze up.

If she would only loosen up that anxiety of hers, she could probably be really useful, even if her stats were low.

"Hit the eye!"

"Okay!"

She did as I said and finally killed the monster.

Watching her flail about didn't exactly fill me with confidence.

Judging from the way the monsters moved, their speed, their attack power, and the way that they held their own against Keel, I guessed that they were around level 35. That was kind of strong.

Raphtalia, Filo, and the old lady were able to defeat them with a single hit, but Eclair and Rishia had to stab them in the eye a few times to take one down. Eclair had special attacks. When she used those she could kill the monsters with only one hit. Keel definitely was not strong enough. He could only manage to defeat monsters that were already weakened.

"I'm doing my best!"

Rishia was putting her weight behind her strikes. She must have been preparing to use one of the special attacks she'd pulled off once or twice during training.

"Hya!"

There was a sharp, piercing sound as she pushed her sword through a monster's eye. The blade came out the back and stuck through the monster's shell.

To put it in gamer terms, she'd scored a critical hit.

I was impressed. She was doing pretty well.

"Whew."

"Did we get them all?"

"I think so."

I quickly looked around the village.

There didn't seem to have been any damage to the buildings. It was like the monsters had only been interested in targeting the people.

I guess that meant that there was someone out there intentionally targeting the villagers. During the waves the monsters would normally destroy buildings and structures too. So these were behaving differently.

I walked off in the direction that the monsters had seemed to come from.

"?"

Just a little ways down the road, I found the corpse of a monster that normally lived in the area.

"Hey, these monsters seem to be attacking things besides humans."

That made me think that maybe this was territorial behavior.

"Well, they weren't all that powerful on their own. Everyone but Keel, go take a look around and see what you can find. If you see anything strange let me know. Villagers, take care of the wounded."

"Yes!"

"Roger!"

And that was the end of our first battle with the mystery monsters.

Raphtalia and the others were investigating as best they could, but I didn't think we were going to find whoever was controlling the monsters.

Our best chance was Filo and her sense of smell, but she hadn't found anything.

The sun fell low in the sky and the village began to get dark.

The villagers hadn't been able to sleep through the night for the last few days.

"Is there anything else you can tell me about what those things might be?"

"Unfortunately not."

"We've kept a lookout and gone searching for them before, but we've never found anything of interest."

So the villagers weren't going to be much help.

I considered going back to the castle with the information we had. But I didn't think it was safe to leave the villagers alone without protection.

It was possible to defend against the monsters, but how were we supposed to attack them? We were missing something.

"Except . . ."

"What? Do you know something?"

"The monsters always fly in from the east."

The east . . .

The mysterious woman that I saw before we left the castle had said something about coming from the east, too. Could they have been related?

"I'm going to the castle to share the information we've gathered. Raphtalia, you and the others stay behind to protect the village."

"Understood."

"Okaaay! Hey, master?"

"What?"

"Those monsters have killed a bunch of other monsters!"

That's right. Filo had mentioned it on the way into the village. We hadn't run into any wild monsters on the road.

She was right. There were way less monsters around than I would have expected.

Raphtalia reported that they had found a lot of monster corpses while they were investigating the area.

"Right, got it. Okay, I'll be back."

I had to go share what we'd learned with the other heroes. After watching the sun go down, I opened a portal and teleported back to the castle.

Chapter Twelve: Getting Ahead of the Enemy

"So those are the monsters we found."

When I got back to the castle, the queen called for all the heroes to come together.

Just as I expected, the other heroes had also come across monsters with strange shells on their backs.

"How could they be appearing over such a wide area?" the queen asked, after hearing all of our explanations.

The queen knit her eyebrows and fell to thinking.

After a minute, she spoke again.

"If the same thing is happening in so many different places at once, it must be safe to assume that something unprecedented and strange is afoot."

"Like the waves?"

"Perhaps. And yet . . ."

The monsters were not behaving the way that the monsters did during the waves. And besides, we still had another six days until the wave came.

Sure, the waves were strange. But even at that, these monsters really took the cake.

"Have you three figured anything out?"

I asked the other heroes.

They all looked as though they had been thinking about something.

But . . .

"Nope."

"Nothing."

"That's right. I haven't figured anything out."

They answered calmly and carefree. It was like our earlier argument had never happened.

Something was up.

"I couldn't figure out what kind of master the familiars serve. Know anything from your games?"

The other heroes based everything they knew about the world from the games they had played.

"No idea."

"I can't think of anything."

"Sadly, no."

They all answered lightly, as though they weren't concerned. Come to think of it, they answered very quickly, too, even though they'd been stressed and ready to snap the last time we'd been together.

They nodded to each other. What was going on?

"You . . . Are you sure you really don't know anything?"

My intuition was telling me that something was up. They were hiding something.

"I said we don't know anything!"

Ren had been so cool and collected just a second before, but he leaned forward and yelled at me before turning his back.

What was that about? He'd just made himself look even more suspicious.

"Naofumi, what makes you think you're the leader of the heroes? Back off already—we said we don't know anything."

"Maybe you should learn to trust people."

Each of them spouted an obnoxious phrase and turned their backs to me.

Did they think I was trying to act like their leader? Ha!

I just wanted to know why they were acting so weird! I should have expected as much from them.

They were still pissed from before, so they were basically refusing to talk to me.

"Anyway, we need to protect the areas we've been assigned. So if the report is finished, I'll be on my way!"

Ren shouted. Motoyasu and Itsuki agreed. Then they all left the room.

Through a window, I saw them open portals and teleport away.

Well, that was weird. Something was going on, I could tell.

"Queen."

"I understand. I will send shadows after them to see if we can learn anything else."

If she overdid it, we might end up in deep trouble.

I didn't know if we could still depend on the other heroes, but all we could do for the time being was to try and figure out the reason for their strange behavior.

"A familiar . . ."

"Similar reports are coming in from our neighboring countries."

The queen opened a map and indicated all the places that the monsters had been spotted.

The range was larger than the entire country of Melromarc. It looked like they were all over the known world.

And then . . .

"They're moving from east to west?"

"It appears so."

The sightings were organized by date, and it seemed like the monsters were moving.

Which reminded me . . .

"Before we left for the village, a strange woman approached me."

"Really?"

I told the queen about the woman that had asked for me to defeat her.

She had mentioned the east. Then she had vanished. I'd thought that maybe it had been a hallucination, but it was starting to seem like something else.

"It sounds like there might be a connection. But what was

this talk of holy weapons? Was she referring to the four holy heroes?"

"That was my guess. Maybe it's an older mode of address?"

"But why would she ask you to destroy her? Regardless, I will look into it."

"Thanks."

My report was finished, so I teleported back to the village where Raphtalia and the others were waiting.

"I'm back."

"Oh, Mr. Naofumi!"

The second Raphtalia caught sight of me she ran at me full speed. She seemed very anxious.

"What's wrong?"

"It's Keel!"

"What?!

Raphtalia took me by the hand and led me to the village clinic.

Keel lay on a bed, writhing in pain as a nurse applied a salve to a huge burn on his back.

"Oh . . . Mr. Shield."

"Are you okay?!"

"Y . . . Yeah. It really hurts, but I'm not going to die or anything."

I helped the nurse cast healing magic on his back. Then she went on to apply more ointments.

"What happened?!"

"I saw one of the monsters flying by. I thought that if there was only one, maybe I could handle it . . ."

"That was foolish! What if you had been killed?!"

Raphtalia's eyes were brimming with tears.

Eclair and the old lady, overcome with concern, were also angry with him.

"I know, I know! I won't do it again!"

The wound was deeper than I would have thought. What was wrong?

What now? It looked like there was something buried under his skin.

Symptoms like that meant . . .

"Keel, did the monster do anything to you?"

"Huh? It shot me with its heat beam. Then I fell over and the monster came and landed on my back. Raphtalia and the others showed up and saved me right after that."

Damn! This wasn't good!

That explained why there were so many monsters. The mystery was unraveling before my eyes.

"This might hurt, but you have to bear with me!"

"What are you going to do!?"

I took some medicine out of my pocket, popped the lid off, and dumped it over his wounds.

"Kyaaaaaaaaa!"

Keel screamed in pain.

But that wasn't the problem! If we didn't do something, his life was in danger.

There was a cracking sound, and something like a tortoise shell began to rise to the surface from under his skin.

"Huff . . . Huff . . ."

"Mr. Naofumi? What's going on?"

"This is what has been causing all the trouble in the village."

The minute I said it, Raphtalia understood what I meant.

The southwestern village was taken over by the crazed bioplant. Then the bioplant planted its seeds into some nearby humans and grew to the point where it was able to control them.

That's right. The mystery monsters had just planted its eggs into Keel's back.

"Ugh."

"He was taking so long to heal that I figured something else was going on."

But this had all happened so quickly. We were dealing with something very dangerous.

"Master!"

Filo suddenly screamed. She'd been on lookout outside.

"What?!"

"I just saw one of those monsters come out of a different monster's body! I saw it!"

What?! So the monster's numbers kept growing because they were reproducing in the bodies of the monsters and people they killed.

"Hurry! Get all of the dead monsters together in one place! We need to burn them!"

There was no guarantee that it was going to work. But if we didn't get all those bodies burned, we were going to be in real trouble—that much was certain.

"Keel, are you okay?"

"Of course I am! But I . . ."

Keel tried to climb out of bed, but he collapsed again immediately.

"I can't . . ."

"Just focus on getting better for now. You're not going to be able to help us in that state anyway."

"But I want to fight with everyone!"

"You're not in any condition for battle. Just make sure you are rested up and ready to help us when the wave comes!"

"Ugh."

Frustrated at his inability to help, Keel buried his face in his pillow and whined.

Raphtalia stroked his healing back.

"Master!"

"What now!?"

"It's a different monster! Not like the other ones!"

"Dammit! They don't let up!"

I ran outside to see what Filo was talking about.

Raphtalia and Eclair and the old lady came with me.

"Fehhh . . ."

Rishia had been on watch with Filo, and she was tottering there, terrified, before the monster as it emerged from the dark of night.

I followed her gaze.

It was about two and a half meters tall—about as tall as Filo in her filolial queen form. It looked like a yeti, and its entire body was covered in fur. Its back was covered with a tortoise-like shell.

——'s familiar (yeti form)

Damn! I still couldn't see the name!

The yeti with the shell on its back raised a heavy fist into the air and came running for us.

It was clearly trying to attack the weak villagers.

"Everyone run!"

"Okay!"

Everyone nodded their agreement and started running.

I stopped the massive fist when the beast swung at us. When I stopped it in its tracks, the others rushed in and killed it.

It wasn't a tough fight at all, but the experience we got from it was on par with what we got in Cal Mira during the activation event.

"Eclair, old lady, what level do you think a normal adventurer would need to be at to fight and defeat a monster like this?"

"Um . . . I would guess around level 45."

"Even if they were a talented fighter, they would probably need to be around that."

Level 45. And that was assuming they were particularly skilled.

So to be safe, a normal person would need to be at level 55.

That meant that anyone that hadn't been approved to go through the class up ceremony wouldn't survive an encounter with a monster like this.

Sure, it's not like these monsters were all over the place. The villagers hadn't seen them before.

But they existed.

"Fehhh . . ."

Rishia, quaking with fear, examined the dead monster. What was she looking for?

"Um . . ."

She appeared to want to tell me something.

If I looked worried as I listened, it would only scare her.

So I made a face like nothing was wrong.

"What is it, Rishia?"

"This monster. I think I've seen it before. I think I saw a picture of it in a book I once read."

"What?!"

"Ahhhh!"

I'd tried not to scare her, but she was who she was.

I had to calm her down—she was still easier to deal with than the other heroes.

"Sorry. So? What kind of book?"

"Fehhh . . . I'm . . . sorry. I can't remember!"

I was a little annoyed with her whimpering, but at least she was sharing information with us.

If she could help us solve the mystery, then she was proving how useful she could be.

She was bookish as hell, but still hadn't been much use in battle.

"Well, what kind of book was it? I'm sure you can remember if you think about it. When you remember, come tell me. That will be our ticket to beating this thing."

"Okay!"

It was best if we took turns keeping watch over the village through the night.

The real problem was that the monsters were all over the country. So even if we protected this village . . . But no—there was no point in thinking that way. It was better to protect them than to leave them.

I'd go report to the queen first thing in the morning. There was the matter of the other heroes to attend to as well.

But the heroes never returned to the castle to give their reports.

Chapter Thirteen: Game Knowledge Bares its Fangs

"Those idiots!"

It was our third night in the village.

The other heroes had come on the second night to deliver their report.

The report from the shadows that had been trailing them came on noon of the third day. The shadow reported that the heroes had left the lands they had been sent to secure.

I had been out investigating during the day, so I didn't hear the report until I got back in the evening.

Keel had been moved to the castle clinic and was recovering quickly.

Rishia thought that she was going to figure out what book she had seen the monsters in and was studying in the castle library.

The mystery monsters were growing rapidly in number, moving to the west, and attacking everything in sight.

The bat-like monsters weren't so powerful on their own, so the country was doing its best to manage them. As for the yeti-like monsters, there weren't as many of them, but they were too powerful for normal humans to handle.

We used the adventurer guilds to recruit adventurers that could help us fight them off.

Anyway, about the other heroes, I'd thought they were hiding something, and I'd been right.

They had attacked the Melromarc border and broken through.

"We have reports of what they said as they stormed the border, which went as follows: 'we have to get through to stop the monsters! Why are you in our way?!'"

I turned that over in my head for a minute and then I realized what it meant. They really had known something about the mystery monsters.

The report said that they had also said things like, "We aren't breaking our promise to the queen," and, "This is necessary to carry out the job we've been tasked with."

"What do you want to do? Should we go after them?"

"Yes, but if we go after them now, we may suffer for it."

"How so?"

"I've heard that they are using filolials and flying dragons— pressing on and on without rest."

What were they after?

Filo was the fastest form of transportation I had access to. Filo was very fast, much faster than normal horses or filolials.

But Filo was a living thing, not a car. She had to rest from time to time.

And if the heroes were really using flying dragons, then we would really be in trouble. They didn't even have to worry about the terrain.

If they used dragons and filolials, then that probably meant they were going places that Filo couldn't get to on her own.

If we wanted to match their speed, then we could keep switching to new animals when one of them got tired. We could match their speed that way, but they had a head start, so we wouldn't catch up with them.

Maybe if we kept Filo on running shifts we could catch up—she was really fast.

Still, we didn't know where the heroes were going.

Even if through some miracle we were able to catch up with them, we still didn't have a way to stop them.

If we tried to force them to stop it would only cause more animosity, and we only had four days until the waves came.

Come to think of it, what would we do if the wave came in the middle of our chase?

Maybe they are going to a wave in another country? But aren't the heroes supposed to come back to Melromarc for the wave?

Regardless, we had to prepare for the wave here. It was our only real option.

Judging by the direction they were last seen traveling in . . .

The queen pointed to a spot on a map. It was a country very far to the east of Melromarc.

Again, the east. That pretty much made it clear. The answer to the mystery lay to the east.

"Based on their speed, it's safe to assume they will arrive three days from now."

"That only leaves them one extra day before the wave comes. What do you think they are up to?"

"I only know that we should stay on our toes. And yet these monsters, could they be . . . ?"

If only we could teleport there. But we couldn't.

We were only able to teleport to places we had already visited and registered.

Huh?

"I just thought of a way to catch up with them. Hold on a minute."

I met up with Raphtalia and the others and found Filo.

"What is it, master?"

"I want to speak with Fitoria."

"Kay!"

Raphtalia, Eclair, and the old lady were confused.

"She says, 'what?'"

I unrolled a map on over a table and indicated where the heroes were headed.

"You have a teleporting ability. Can you teleport us to this spot? The other heroes are heading there. We have to catch up with them and figure out what they are up to."

Filo's cowlick started twitching.

"Uh-huh. Yup. Mkay. She says that area is outside of her jurisdiction, so she can't take us there."

"Huh? Wait a second. Does she know what the other heroes are up to?"

"Yeah. She says she actually wants to help, but that if the heroes are really on such bad terms with each other that it would be better for the world if you just gave up."

Could it be what Fitoria had mentioned before? That after a number of the waves passed there would come a time when all the life in the world would be threatened? Was she saying that the time had come?

She'd said, "You can save the people or you can save the world. If the other heroes really can't get along with you, and they want to abandon their purpose, then you need to survive. Then you can choose to save the world. It will entail great sacrifice, but you will be able to fulfill your purpose."

Was now the time she'd been talking about?

"Is she saying that if all goes well, it could be the end of the waves?"

"Is she saying this is it . . . ?"

"Mr. Naofumi. You're not talking to Filo, are you? What are you talking to Fitoria about?"

"Something that we talked about in private once. She said that there would come a time when all life would need to be sacrificed to save the world."

"Are the heroes trying to save the world?"

Eclair leaned forward and asked me. She found it hard to believe.

"Regardless, we don't know what's happening with these monsters. But it sounds like whatever the heroes are up to might have something to do with ending the waves for good."

"Will it be alright?"

"I don't know, it makes me nervous. We have our hands full trying to protect the country. And yet . . ."

I turned back to Filo's cowlick.

"We can't give up. We're going after them."

"She says, 'Good luck then! I'll be watching from afar.'"

The queen of the filolials didn't seem to care a lick about humans. She wouldn't even tell us where they were going.

Maybe she had realized that she'd done all she could for heroes like us.

I guess I couldn't disagree with that.

The situation was looking dire, but the heroes that were supposed to save everyone were fighting each other.

If I was Fitoria, I'd have been disappointed too.

But I bet she was really waiting for us.

Waiting for us to learn to fight for the sake of everyone. But she wasn't going to do it for us. Maybe that's what she meant.

We all went to go meet with the queen. I explained the situation.

"I see. Well, now we know what the heroes are after, don't we?"

"What is waiting for them there?"

Rishia came running into the throne room and shouted at me.

Her face was pale.

Like the queen, it looked like Rishia had figured something out.

"Feh!"

"What is it?"

"Fehhh . . . Right . . . I . . . Um . . ."

"What is it?"

"When I heard where Master Itsuki was headed to, I remembered where I'd seen those monsters."

"Where?"

"Yes. I saw them in one of the ancient legends about the heroes. Those monsters were the familiars—the servants—of the Spirit Tortoise."

"I believe she is correct."

"Spirit what?"

Come to think of it, there was a legend in my world about a Spirit Tortoise too. It was a mysterious monster.

The four benevolent animals showed up in games sometimes, but the tortoise was one of the more minor ones.

They were four symbolic animals that protected the different cardinal directions.

They were similar to the four symbols, the azure dragon, vermillion bird, white tiger, and black turtle. The four benevolent animals somewhat paralleled the four symbols and were made up of the kirin, phoenix, Spirit Tortoise, and dragon.

They were the same kind of creatures, so a lot of people confused them for one another, but they were different.

The Spirit Tortoise was a giant turtle that wore Mount Penglai on its back.

But the black turtle of the four symbols was different; it has a snake for a tail and stood on long legs. It was the protector of the northern direction.

Mount Penglai was a famous mountain for ascetic training in the east, so a beast that wore it on its back wasn't necessary the protector of the north.

"So? The monsters that are flying around Melromarc are the servants of the Spirit Tortoise?"

"Perhaps . . ."

That didn't sound good. I was probably going to have to step in.

"Hm . . ."

The Spirit Tortoise in my world was a protective spirit that had something to do with floods or something.

I think it was also believed to issue prophecies about the future.

"So there is a giant monster behind all this?"

The other heroes were rushing there without waiting for us because they wanted to feel like they were getting ahead of me.

I didn't want to think about what kind of ideas they had.

They probably just thought that they would get their hands on some good equipment by defeating the Spirit Tortoise.

If everything went well, they would get good equipment and they'd put an end to the newest threat to the world.

They probably thought everyone would love them and praise them night and day.

"But ancient heroes sealed the tortoise away and took the secrets of the sealing process with them to their graves."

"The other three heroes think that they know what to do about it, just because of the games they've played."

If they really did know about the seal from the games, then maybe they knew how to undo the seal, even though that knowledge had been lost in this world.

Come to think of it, Itsuki had said something that made sense in hindsight. He'd said that I wasn't going to be able to be high and mighty for much longer.

When he'd said it, I thought he was just whining. But now it all made sense.

If all three of them were heading for the same place, that meant that the enemy could probably be defeated by people around level 80 or so. Either that or they already knew what to do.

So that's what their game knowledge had gotten them. I wished they would calm down.

I felt like I was going to have to give them a piece of my mind.

"But there are already so many servant monsters. Could the seal already be broken?"

"Maybe."

And if it was, it wasn't the heroes that had done it.

"Let's get prepared for battle, just in case."

If what Fitoria said was true, then the waves might end if we just did nothing and let all this run its course. But there was no way to tell what that would lead to.

She'd said there would be sacrifices. But only Fitoria knew what that really meant.

And besides, I couldn't just sit back and do nothing.

"We're going after the heroes."

"Understood. Thanks to your cooperation, we have discovered the cause of all this. I have asked the guilds for assistance. I hope that they will prove useful."

"I'm really getting tired of the other heroes' behavior."

"I understand. I will try to buy you some time to intercept the heroes in the country where the Spirit Tortoise is sealed."

That would help. We had to find a way to make up for their head start.

But how were we going to deal with the wave in Melromarc?

Hopefully our training would pay dividends when the time came.

Plus Eclair and the old lady were helping us now. So we were in a better position than we had been.

We left the throne room, teleported back to the southwest village, and hitched Filo up to a carriage. Then we departed.

We were about to enter the fray of the real battle, the battle that would determine the fate of the world and the waves.

We crossed the border into the neighboring country at dawn on the fourth day.

Filo had run all through the night. We had just reached the closest border. There was still so far to go.

Eclair and Rishia had both gotten terribly motion sick during the night.

"Sh . . . Shield Hero, please . . . stop the . . . urp!"

"Fehhhh. Burp!"

"If we stop, we won't catch up to them."

They'd been saying stop all through the night. And they had already thrown up everything they had eaten. They were still trying to throw up.

Filo was starting to tire out.

"Guess we don't have a choice. Let's rest."

"Whew! I'm tiiiiired!"

I stopped the carriage and Filo immediately began to snore.

She must have really pushed herself.

We met some shadows on the road and asked them where the heroes had gone.

We weren't even in the right country yet.

They were going to arrive at their destination with only one day to spare before the wave came.

Which meant that we probably weren't going to make it in time.

We stayed on the road though and when there were only two days before the wave . . .

Suddenly, the air was filled with the sound of shattering glass. A shockwave rocked the carriage so strongly it made me dizzy.

It sounded like the beginning of a wave, but it was somehow different.

"What was that?!"

"What?"

I surveyed the area.

For a second I thought we'd been teleported, like what happened when the waves came. But a look outside the carriage proved otherwise.

"What's going on?"

"I don't know yet. Filo, could that . . . could that have been the seal breaking?"

Had the heroes arrived?

A window appeared in my field of view that contained the countdown clock for the wave.

It had stopped ticking but indicated that there were still two days left.

Then, next to it, another icon appeared. It was a blue hourglass with the number "7."

"There's another hourglass, and it says seven. I don't know what it means."

I opened the help menu to see if there was any new information.

But there wasn't.

I realized that this might be a chance to escape from my duties as the Shield Hero. But if I did, if I ran away, how many people would suffer? How guilty would I feel?

"What should we do?"

"We have to find the heroes."

I didn't know what was happening, but we couldn't sit back and do nothing.

"Can we use a portal?"

I used portal shield to check.

Apparently we could.

But I still had no idea what was happening.

Something must have happened in the eastern country.

What had the heroes done?

We all got back in the carriage and spent another day on the road.

We passed through a town on the way, and a shadow appeared to stop us.

"Shield Hero, you must return to Melromarc."

This shadow spoke normally.

The shadow I'd spoken with before had an idiosyncratic way of speaking.

But he looked just like the other ones.

"What happened?"

"You see . . ."

It was the start of everything, of Fitoria's suspicions, of all I'd been thinking about, and of the other heroes' belligerence. Everything was coming to a head, and what happened next would shake the world to its foundations.

Chapter Fourteen: What it Means to be a Hero

"The Spirit Tortoise is moving towards heavily-populated areas. The queen has requested your return to Melromarc."

"What?"

If it was powerful enough that it needed to be sealed away, then it couldn't be good that it was moving into a populated area. Not good at all.

"What have you heard from the shadows tailing the heroes?"

"We haven't heard anything from them recently."

"Hm. Okay, we'll head back."

I used portal shield to return to the castle, then went to meet with the queen in the throne room.

"This had to happen right after we hit the road, didn't it?"

"My apologies."

"So what have you heard about the other heroes?"

I assumed they had reached their destination and used their game knowledge to go and break the seal on the monster.

"It seems the monster was already on the move by the time they arrived. In the midst of all this chaos, they continue to chase after the monster."

"And?"

She hesitated. That meant I wouldn't like what she was going to say.

"We haven't heard anything since."

Idiots. They thought they knew *everything*. They had to go and attack it.

Well, at least they hadn't broken the seal themselves.

I bet they would have done so, thinking they were more than powerful enough to defeat whatever monster came out.

The queen looked pale. I guess her daughter was with Motoyasu—of course she would be worried.

"Master Itsuki!"

Rishia ran off to save him, though she had no idea where she was going.

"Filo, go get Rishia."

"Okaaay!"

Filo took off running after the fleeing Rishia.

"Let me go! I have to save Master Itsuki!"

I wondered if it would make Itsuki happy to see her like this.

"Calm down."

"Fehhh!"

"Stop whimpering!"

"Feh?"

"We don't know what sort of monster we are dealing with,

but we also don't know that the other heroes have died. Don't lose hope."

"B . . . But . . ."

"They always seem to make it out of these things fine. So just calm down."

It was true. They'd lost to Glass, were knocked out by the high priest, and knocked out by one of L'Arc's attacks. But they were still alive.

That was three major battles they'd survived. Maybe they had survived this one, too.

I bet they were all passed out at the tortoise's feet. Maybe.

I had to give them the benefit of the doubt and hope for the best.

"Oh, okay! I hope Master Itsuki is alright."

Rishia sighed, as if in prayer. She was so simple, as fragile as a block of tofu in some ways, but with a spirit like hardened steel.

She was a strange girl—that much was sure.

"I guess we better go see what we can do about this turtle."

"Call it a rescue mission. We must keep the damage under control—we cannot afford necessary loss of life."

Two days later.

I rode out with a group of knights the queen selected, and we formed a coalition army with a neighboring country.

I would be attempting to hold the front line.

As we were setting everything up, we began to get news of the Spirit Tortoise's advance.

Already five cities, three forts, and two castles had fallen. Many, many people had died.

The tortoise itself was gigantic. It was surrounded by flocks of servant monsters.

It sounded like the tortoise was knocking everyone down, and its servants were finishing off any survivors. The reports suggested that the monster was purposefully targeting human life.

"Do you think the heroes are still alive?"

"I'm sure of it."

"How can you be sure?"

"The Church of the Four Holy Heroes in Faubrey has a device that can confirm the status of the heroes. I had them look into it, just in case, and received an answer that they were still alive."

That was good news. Rishia looked relieved.

If we could find some way to defeat the Spirit Tortoise, then there might still be hope for them.

The worst situation would be if the other heroes died and I had to find some way to defeat the monster on my own. Even if I won, Fitoria would come hunt me down and kill me.

"Where are the seven star heroes?"

"I've sent for them, but it may take them a few days to get here."

We could wait for them, but a lot of people would die in the meantime.

And we didn't know if they were going to be powerful enough to even help us.

I didn't know if I was powerful enough to defeat it either.

If we did nothing, it would be the end of the waves, but we couldn't just let it rampage and kill everyone.

We had to fight back.

Was Fitoria even telling the truth? If we let the Spirit Tortoise do what it pleased, would the waves actually stop coming?

"We have to fight back. What can we expect from these soldiers?"

"Our neighboring country has supplied us with knights, soldiers, and adventurers to fill out the army. But another country has already launched an offensive, and they were unsuccessful."

"They attacked before the heroes got there?"

"The Spirit Tortoise had already entered their lands. Their cities were in danger."

"Right."

It might have been reckless, but they hadn't had a choice.

I understood how they must have felt.

"So I'm the only hero we can count on."

I really wasn't fond of heroics.

Wasn't it foolish for a single hero to go up against a monster that was so destructive, especially if that hero was a shielder and incapable of attacking? Was I being foolish? Regardless, the first step was to go see the monster in person.

"There it is."

The queen pointed from the rattling window of the carriage.

I squinted at the horizon—I couldn't believe my eyes.

"I think I can see a mountain on the horizon. It seems to be moving."

THAT was what I had to fight against?

It was so far away that I couldn't really make it out. But it was like when a giant, mountain-like dragon appears in the game where you hunt monsters. Only it was bigger.

It made me think of those ancient myths where people thought the entire world was supported on the back of a tortoise.

Its shell was like a mountain and it looked like there was a ruined city on its back.

So that was the Spirit Tortoise.

"Queen, in the legend of the heroes, when they fought the Spirit Tortoise, how did they defeat it?"

"They were able to get inside the shell through cracks in the mountain range on its back. Then they attacked and sealed its heart, to seal the whole monster away."

So the way to stop it was from inside. But it was so large! Stopping it looked impossible. While we tried to get inside of it, it would decimate the army.

"Do you have a plan?"

"A basic one. It appears to target human life, so we are evacuating all the towns, villages, and forts in its path. We will attempt to lure it into an area where it will be easy to attack."

"I'm sure there's more to your plan, right?"

"Yes. Just like in the legend, the heroes will find a way inside of its body, then attack its heart."

What was I supposed to do? Use the Shield of Wrath and then iron maiden and blood sacrifice?

I had just gotten rid of the curse from the last time. But if the enemy was as powerful as it appeared, then I suppose I didn't have a choice.

"Won't there be a lot of casualties?"

The beast would probably rampage the whole time we were inside of it.

Which meant a lot of people would die before we took it down.

"Yes."

"Let me go! I won't fight! Shield! Send the Shieeeeeeld!"

". . ."

Trash was writhing in the seat next to the queen.

She grabbed his chin and used ice magic to create a frozen mask over his mouth.

Things weren't looking good.

"I understand that. But we do not know of any other way to defeat the monster."

Trash had put me on edge.

What was he there for? He was supposed to be a military general of some kind, but what good would his experience be against an enemy like this?

"No, it won't work."

"What do you mean?"

"Obviously your husband will be no help. I mean, we can't allow the monster to continue its rampage. Too many people will die."

If we didn't know what the Spirit Tortoise's attacks were like, we couldn't come up with a strategy to defeat it.

We had to find out how the fallen cities had lost their battles. We needed to know exactly what had happened.

"I will call the army leaders together for a meeting."

"Good."

I told Raphtalia and the others to wait for me at camp. Then I went to the assigned meeting place for the coalition army.

"Oh! Shield Hero!"

"You must save the world!"

"Please help us. That thing destroyed my country."

The assembled military commanders looked ragged and pale. The situation was looking desperate. If I ran away now, they'd be left without options.

"First we must come up with a plan for how to fight that giant."

The queen addressed the room. Trash was nowhere to be seen.

Had he come he would have just been in the way.

"Right. What are the heroes supposed to do against a threat like that?"

I was a hero myself, but I had to ask.

In the past, I'd managed to defeat a very large monster myself: the Inter-Dimensional Whale.

But this thing was much larger than that. I had no idea what to do or where to start.

"Let's start at the beginning. Does anyone know how to seal the monster away?"

"Yes. We held an investigation and discovered the method."

"And is it a type of magic that we can use?"

"Well . . ."

The queen fell silent. I guess not then.

So no easy solution was going to fall into our laps.

"Oh!"

"But the coalition army wizards can cast it if they all work together."

"So we need to weaken the Spirit Tortoise so that the wizards can seal it away?"

"Yes."

There was a map on the table. I looked at it to see what city was closest to the tortoise's current location.

It was very close. If we didn't do something, the city would be in danger.

"Have you evacuated the city?"

"Not completely. Not yet."

"Damn. So we need to find a way to buy some time."

I didn't know how we were supposed to fight the thing, but it was looking like we didn't have a choice.

The earth was shaking beneath our feet as it walked.

Had we been any closer, it probably would have felt like an earthquake. What were we supposed to do?

And the monster seemed to have a clear goal. We needed to get that city evacuated.

"How advanced are the evacuations?"

"They will not be able to finish before the Spirit Tortoise arrives."

There would be casualties. A lot of them.

Sacrifice for the fate of the world. If I ran away, I'd survive the waves with only a ruined name.

But I had to help. I had to do what I could.

It wasn't for justice or anything like that. It was for the people who believed in me, for Raphtalia . . .

I had fallen silent. The queen took the opportunity to explain what she knew about the Spirit Tortoise.

"But that . . . Can it be?"

"You speak the truth?"

"Yes. If the Spirit Tortoise rampages over the land, it will put an end to the waves."

"Who could believe that? Where did you hear such unfounded absurdity?"

"But what is better? A destroyed world or a world with survivors that can carry on our civilization?"

It was hard to call that optimistic.

Did we force people to die and save the world? Or did we save the people and destroy the world? Weren't there any better options?

I looked through the flap of the tent at Filo, who was resting outside.

Fitoria could have taken the beast down.

But there was no point in thinking about it. She'd given up on the heroes.

The other heroes were still alive, but there was no guarantee that we could all get along.

But if they had lost, if they came to understand that they

really were weak, then maybe they would be more willing to listen to what I'd been trying to tell them. With any luck, Fitoria would change her mind, too.

"What do you think?"

"What is Faubrey doing?!"

"That country is always slow to enter the fray. They only take steps after the problem is already there!"

"We must wait here with the Shield Hero for the arrival of the seven star heroes!"

"But how many cities and forts will we lose while we wait for them?"

"That's easy for you to say. Your country hasn't taken any damage yet! We have to defeat the beast as soon as possible!"

"For the sake of the world?"

"The Sword, Spear, and Bow Heroes have already gone missing!"

The tent was in an uproar.

What was I supposed to say to make them feel better? The heroes had already lost a lot of respect.

There would be resistance to what I said, no matter what it was. I had to be prepared for that.

If the other heroes were still alive, then I was going to have to clean up this mess.

To tell the truth, it didn't matter how many of these people died. They had never been decent to me.

But I had promised to fight for the people who believed in me.

Raphtalia believed that I would fight to save the world, that I would fight to limit the casualties. She was like a daughter. I wanted her to be proud of me.

If this was the only way to save the world, then what good was a world like that?

Fitoria knew it.

"We have to defeat it and save everyone we can."

If this is how things were going to be, then I couldn't act the way that I had up until now.

I had to play the role. I had to be the Shield Hero that saves the world, the champion of justice.

Even if I didn't really believe in it.

I had to do it for those that believed in me.

"The only reason we are in this situation in the first place is because the heroes are so undependable! Look, only one of them is here! Where are the other three?!"

"The other three are currently unaccounted for."

"See! It's all just empty talk! What is the Shield Hero supposed to do for us anyway? He can't even attack!"

"Then you tell me: what is a hero?"

"W . . . Well . . ."

Everyone fell silent, unsure of how to answer.

"A hero has strength and uses it for justice. A hero is brave."

The queen understood what I was saying and supplied the answer.

Perfect. If she understood, I'd carry on.

"Heroism is a matter of the heart. It is the hero that doesn't give up in the face of despair. Heroes fight to protect the people!"

What was I saying?

The words sounded strange in my mouth. I felt a chill.

I was not the sort of person I was pretending to be.

But everyone likes that kind of thing, don't they?

Justice, protection, and willpower and so on . . .

"If all of you in this room together do not have enough strength, then I will lend you mine. I will be your shield."

"Shield Hero . . ."

Some of the generals appeared moved and speechless.

I spoke as loudly as I could. People outside the tent had probably heard me, too.

"Shield Hero. Please forgive my earlier grievances."

"Not a problem. The nobility's . . . Everyone's complaints about the heroes are fair. I accept your anger and frustration."

I held my hand up and spoke to the whole tent.

"But for now, please, lend me your strength! We must work together! We must defeat the beast!"

"Yes!"

A general ran forward and grabbed my hand. He shook it and nodded.

Piece of cake.

That got rid of the problems that we'd face after the Spirit Tortoise fell. And it got the whole army into a fighting mood.

Now we just needed to make a plan to defeat the monster. I would just have to play the part of the hero of justice, like I'd announced.

"Back to the matter at hand. Everyone, don't give into despair. We must think of a way—any way— to reduce the casualties. Even one person saved is a success."

The queen was regarding me strangely.

Anyone that had known me before would immediately know that I was faking all this.

She nodded and the meeting was back on.

"We will implement the strategy once the preparations are complete."

The meeting ended. I left the tent to see Raphtalia stalking over to me, sighing deeply.

"Mr. Naofumi, what did you do this time?"

I'd spoken as loudly as possible, hoping that people outside the tent would have heard me, too.

But judging by her sigh, she must not have heard what I'd said.

"Nothing. It's just like when I taught that charlatan in Cal Mira a thing or two."

"Well, I don't know what you mean. But okay."

"Sis! Master said that all the people in the world . . ."

"Shut up, Filo."

If Raphtalia hadn't heard me, then that was just fine.

She would just worry anyway.

Hm? Rishia was gazing up at me with sparkles in her eyes. What was that all about?

"I was very moved! I'm scared, but I'll do my best!"

I guess Rishia had heard me, too.

Then why hadn't Raphtalia been able to hear me?

Apparently she had been off fetching water.

By the time she came back the tent was in an uproar like I'd caused a fuss.

Up until now, every time she found me in a situation like that, I'd pissed someone off. So it was only natural she'd think the same thing had happened.

"I was quite moved by it as well. The Shield Hero has a dirty mouth, but he sure can give a speech when one needs to be made."

That was Eclair.

She was unbelievably serious and severe, so I'd assumed that she thought little of me this whole time.

"What are you talking about? Hurry up and tell me."

"The Shield Hero . . ."

"Don't tell her. I was only bluffing."

"Bluffing?"

"If I'd run away from the responsibility, the heroes would have lost face. So I just lined up some pretty lies for them."

"Mr. Naofumi, what did you say?"

Raphtalia was sighing again.

But Eclair was speechless.

"I just say what I have to say to get what I need from a situation."

"Even if you act like you're proud of . . ."

"I was moved! Take it back!"

Eclair was acting offended by the whole thing now. I didn't care.

"I've been framed and oppressed. I've been lied to. I learned not to take people at their word without proof. You have to learn that bluffing can be important."

"Ms. Eclair, Mr. Naofumi has a harsh way of speaking, but he always acts fairly. So please believe him."

"Hrm . . . If Raphtalia says so."

Eclair calmed down when Raphtalia talked to her. It made me feel a little strange.

Was I jealous? I was normally the one that Raphtalia had to talk sense into.

"Yes, sometimes one must bend the truth," the old lady said, nodding. "I know of a seven star hero who once did the very same thing."

The old lady knew one of the seven star heroes?

"If only the other heroes would awaken to their true calling."

Who was she talking about?

Whatever. I'm sure we'd meet this hero friend of hers someday.

"Alright, I'll tell you what we decided in the meeting."

"Okay."

"We attack the Spirit Tortoise, and I take the lead. The coalition army will follow behind us, casting powerful magic to support us."

"Just like how we've battled the waves?"

"Isn't that the simplest way? The thing looks really big, but first we have to see how it fights—that will help us buy some time. There is a town in its path that hasn't been evacuated yet."

"Then I guess we don't have a choice."

"Okaaaay!"

"Understood. But Mr. Naofumi, are you going to be okay?"

"The servant monsters can't hurt me. Now, I just need to find out if I can withstand an attack from the Spirit Tortoise."

I could always switch to the Shield of Wrath and use it to block the monster's attack.

But could I control my emotions? I'd have to rely on Raphtalia and Filo to help me there.

"Rishia, get it together."

"Okay! I'll do my best!"

Young girls in love just say whatever they want.

"That reminds me. You need to stop whimpering about everything."

"Fehh . . ."

"That. That little whimper of yours is going to make trouble for you. It's annoying."

"Fehh?!"

"Are you trying to piss me off? If you would toughen up a bit you'd be stronger. That whimper is a good place to start."

"I'll try."

If she couldn't stop whimpering, she'd never really grow. All growth started from inside.

Raphtalia had been like that in the beginning. She was proof that change was possible.

"Rishia, depending on how the battle goes, I may need you to act as the queen's messenger."

"Bu . . . But . . ."

"I know. But that kigurumi has given you a speed boost, and we still need to see how you handle yourself in battle."

She didn't look like she could hold her own in a battle with heroes.

But I couldn't have her getting scared and running away either.

Even in that game where the monsters are the size of mountains, you couldn't defeat the monsters by getting scared and running from them.

First we had to see her fight.

"Understood. We will update our strategy depending on the way the battle goes."

"You're in charge of the support troops. In a worst case scenario, we retreat and wait for the seven star heroes."

"Understood. Mr. Iwatani, you are a source of morale for the troops. You must return from this fight."

"Got it. Filo, run at that big thing."

"Okaay!"

"Raphtalia, it's just like we always do."

"Understood."

"Rishia, just focus on yourself. If things get messy, leave the front line and assist the queen."

"O . . . Okay."

"Eclair. You know how to handle yourself, so you'll be fine. Just fight like you did when you dueled Ren."

"Understood. But why do you mention Ren?"

"Old lady. I don't have to tell you anything. Just do what you want."

"Roger!"

I gave everyone their orders and we started our preparations.

"Here we gooooo!"

Filo took off running and our battle with the Spirit Tortoise began in earnest.

Chapter Fifteen: The Spirit Tortoise

"It's so big once you get up close."

The enormous tortoise was before us, advancing step by step.

When its feet hit the ground, earthquakes occurred. I felt it rattling my bones.

"It sure is."

"It makes me want to run away."

"I know how you feel."

A little over a month ago I was doing all I could just to try and keep up with the other heroes. Now I was facing off against an enemy they couldn't defeat.

It was a real test. If we were in over our heads, we'd have to retreat.

It wouldn't hurt me. If it would end up saving the world in the end—not that I was on Fitoria's side here—that was always an option.

I hadn't saved it for the Spirit Tortoise, but I went ahead and switched to the strongest battle shield that I had.

Whale Magic Core Shield (awakened) +6 45/45 SR: abilities unlocked: equip bonus, skill "bubble shield":

naval combat ability 2: special effects: water element, heat beam shield (medium), magic assistance, magic recovery (small), underwater time increase: mastery Level 65: item enchantment level 6, fire resistance up 15%: karma pengu familiar spirit, water element equipment abilities up: status enchantment, magic defense up 25

The abilities that came with the Inter-Dimensional Whale type shields ended up being better than the Soul Eater Shield.

The whale had used a heat beam attack and had shot it from a spherical crystal type organ. So the shield was like a semi-spherical crystal, and its counter attack was that same heat beam.

It was also a water-elemental type shield, so I expected it to defend well against fire and water type attacks.

I can only really explain that in terms of games that I'd played, but it would mean that water attacks didn't work well against fire-based enemies and vice versa. Some games had elemental effects like that.

If I had a number of shields with different elements to choose from, then I could theoretically choose the shield with the best element for battle against each specific enemy.

The magic assistance and recovery effects would make it easier to cast expensive spells.

And if my magic power replenished itself, that would be much easier than trying to use soul eat to recover lost energy.

"That is one big turtle."

"Fehhhhhh! Master Itsuki!"

The turtle was surrounded by clouds of bat-like servants.

That's right—now that we know the name of the real enemy, I was able to see the servant's real names.

"Shooting star shield!"

I deployed the force field and pushed Rishia behind me.

"Hate reaction!"

I used a skill that caused all the monsters in the area to focus on me. The bat-like creatures all responded by swarming in my direction, firing heat beams from their eyes.

There were so many of them. When they descended on us they blocked out the sun.

I could hear the sound of the shooting star barrier beginning to crack.

It wasn't going to break yet, but it was definitely taking a beating.

"Leave it to me! Hi-yaaaa!"

The old lady jumped out of the barrier. She was spinning like a top, kicking anything that got in her way.

A tornado formed around her and blew away the tortoise's familiars.

"You can't have all the fun! Hya!"

Eclair held her hand to her blade, imbuing it with magic. Then she used the point to draw an "X" in the air.

It remained in the air, flashed, then flew at the enemy.

But there were far too many of them to be beaten back by the old lady's attacks. Every monster she hit fell, but there were many left behind.

But she quickly used the attack again. Come to think of it, her attacks may not have had a cool-down time like the heroes' skills did. If they did, it must have been very short.

It was a good attack. I didn't know if it had levels, but if you worked with it from level one, it could probably end up really powerful.

If we made it out of this battle and ended up with time on our hands, I would love to make her my slave.

I almost couldn't believe my own thought process. If I found a stronger fighter, I wanted them to be my slave.

If I said that out loud, someone would probably slap me.

If both of them had been with us when the wave came to Cal Mira, maybe that battle would have ended differently.

"Hatcho!"

"Hi-ya!"

Raphtalia and Filo left the protective barrier and started to attack the swarming familiars.

"Kiiiii!"

Each time a hit connected, the bat-like familiars let out a squeal and fell to the ground.

I was surrounded by excellent fighters. I could depend on them.

If everything went well . . . But before I could finish my thought even more monsters surged into the air.

"Ta!"

"Hyaaa!"

Raphtalia and Filo were batting them out of the air as fast as they could.

Was it safe to assume the fight was going in our favor?

If they weren't able to break through the shooting star shield barrier, they weren't really anything to worry about anyway.

"Are you okay?"

"Yes. There are a lot of them, but they are not very powerful. We can handle them."

"Good."

I heard something like a heavy explosion and noticed that something seemed to be leaking from the Spirit Tortoise.

I soon realized it was hordes of monsters. They were like gorillas with shells on their backs, and they were running straight for us.

They must have been the yeti-like monsters we saw back in the village.

"Zweite Aura!"

I started casing support magic on everyone.

"First Guard!"

Rishia cast a defense-boosting spell on me.

That was a pretty good idea. Her stats may have been low, but she wasn't an idiot.

"I'm going! Illusion sword!"

Raphtalia's sword flashed black and white as she swung it at an approaching monster.

The monster she hit was sliced clean in two, then those two pieces turned into black and white balls before running into other monsters and destroying them.

Two birds with one stone?

"That was great, Raphtalia!"

Eclair thrust her sword through a nearby familiar and shouted at Raphtalia.

"Yes, I did just as you instructed."

"Let's see if I can't still show you a thing or two!"

"Alright!"

Raphtalia swung her sword in time with Eclair's attack, and their attack effects seemed to synchronize. The monsters around them dispersed.

That was some impressive teamwork.

"Buchikuikku!"

Filo was running through crowds of monsters and kicking the life out of them.

"Ah-cho!"

The old lady followed behind Filo and took out any monsters that had survived her attacks.

"Fi . . . First Water Shot!"

Rishia, somewhat hesitant, shot a ball of water magic from within the safety of the force field.

It didn't kill the monster it hit, but it did cause the monster to stop in its place.

"This isn't so bad!"

It wasn't, but then again, if we'd had trouble with just the servant monsters, then we'd have no chance against the tortoise.

What were we going to do about that thing? The other heroes had probably tried to battle it directly. Since they had gone missing, there was a chance that maybe they were still fighting inside of the giant's body.

"Keep it up everyone!"

"Okaaay!"

"Yes!"

"Fehhhh!"

We kept battling the servants and advancing until we eventually found ourselves standing in front of the Spirit Tortoise.

It seemed even larger up close. Its face alone must have been the size of a village.

What was the next step?

The Spirit Tortoise looked down, directly at us.

"_____!"

The tortoise roared so loudly we had to cover our ears. It didn't look friendly.

The shooting star shield force field looked ready to cut out, so I used the skill again. Within it we were safe from the familiars. I looked up at the tortoise.

It was looking directly at us. It raised its front foot into the air.

"Dammit!"

The foot was swinging at us. I readied my shield.

The shooting star shield barrier broke with that same shattering sound I'd heard during the fight with Glass. Immediately after the field broke, the foot swung straight at me. I held up my shield.

The attack rattled my whole body.

"Ugh."

I was pushed back a few steps. Sure enough, shooting star shield wasn't going to be enough to protect us against the tortoise.

Seeing that the barrier was gone, the familiar monsters crowded towards us.

"Not this time!"

Raphtalia and Eclair jumped ahead of me and beat back the encroaching horde of monsters with a blur of techniques.

Rishia crouched behind me, under my cape, understanding nothing of the situation and whimpering.

"Here it comes again."

We'd been able to survive a direct kick and the tortoise's advance.

Things were looking good.

"Hyaaaa!"

"A-cho! Holy saint, be careful!"

"Yeah! If you get in trouble, I'll protect you!"

The old lady and Eclair fought the hordes of monsters back and made attacks at the Spirit Tortoise's head whenever there was an opening.

I saw a spurt of blood issue from one of their attacks, so the tortoise must have taken damage. It didn't seem to mind though.

The shooting star shield force field ran out again. I deployed another.

"Everyone, get over here!"

"Roger!"

"Understood!"

Immediately after we moved, the sky filled with heavy clouds. Bolts of lightning fell on the familiars as they rushed to attack us.

The smell of burning flesh filled the air as the monsters fell to the ground, electrocuted.

The lightning immediately killed whatever it hit, but the shock also spread out from the target monster, causing other monsters to fall.

It was the support magic from the queen and her troops.

If they didn't get the timing right, the spell could have hurt Raphtalia and the others.

They must have waited to see my shooting star shield barrier go up before casting it.

"Alright everyone! Back on the attack!"

I shouted as the lightning subsided.

I didn't know if our attacks would have any effect against the giant monster, but maybe it was weaker than it looked.

Maybe it was because of the queen's magic, but there appeared to be much fewer familiar monsters than there had been.

We decided to ignore the servants when we could and started to direct our attacks at the Spirit Tortoise's face.

"Take THAT!"

Filo charged up all her strength and kicked the tortoise hard across its giant chin.

"_____?!"

The Spirit Tortoise raised its massive head to dodge her attack.

"Oooh, it's so heavy!"

"My turn!"

The beast's head was raised high to avoid Filo's kick. Raphtalia dashed at the exposed neck and sliced at it with her sword.

There was a sound like a tomato being cut, and a cut appeared at the base of the tortoise's throat.

Blood sprayed out.

But the tortoise didn't seem hurt. The wound quickly

closed itself, and the furious Spirit Tortoise turned its gaze to Raphtalia and Filo.

"I won't be shown up by my students! Hengen Muso Style essence! Full moon!"

The old lady began to furiously kick in circles. Something shaped like the full moon appeared in the trail of her kicks and flew at the Spirit Tortoise.

It slammed into the tortoise's face and exploded.

So that is what everyone was trying to learn how to do when they were practicing with the boulders.

It was too powerful for Raphtalia and Filo alone, but it had to deal with too many attacks.

"Now!"

"Magic thrust!"

Eclair filled her sword with power before thrusting quickly forward.

Her sword was glowing. The end of each thrust produced an impressive concussive force that slammed into the tortoise's head.

The attack was weaker than the old lady's, but the Spirit Tortoise was hurt by it.

"Fehhh!"

Rishia was also rushing to cast attack spells, but they were too weak to be of any use.

Still, she was trying.

Raphtalia and the others had become very powerful though. Thinking back on it, L'Arc and his crew had been oddly powerful, but the monsters you encountered in a typical wave weren't. So even if the Spirit Tortoise was a very strong monster by comparison, was there any reason to think we wouldn't be able to handle it?

"_____!"

A huge magic circle appeared before the tortoise.

I didn't like the look of that.

A second later, everyone outside of the force field fell flat to the ground.

"Ugh."

"What . . . What's happening?"

"I feel so heavy. It's like I'm being crushed!"

"Control your energy!"

Only the old lady was still on her feet. The Hengen Muso Style must have really been powerful!

"What happened?"

"I don't know. It feels like I'm being sucked to the ground. I can't move."

Damn! I didn't know what was going to happen, but it wasn't good. Raphtalia and the others were in danger!

"Fehh?"

Rishia was still whimpering and hiding under my cape.

What was her problem?

The force field was shaking, which must have meant it was still protecting us from something.

I moved to try and get everyone into the boundary of the force field.

"That feels better."

Once they were within the barrier, all three of them stood up.

Had the tortoise used some kind of gravity magic?

But the tortoise's magic hadn't been able to break through my barrier.

"_____!"

"Wh . . . ?!"

The tortoise opened its mouth and howled.

Actually, no. I saw a shining object travel from its torso and up through its throat.

That made me nervous.

I quickly ran to the head of the group and redeployed the shooting star shield barrier.

Crackling electricity issued from the beast's mouth.

Electricity?

Damn! I was using a water element shield!

I switched to the Soul Eater shield as fast as I could and used shield prison.

The monster's mouth was filled with electricity now, and it roared, sending out a cloud of lighting in a straight line.

The stream of electric breath caught up any servant monsters in its path as it flew towards me.

It was like a particle cannon from an anime!

"Ugh."

"Mr. Naofumi?!"

"Waaa!"

"Fehhhh?!"

The force field collapsed immediately, and I could smell burning skin.

Pain overtook my whole body, but I didn't lose consciousness.

There was a second that seemed to last an eternity. I couldn't tell how much time had passed.

"Huff . . . Huff . . ."

It was hard to keep focused on what was going on, but I could tell that the tortoise's attack had ended.

I felt like my muscles were burned.

The last time I'd taken damage that bad was when I'd used blood sacrifice.

Actually, it felt worse than that.

That was close. If I'd still been using the Whale Magic Core Shield, I probably would have been vaporized.

"Master?!"

"Mr. Naofumi?!"

I wanted to cast a healing spell on myself, but I couldn't concentrate.

A second later a warm, healing light fell on me.

I saw my wounds heal themselves, but it would still be a while before they healed completely.

"Zweite Heal!"

I cast a healing spell on myself and blocked the tortoise's foot that was swinging at me to finish me off.

Yes, I could think again. I assumed that the queen had cast a spell to save me.

Someone had saved me anyway. Apparently the Soul Eater Shield wasn't powerful enough to block that last breath attack.

Luckily, the tortoise needed to recharge if it wanted to use that attack again.

I turned to survey the damage. Everywhere aside from where I'd protected was completely uprooted and destroyed. A mountain in the distance had been ruined. It had been reduced to a pile of rocks.

"Filo, charge up your magic power."

"Okay!"

I had a bottle of magic water prepared for times like these. I tossed it to Filo.

The Spirit Tortoise had noticed that we were still moving. It formed another magic circle in the air and raised a foot to crush us.

But I wouldn't let it!

"Shield prison!"

A cage of shields appeared around the force field.

There was a cacophony of clanging against the shields, but when the shield prison broke, the force field beneath it stopped the foot.

I wasn't sure if it could withstand the tortoise's bodyweight though.

The barrier started to crack—it wouldn't hold out much longer.

"We're moving. Stick with me! Whatever you do, don't step out of the barrier."

There was no need to just stand there and let the monster step on us.

"Okay!"

"Okaaay!"

"Fehh . . . Alright."

Once all five of them agreed, we took off running from the Spirit Tortoise's foot.

There was a crash and an earthquake where the foot came down. Clouds of dust billowed up around it.

None of the dust crossed the shooting star shield barrier.

"Well, we were able to withstand it, for now."

"It looks like he can't find us in all the dust."

"It looks like he thinks he already got you, doesn't it? Is your magic already depleted?"

Maybe he could sense our magic power to find out where we were.

You could tell just by looking at the tortoise that it had lost us in the dust clouds.

Or I wondered if it used the eyes of its servant monsters to figure out where things were.

"Ugh . . . But our chance to attack . . ."

Familiars were dropping heavily out of the air all around us.

The tortoise was unsure. Maybe it was trying to check and see if we were dead.

There was no time—what to do?

"We don't have another attack, do we?"

"We do, but it's not ready."

"Right. Using it once is exhausting."

It sounded like they had a plan.

But if they could only attack once there could be a problem. If the attack didn't kill the monster, we'd have to retreat.

"Raphtalia, can you use that thing again?"

"Yes, you mean the special attack I do with Eclair?"

"Yeah. Do your best!"

"Okay!"

"I'll help the bird god loosen up a bit!"

The old lady ran around Filo and punched her here and there.

"Ouch! Stop that!"

"Old lady, stop being a pain."

The old lady seemed to enjoy causing Filo pain. Creep.

"Huh? I kinda feel good! Master!"

"Oh yeah? I guess those were pressure points or something."

She was a teacher of an impressive school of martial arts after all. And this was a different universe. I guess she could do things like that.

So that was good news.

"Can I leave this up to you two?"

We'd gotten in a good hit at its throat before. With any luck, maybe we could finish it off.

"Leave it to us."

"Yeah."

Raphtalia and Filo both crouched into position for their strongest attacks.

I recognized Filo's immediately.

She started to flap her wings.

She was focusing her magic power, and it was strong enough to see with the naked eye. A whirling vortex of wind appeared behind her.

"I'm almost ready, sis!"

"I need more time."

Raphtalia's tail was all puffed up.

Then it grew even puffier. A number of magic circles, like mandalas, appeared all around her. She was condensing all of her magic power.

"_____!"

The tortoise noticed them and started to lurch in their direction.

Damn. The dust had started to clear. He must have seen us!"

Just like last time, the Spirit Tortoise opened its mouth wide and howled.

Its torso started to glow, too. It was definitely about to use that electric attack again.

I thought we'd have more time!

"He's attacking! Are you ready yet?!"

"We just need a little more time!"

"Fine. I'll block it again. Use the extra time to charge your attacks as much as you can."

"Okaaaay!"

"Understood."

To survive the attack I would need to have the shooting star shield barrier in place.

I tried to recall what I'd learned in my week of training.

I didn't know if I could do it yet, but I needed to try.

I focused all my magic into my hands.

"Shooting star shield! Air strike shield! Second shield! Dritte shield! Shield prison!"

Before me three shields expanded to protect us from the front. Behind that line of shields the shield prison cage appeared. Our defenses were set.

It was the most defensive position I'd ever taken. Last time the tortoise used this attack the barrier and shield prison had broken. Let's see what it could do this time.

When the skills deployed I felt my magic power drain away.

I didn't know what that meant or if it would help.

I wasn't sure that I understood what the old woman's energy was or if I could use it.

But I bet I could survive one more attack from this monster!"

"_____!"

A dense stream of particles flew from the tortoise's mouth.

The attack broke the air strike shield, then the second shield cracked, and finally the particles burst through the dritte shield.

It was a very powerful attack, but it lost power each layer it went through.

It hit the shield prison next.

It stayed put for a few seconds before a hole appeared on one side. The stream of particles flew into the hole.

The interior of the prison filled with light for a moment before breaking.

I held my shield with both hands and readied for impact.

". . . !"

The power of the stream as it slammed against the shooting star shield force field was amazing, but it wasn't as strong as last time.

A crack appeared, and then the barrier fell.

The attack was coming straight at me.

I moved my magic power into my hands and gripped my shield with all my might.

"Ugh!"

The shield conducted the charged electric particles. My whole body, inside and out, sizzled painfully.

I grit my teeth against the pain and pushed forward with my shield.

The attack ceased a few seconds later. I had survived it.

My shield was smoking in my hands.

But Raphtalia and the others were safe behind me.

"I'm ready! Filo?"

"Yes!"

Raphtalia climbed on Filo's back and released her charged up magic power.

"Spiral . . ."

"Directional . . ."

Dust and light began to swirl around them.

The light split into eight black and white balls.

Raphtalia's attacks always had a somewhat eastern flair to them.

"Strike!"

"Sword of heaven!"

In a flash, they flew straight through the tortoise's throat. They moved like a beam of light.

The Spirit Tortoise was shocked.

But no, its body was already sliced apart. It didn't even have time to react.

That's right. The massive head was torn clear from its neck, and it flew through the air, showering the whole area with hot blood.

The tortoise's torso fell to the ground with a heavy thud.

"We did it!"

If its head was gone, it was safe to assume we'd won.

The battle had been easier than I'd expected.

I guess we didn't really have to get inside it and seal its heart away.

The army behind us was cheering.

"Fehhh . . ."

Raphtalia and Filo landed and then collapsed.

"We did it."

"Yeah, you did it. Good work."

If we could come up with attacks like that, then we weren't going to lose.

We were definitely much stronger than the other heroes now.

"Yes, that was amazing. Even after all the training we did together, your power was astounding, Raphtalia."

"Only because you taught me how to do it, Eclair."

"No, your attack was very surprising. You must be more powerful than even the Sword Hero."

Compared to Ren? Actually, yeah, she probably was. The other heroes were far too weak.

But he could still power-up, if he'd only listen.

But where were they, anyway? What were they doing?

"And the Shield Hero, Mr. Iwatani, you were amazing. You defended against that terrible attack not once, but twice. You truly are the Shield Hero."

"Yeah well, that's all I *can* do."

Glass's attacks in the last wave had been very powerful, but the Spirit Tortoise was no pushover either.

How much longer could I count on being able to defend against these attacks?

If the day came that I couldn't stop an attack, I wouldn't be the only one to suffer for it. All my friends would die, too.

I had to remember that.

I didn't tell anyone, but I promised myself not to let that happened.

"I'm glad that's over."

"You were amazing."

Rishia was very impressed.

I wanted to say something, so I opened my mouth.

"Rishia, you can do everything we did if you work at it."

"Fehhhh . . . I could never!"

"You can. You will!"

"I could never!"

Rishia just kept saying that she could never do it. I guess we would have to start working on her attitude, too.

We went back and forth for a little while, savoring our victory and the defeat of the Spirit Tortoise.

Chapter Sixteen:
The Country Above the Spirit Tortoise

"Mr. Iwatani, I cannot begin to express my gratitude for your efforts in this latest battle."

I went back to the meeting tent of the coalition army after the battle. The queen and foreign generals there all offered words of gratitude to me.

The crowd of soldiers and adventurers in the camp had also shouted their thanks to me when I walked over.

I have to say, I didn't hate it.

The only strange thing was that no one had said thank you before.

There had been times when those directly affected by the destruction of the waves had offered their thanks, sure, but no one had ever cheered for me and meant it.

As for the wave in Cal Mira, we hadn't had the time to celebrate because we'd been so worried about what was coming next.

For the time being, I wanted to immerse myself in the joy of victory. I wanted to savor it, just once.

Recognized as the MVPs of the battle, Raphtalia and Filo were surrounded by enthusiastically cheering soldiers.

"Wow! Mr. Naofumi!"

"Yay! Master! They like us!"

Considering I was a hero, I thought it would be best to avoid the limelight.

Then the crowd split and bowed, forming a path for me to enter the meeting tent.

Eclair, the old lady, and Rishia were standing off to the side, watching.

I guess I was the only one that really needed to stand before the crowd.

"This is all well and fine," I said, acknowledging their cheers.

I looked through the flap of the tent. I could see the massive body of the Spirit Tortoise where it lay on the battlefield.

It was just lying there, not even twitching, on the silent ground. Clearly, we had won.

"But there is still a problem."

"What's that?"

The queen and the others hadn't noticed yet.

I guess only a hero could really check anyway.

I looked at the icon flashing in my field of vision. The blue hourglass was still there.

The countdown to the waves always appeared immediately when the current wave ended.

So if the icon was still there, what could it mean? The blue hourglass was silent but present.

"The blue hourglass . . . It wasn't caused by the Spirit Tortoise."

Something else was going on.

The Spirit Tortoise had fallen easier than I would have expected, and the blue hourglass was still there.

What was it trying to say? It was saying that whatever was going on wasn't over yet.

"But . . ."

The whole tent fell silent. Everyone looked around, their faces growing pale.

We'd dealt with the immediate problem. The Spirit Tortoise was dead. But something else was going on.

"I want to you to look some things up for me. There's still something important we haven't figured out yet."

"Mr. Iwatani speaks the truth. Do not let your guards down yet. We must search out the cause of this."

"I'll leave it to you then."

"Then I will send word to the seven star heroes. They are currently on their way here, but I will have them visit the land where the Spirit Tortoise slept to see what they discover. Besides, they would be able to get there sooner than you could, Mr. Iwatani,"

I didn't know what sort of people these other heroes were, but I don't think it was the sort of investigation that needed a crowd.

Anyway, I had other things I wanted to look into.

"Please leave the Spirit Tortoise investigation to us."

"Yeah, good. We're going to look for the missing three heroes. And the coalition army will probably need help assisting the areas that were damaged in the Spirit Tortoise attack."

"As you wish."

The queen left to go investigate the tortoise's body. The land where it had been sealed away was going to be looked into by the seven star heroes. So what was left for us to do? We needed to backtrack, following the path the Spirit Tortoise had taken, to try and discover what happened to the other heroes.

Still, if we helped the damaged areas we came across along the way, people would start to think better of the Shield Hero.

I wanted the other heroes to understand how different I was from them.

The four heroes had to fight together, and yet I was the only one, along with Raphtalia and the others, who helped the coalition army in this fight. I should let them know how different we were—I had the right to do so.

There was a feast that went all through the night. I spent a little time there before meeting up with Raphtalia and the others.

"It looks like we are going to go searching for the other heroes pretty soon. We'll assist any communities we pass through on the way."

I told the queen to send word if they found anything of interest.

The investigation of the tortoise itself was very important. I wanted to help if I could, but it was also essential that we find and secure the other heroes as soon as possible.

If they were just out wandering around the countryside, I'd have to drag them back to the castle. And if they were hurt or unable to move for some reason, I'd have to find a way to rescue them.

Apparently they weren't dead—which meant I was going to have to go after them.

They had probably just run away when they realized that they weren't a match for the Spirit Tortoise.

They did have bad luck with that sort of thing, after all.

"We should check out the back of the Spirit Tortoise, too."

"You want to climb up on the back of a dead monster?"

"The shell is like a mountain, I think we can get a lay of the land and look for affected towns from up there."

"Understood."

The earlier we got started, the better.

They queen had mentioned going inside the tortoise's body. I hoped that we'd find the other heroes in there.

I had no doubt they realized they were in over their heads when they found themselves face-to-face with the tortoise for the first time.

Maybe they would have decided to sneak under its shell and to fight it from within.

They'd probably come crawling out and find some way to complain about the fact that we had defeated the Spirit Tortoise. That's just the sort of people they were.

We started the climb up onto the Spirit Tortoise's shell.

I took a look around. There was a small town nearby.

I wondered what the residents of the town had thought when they realized their homes were actually built on the back of a giant monster.

There was a building that looked like a castle of some kind.

The town itself had a Chinese aesthetic. People said that the Spirit Tortoise had Mount Penglai on its back, so I guess that made sense.

I wondered if there might be some mountain-dwelling ascetics up there too, but we didn't run into any.

The coalition army followed us up to the tortoise's shell.

The town we found on the shell was completely ruined, and there were corpses scattered around the streets. The Spirit Tortoise's servant monsters had probably killed them.

The smell of putrid rot stung my nose.

There were no servant monster bodies to be found. All we found were the bodies of the townspeople.

But the familiars infected the people they killed. We had

to be careful of the remaining bodies while we took a look around.

After a short walk, we came upon a building that looked like a temple.

It looked like the sort of place that would give us an important clue. Any gamer would think the same thing.

"Let's check out that building."

"Okay."

"Yay!"

"Oh, yes. I believe that temple was very famous in the area."

"You know your stuff, Rishia."

Eclair was saying short prayers over the bodies we passed.

"I read about it in an old travelogue."

"I came here once, many years ago. It's like there is nothing left. This is horrible."

We couldn't rely on the old lady's knowledge about the place then.

But at least she had been there once before. That was better than nothing.

I walked up to the temple and looked inside. The building had been severely damaged in the Spirit Tortoise's rampage.

I looked around the interior, but the only thing of interest I found was a mural depicting the Spirit Tortoise.

"What's that?!"

There was writing in the lower corner of the mural.

It was Japanese.

"What's it say?"

Those summoned from Japan . . . If you can read these words . . . Know . . . Please . . .

. . . Monster very dangerous . . . After the seal . . . Seventh . . . Destroyed . . .

After looking into it . . . The goal . . . Of the world . . .

Please . . . Intent . . . Do not break the seal.

Those that sacrifice all do so for the world.

Their sacrifice will be rewarded.

Yet pride . . . no . . . Can read these words . . . Then . . .

You must for . . . defeat . . .

The way to defeat it is . . .

Eight . . . Hero . . .

—Keichi

Much of the message was too degraded to make out.

But I could fill in some of the blanks myself.

The seventh would break the seal.

That fit with the number on the blue hourglass. Did the seal number count down to this?

The writing was too faded to make out the important parts. What was the "goal" it referenced?

It mentioned sacrifice for the sake of the world, and that lined up with what Fitoria had said.

Hey, this wasn't an anime or a manga or anything—why were the important parts all missing?

If I hadn't spoken with Fitoria before, I wouldn't have been able to make heads of tails of most of it.

I looked closer. Most of the writing had faded, but the section after "the way to defeat it" looked like it had been purposefully erased.

The scratch marks looked too old to have been created in the recent awakening. The writing itself looked ancient—so I couldn't complain about its illegibility. That didn't make it any easier to read though.

The only other thing I could get from it was the name at the bottom.

I didn't know his last name, but there must have been a hero named Keichi.

But it was all very old. There was no way to know what sort of person he had been.

Still, I knew there was a high likelihood that he had come from an alternate version of Japan, just like me and the other heroes.

There was no way to know how long ago that mural was painted. And all of our worlds might have been on different timelines.

Ren seemed like he was from a different time. Still, there was no point in guessing at random.

And what was this "eight" that was mentioned at the end? That couldn't have been referring to the seven star heroes.

It must have said something important, but it was too degraded to read.

Hm . . .

"Can you read it, master?"

"Yeah."

"Wow! The writing is so strange."

"Yeah, I guess they don't write like this in Melromarc."

"Is this the kind of writing system they use where you are from, Mr. Naofumi?"

"Yeah. Remember how I read that other thing?"

"Oh yes, that's right."

"Hero writing?"

Eclair whispered as she ran her hand over the letters.

Hero writing? That was the sort of thing an otaku would flip over. It did sound kind of exciting.

"Hero writing?"

"Yes. You probably know about it already, Rishia. It's the kind of writing that the ancient heroes left behind. It's from their world."

"It's just normal Japanese. Nothing special."

"The writing means something different depending on

the hero who wrote it. Deciphering the messages can be very difficult."

I could sort of understand what she meant.

So Ren and I might use the same characters to write, but there was always the chance that the words themselves could be different.

Words and their meanings change and evolve over time. Something that was said a long time ago could carry a different meaning when spoken in the present.

So the writing could mean different things, even if it was written with the same characters, depending on who wrote it.

It was possible to study the writing, but how would you even know if you were interpreting it properly?

"Has this been analyzed?"

"Um . . . Well, this land has adhered to isolationist policies for the last hundred years or so. It was very difficult to enter or leave it. So I don't know."

"Oh yeah?"

"Yes. They wished to protect their unique culture. Our own land was running out of resources due to all the wars at the time."

Did that mean this was the only chance anyone had yet had to read the mural? And was I the only person who could read it?

I'm sure someone else, some studied expert, could read it too.

But could we really be sure that all the heroes had all come from Japan?

If we found messages in English, that would be fine too, but what if they were in another language?

But then there were the characters themselves.

My shield could translate languages, so I'd been doing alright this whole time. Written language, on the other hand . . .

"It doesn't look like there is much else for us to learn here."

"No, it doesn't it."

"This temple was famous. What a shame that it was ruined by the Spirit Tortoise."

"Feh . . . Yes, it's very sad."

I turned to the two of them and indicated it was time to move on.

"Where shall we go next?"

"To the castle we saw earlier? It might be filled with useful materials."

"Wait, Mr. Iwatani. What do you intend to do with the castle's treasure?"

Eclair shot me a suspicious look.

Raphtalia gave an exasperated sigh.

"The owners are all dead, so I thought it would make the most sense for us to take what is useful."

"Isn't that just like looting a disaster area?"

She was technically right . . .

But there were sure to be people out there that needed those materials more than we did. They could be used to help other towns rebuild.

"We can distribute the materials to communities affected by the Spirit Tortoise's rampage."

"I suppose you are right."

"Or shall we surrender it all to the coalition army? They are heading for it as we speak."

"What?!"

Eclair gazed at the castle. A line of coalition army soldiers was heading for the doors.

Say what you want. Armies always behaved this way.

I hadn't been face-to-face with this stuff much lately, but the army was full of jerks. Not that I was one to talk.

"We cannot permit such barbarism! Mr. Iwatani, we must go stop them."

"Oh, yeah, right, right. Filo, take Eclair over there."

"Okay! Let's go, lady! Your hair is like red veggies!"

"Red veggies?"

Eclair was stunned by Filo's "special" way of viewing things.

Granted, most of us wouldn't take kindly to being called vegetables.

If she'd talked to me like that, I would have given her an earful.

"Listen up. My name is Eclair. I expect you to remember that, Ms. Filo."

"Um . . . Declaria?"

"No! Did you even listen to me?"

They both looked crazy to me.

I decided to tell the queen about what the coalition army was doing.

"Hey, old lady! Do me a favor and tell the queen about this."

"Very well. When I return I will accompany my disciple, Eclair, and help her defend the treasure."

She quickly ran from the temple ruins.

That just left Raphtalia, Rishia, and I.

"Let's continue looking into this."

"Alright."

"Fehh . . . It's so quiet. It's kind of scary!"

She was right—temples were kind of scary. They always made you feel like you were going to run into a ghost.

I guess ghosts were just ordinary monsters in this world.

"Hope we don't run into any ghosts or undead monsters!"

"Fehhh!"

The sun was starting to set, which helped with the creepy atmosphere.

"Mr. Naofumi, you're scaring Rishia. Please don't get her too excited."

"I know, I know. Let's leave the town to the army. Want to go check out the mountain?"

"Yes."

We went to the mountain and looked around for a little while. But we didn't find anything of interest, so we called off the investigation.

We did find a cave, and it seemed to lead into the inside of the tortoise's body, just like the legends had said. When the sun rose the next day, we went back to check the cave out in more detail but were not able to find a passage that led to the inside of the monster.

In the end, all we found during our investigation of the Spirit Tortoise was an eerie, empty mountain, and a town full of the sleeping dead.

Epilogue: A Disquieting Place

We didn't find the heroes, but we eventually made our way to the town where they were last seen.

Eclair and the old lady were off searching for the heroes on their own.

Rishia had wanted to go with them, but she was a bookish girl, so I figured she'd be most useful back at the Melromarc library researching the legends about the Spirit Tortoise.

The new town we found ourselves in had been damaged in the Spirit Tortoise's rampage, but there were a number of survivors, and they had already begun the rebuilding efforts.

Oh, and while we'd killed all the ones that were hanging around the tortoise, off in other places, the familiar monsters were still causing trouble.

We saw them from the road sometimes. They must not have been completely dependent on their master.

"Hey! Ren! Motoyasu! Itsuki! If you're around, come on out! It's not your fault that you lost to that thing!"

"Mr. Naofumi, you don't sound like you actually want to find them."

"I've been yelling their names for how many days now?"

Three days had passed since we defeated the Spirit Tortoise.

I still had no idea where the other heroes were wandering about, but I wanted to hurry up and find them.

Their party members were also still unaccounted for. All in all, we were looking for a pretty big crowd of people. How could so many people have vanished without a trace?

"But I heard that the only one that helped in the last battle was the Shield Hero."

We were passing through a damaged town center when I heard some adventurers talking about the Spirit Tortoise.

Raphtalia and Filo were resting in the carriage, so I decided to go visit an adventurer's guild and see if I couldn't find any new information.

Considering how major all the recent events had been, I thought there was a good chance that someone would know something.

"Really? What about the other three heroes? They call them the four holy heroes, so there must be three more, right?"

"I heard they tried to take the tortoise on by themselves and ended up disappearing."

"Did they lose or did they run away? Maybe it was just other people pretending to be heroes."

I eavesdropped on their conversation as I walked up to the reception counter of the guild and showed the staff a portrait of Ren and the others.

In the end no one knew anything.

Where the hell had they gone?

"If that's true, then we really can't count on the heroes for much, can we?"

"I know. Anyway, I'm gonna get going. I guess we just met, but you look out for yourself, you hear?"

"Yeah, thanks for the chat."

The adventurers finished their conversation.

They were complaining about the heroes, but I guess that's just how people talked.

There was no point in trying to correct them. I decided to just let it go.

I left the counter and starting thinking about whether or not we should move on to the next town. Then I heard it.

"You might be the strongest of the four holy heroes, Shield. But this isn't over. Next time more people will die."

"?!"

I turned to see who was talking, but there was no one there.

I thought I saw a few slips of paper fluttering to the ground, as if the speaker had just disappeared with some kind of trick.

What was that? The voice sounded like it might have been one of the adventurers I'd just been eavesdropping on.

I was carrying a shield, but I hadn't announced to anyone in that town that I was the Shield Hero, and no one in the area should have recognized my face.

I showed the guild staff a paper that the queen had given me, but it didn't indicate anywhere that I was the Shield Hero.

So how had the voice known who I was? Had I just imagined it?

"A hallucination? Or maybe I was talking to myself?"

I had a bad feeling about it. The ominous words hung over my head for a while.

It felt too ominous, too bad to brush off as a hallucination.

The blue hourglass was still blinking in my peripheral vision too. Something wasn't right.

There must still be something important about the Spirit Tortoise that we didn't know. We'd looked into it all we could. The queen and the army were still investigating.

I still needed to focus on finding the missing heroes.

When I found them, I had to find a way to make sure they understood how weak they were. That was the only way that they would listen to what I had to say.

But if they would listen, then maybe we could power-up enough to survive whatever was coming.

If they were alive, I wanted them to show their faces.

"Did you find the heroes?" Raphtalia asked as I climbed into the carriage.

"No. Nothing."

"Oh . . ."

Raphtalia looked upset.

Of course she would be. The whole world was going crazy. It was hard to smile.

"Hey, master!"

"What is it, Filo?"

She sat there, gripping the reins and pointing to a collection of stalls that lined the street.

"I've never seen that kind of food. I wanna eat it!"

She was the same pig she'd always been.

"Right . . ."

Were they selling local delicacies? I saw a dish that looked a lot like *yakisoba*.

It was like the Napolatta that Raphtalia had when we went to that lunch spot a long time ago.

Napolattta, to a Japanese person, looked just like a pasta dish.

There was a griddle where they fried pasta-like noodles in an original sauce.

"I can make that myself. Just wait a while."

"But—"

She really looked like she wanted to fight me for a second. Give me a break.

The food was more expensive than I wouldn't have expected, probably because of all the damage the Spirit Tortoise caused.

We had so much food in the carriage too. I thought I could make it myself, so I told her we couldn't buy any.

"But I want to eat it!"

"Filo, if you calm down, then Mr. Naofumi will make you some. Okay?"

"Yeah, I'll make you some for dinner. So chill out."

"Really? You promise?"

"Yeah, whatever."

I didn't know what to do about the sauce though. I'd just have to mix some stuff together and hope for the best.

Filo finally settled down and started pulling the carriage.

Hm . . .

"Mr. Naofumi, what's wrong?"

"Huh? What do you mean?"

"You've been lost in thought since you got back."

"I was just thinking how all of this has left a nasty aftertaste in my mouth."

"I know what you mean."

She looked like she'd realized something.

"Mr. Naofumi."

"What?"

She raised her face and looked straight into my eyes.

"Whatever happens, we can get through it. Just like we have until now. We just need to keep training."

"You're right."

We were training to prepare for the unknown, for the unpredictable.

So we had to stay optimistic and hopeful. We had to keep moving forward.

"Let's stick to the plan for now. Let's go find those heroes."

"Yes!"

"Okaay!"

So we left to look for the lazy idiots, wherever they were.

But I wasn't looking to punish them the way they had when they'd chased after me.

I was doing it to help them, because I wasn't the only hero that the world needed.

**Extra Chapter:
Trials and Tribulations of the Bow Hero**

My name is Itsuki Kawasumi.

I was walking home from my prep school, upset, because the results of my last test were always the same. I got another E.

Whenever I felt bad after class like that, I would relax at home by playing Dimension Wave and go for walks in the evening.

You could defeat evil and prove yourself in a game. But this was reality.

If you didn't have power, you could never live true to your sense of justice.

I was at the point where I felt like I would lose my sense of self if I wasn't able to rediscover it in the game world.

If it weren't for games, I might not be alive anymore. If I hadn't learned to enjoy stories, I might have gone crazy.

"How should I try to clear the game this time?" I muttered to myself at a crosswalk. The light turned and I stepped into the street.

Vrrmmm—

There was a bright light and a heavy rumbling sound. I don't remember anything after that.

When I woke up, I was in a stone-walled room I'd never seen before. There were three other young people there with me.

I had a bow in my hand. At first, I didn't understand what was happening.

But then I realized it was a situation I'd read about before in a novel or two. A man dressed like a wizard came into the room and begged us for help.

I didn't want to immediately agree, as I might end up agreeing to unfavorable conditions. And there was always the chance that this was an elaborate prank, right?

Plus, I was pretty sure that I'd just been run over by a truck.

Why would someone pick me up from a traffic accident and then try to prank me?

I guess there might be psychologists out there that would set up an experiment like that to measure my reaction. Maybe?

So I had a number of doubts, but I couldn't suppress my excitement either—I was in my favorite world, Dimension Wave. And I'd been summoned there to serve as a hero with one of the best weapons, the bow.

I decided to ignore all those people that had called me useless or dumb. I decided to use what I knew about the world to become strong, so that I might right wrongs and defeat evil.

I don't like to have the spotlight on me.

Justice is when you defeat evil without announcing it. When you do the right thing in secret.

That's what all the heroes I knew about from books were like.

They would never fight for the praise of others.

I soon realized I would have to hide the fact that I was the Bow Hero.

Besides, if evil realized that the Bow Hero was around, it would run and hide.

Ren, the Sword Hero, and Motoyasu, the Spear Hero, hadn't figure that out yet. They just ran around doing whatever they wanted.

But someday they'd come across an evil that they wouldn't be able to handle on their own.

Like that raping demon, Naofumi.

Right, I'd have to do it alone then. I decided to travel in secret, with my party member Mald, and defeat evil wherever I found it.

I was trying to gather information in town one day.

We often went to the town taverns to see if we could find anything out about corrupted nobility, unsavory merchants, or other people that preyed on the weak.

There were times when the castle requested I deal with corrupt members of the nobility as well.

Evil people were the best at staying in the shadows.

"Master Itsuki, it certainly seems as though the nobility in this town is up to no good."

We were taxed upon entry to the town. It seemed like everyone was on edge.

But it wasn't enough to just go around accusing people of unsavory behavior.

There was always the chance that it was a town that had issues with safety and corruption in the first place. Maybe the nobility had to raise taxes in order to do something about the preexisting problem.

"Up to no good? I suppose we should check into it then."

It was true that there might have been a preexisting problem, but my intuition was telling me that wasn't the case. It was telling me that there was evil in the area.

I went to go check out the mansion that the town's nobility lived in.

"Please! Please let me meet with your daughter!"

"No! Go away!"

"I brought money—we pooled our funds together for this."

People were arguing in front of the mansion of the town's nobility.

When I got closer I could see that it was a well-dressed married couple. They were arguing with the gate guard.

They both appeared to be in their 40s. Perhaps they were laborers. I could see that their well-cut clothes were also wearing fairly thin in places.

"We did receive your payment, but it seems to have just covered your interest."

"That's not what we agreed to!"

"Go away!"

"Ah!"

The guard shoved the man, who shouted and fell to the ground. The guard turned, went inside the gate, and closed it with a heavy, metallic clang.

"Ugh . . ."

"Rishia."

The man climbed to his feet. Along with his wife, he leaned against the bars of the gate and hung his head.

"Excuse me."

I called out to the couple.

They both turned to face me.

"What is happening here?"

"Who . . . Who are you?"

"Just a nosey adventurer."

Things went a little more smoothly when I hid the fact that I was a hero.

I certainly couldn't allow myself to be taken advantage of by those that might want to use the heroes for their own ends.

"Well then, don't worry about it kind adventurer."

"I can't just ignore that, not considering how it looked. Why don't you tell me what is going on."

My justice sense was tingling.

I felt like I could finally exercise it—it had been a few days since it had last been satisfied.

I'd recently disposed a corrupt king in a neighboring kingdom, and I still felt good after restoring justice to those lands.

"There's nothing in it for you."

"We'll see about that. "

"You're not going to leave unless we tell you about it, are you?"

"I guess not."

They both sighed deeply, then agreed to talk. I led them to a nearby tavern.

I bought them both drinks.

"Now tell me what's going on?"

"Actually—"

They were from a powerful noble family in a nearby town.

It was a rather poor place. It was more of a village than a proper town. They said it was a peaceful place.

Their family had fallen on hard times, but despite their relative poverty, they were still tasked with governing the town.

They were technically nobility, but they lived in a normal farmhouse, not a mansion.

They had disagreed with a number of the Melromarc royalty's pronouncements, which led to their authority and power being slowly chipped away. The fees incurred by refusing to be complicit with the demands of the crown was what led to their loss of status.

So they had very little money, but they were respected and loved by their fellow townsfolk.

They lived a poor but happy life, surrounded by friends.

But lately, the lands and fields of the townsfolk that lived under their rule found their crops and buildings sabotaged.

People reported thefts in the night. Con men plied the streets.

The noble family used their own funds to help cover the damages, and that was the end of any remaining savings they had.

"Our citizens are our treasure. So we gave all we had to secure their safety and yet . . ."

One day, merchants and tradesmen stopped visiting their town all together.

With no option to sell their crops or wares, life grew harder and leaner in the town.

The waves had affected their crops and handiwork. They had to use all their medicine to save the lives of those who were attacked by monsters.

Simply staying alive took all they had.

Finally, a nobleman from another town came to visit, saying, "If you give me your daughter and allow her to serve my house, then I will lend you money and appoint guards to watch over your town."

"How absurd! We can survive without your help just fine, thank you!"

They chased him away. But from the very next day burglaries increased dramatically.

The village lived in fear for a short while, but then adventurers appeared to drive the thieves away. A short while after that, however, a bill arrived from an adventurer's guild asking the noble family to pay.

But not only did they not have the money to pay, they had never asked for assistance from any guild.

Apparently, the nobleman from the neighboring town had sent a request in their names, and he soon arrived to encourage their payment.

"Give me what I asked for!"

"Papa! Mama! Fehhhh!"

"Rishia!"

"Hahaha. It's not so bad. I will offer you assistance."

The assistance they actually received was half of the promised funds. They also received a handful of rather rough-looking bodyguards.

It was clear that there was a problem right from the start. The bodyguards matched the description of some of the thieves that had been seen.

"When the issue was brought public, the bodyguards abandoned the town. We immediately ran here to meet with the nobleman, but he says that if we want our daughter back, we'll have to pay for her."

"Have you informed the crown?"

"It was all covered up before we could take our story to the castle. We had no other options, so we brought the money he requested, but he wouldn't even let us through his gate."

"Oh, Rishia!"

The wife started to cry.

It was a terrible story. The sudden uptick in burglaries was suspicious enough, but tradesmen had stopped coming through, and that was especially telling.

"Thank you for telling me."

I stood up and looked to Mald and the others.

They understood my intention and immediately nodded.

"Please, set your minds at ease. I will return your daughter to you," I announced, and we left the tavern.

The first thing on the agenda was to gather information and make sure we understood the situation completely.

If we were to accuse the nobility of corruption, we were going to need proof.

If I accused him based only on my authority as a hero, he might run away and escape. I would need proof.

"Master Itsuki!"

We centered our operations on the tavern and split up to search for proof.

Mald and I were walking towards the market when we ran

into a suspicious group walking haughtily down the street.

They stopped at a business and started eating all the arranged food without permission.

"Look at all this. What are you up to, lining up all this delicious-looking stuff! Eh?!"

"Ahhh!"

"Stop that!"

Mald stepped forward and yelled at them.

"Who the hell are you?"

"I saw what you just did! We cannot allow such behavior to go unpunished!"

"Ha! You want to have a go at it? People that piss us off tend to end up hurt."

I stood behind Mald and drew my bowstring back, fixing my aim.

Mald attacked the front two brutes while I pinned the rest of them to a wall with arrows through their clothes.

"Heh."

"You think you're going to get away with this?"

"I think we already have. Come after us anytime!"

A few of them managed to run away, but there was nothing we could do about that.

We looked around the market, but something was strange. Everyone was looking at us, and they were pale. They looked scared.

"If you guys want to live, you'd better get out of here!"

"Do not worry. We can protect ourselves."

We continued our investigation and ended up with quite a lot of proof.

We went back to the tavern for another meeting.

We had discovered that the nobleman's tax increases far outweighed that which was requested by the crown. Also, he had been accepting bribes from merchants and tradesmen. Furthermore, it seems that he was planning on selling the couple's daughter. That explained the situation in their village.

"Are you sure about this?"

"Yes."

"Hm . . ."

"He severely punishes those who challenge him. We met plenty of people that lost their fortunes paying for 'crimes' they never committed."

"Furthermore, people that couldn't be convinced to see things his way were disposed of by his bodyguards. The haughty jerks we met in the street earlier were a group of his bodyguards."

We'd run into a crowd of self-satisfied jerks on our way back to the tavern.

They were probably bodyguards under the nobleman's employ.

We had the proof we needed. The nobleman was definitely evil.

"We'll have to help him to see the error of his ways."

When I said that, the person sitting next to me nearly fell out of his chair.

But it wasn't because he was scared. It was because I sounded so cool when I said things like that.

"Yes, Master Itsuki."

"Let's get them, Master Itsuki."

"Yes, we will. Now then everyone, let's get going. For justice!"

"Yes!"

We all stood and left the tavern.

A tall, thick, metal wall surrounded the nobleman's mansion. There were guards posted at even intervals around it.

But we had already investigated the premises.

I pulled my bowstring back and pointed it at the gate and used a skill.

It was the perfect opportunity to try out a newly acquired, powerful skill of mine.

"Shooting star bow!"

The arrow shot like a shooting star, then clattered off the thick iron gate with a clang.

A whistle rang out.

It was an alarm being rung. In the distraction it caused, we climbed over the wall and snuck onto the property.

"Who are you? Stay right there!"

The nobleman saw us from his foyer. He pointed and shouted.

When they realized he was shouting, the guards all came running back in this direction.

"I don't know what kind of stupid adventurer you are, but breaking into my property will cost your life!"

"I should let you know, first of all, that we have quite a lot of proof that you have abused your authority as a nobleman, that you have colluded with corrupt merchants, and that you used your money to pay for bodyguards, all while using those guards to insight the fear that necessitates them. Finally, that you have kidnapped and imprisoned a young, weak girl. You are the very definition of evil! We have come to punish you!"

The man's face grew more and more red as I spoke. Finally, he shouted for his subordinates.

"That's some fancy talk from an adventurer. Whatever, it's no matter. Now, send these men to another world!"

The guards readied their weapons and turned to face us.

"Mald, Rojeel, everyone, let us show them the error of their ways."

"Yes, sir!"

My party members all readied their own weapons and began to clash with the guards.

I noticed that someone standing far behind us was trying to case support magic on us.

I fired an arrow to protect them from an attack.

We were doing all this for justice, so naturally I didn't want to kill anyone I didn't need to.

"Argh!"

"Damn, these guys are strong!"

"They aren't normal adventurers!"

"Leave it to me!"

A few of the bodyguards stepped forward to block our advance.

They seemed to be strong enough to block Mald's attacks and still deliver attacks of their own.

Still, if I just stood back and watched, it looked like Mald and the others would win easily.

That wasn't a bad idea.

Or I could wait until it looked like they were going to lose, then waltz in and clean up the bad guys. You had to make an appearance like that every once and a while.

"Master Itsuki!"

The bodyguards were hired as adventurers, which meant they had probably already gone through the class up procedure.

Not a problem.

"Shooting star bow! Arrow shower!"

I shot two of my strongest skills and instantly eradicated the group of guards battling Mald and the others.

Shooting star bow is a powerful attack that shoots an arrow like a shooting star. An arrow shower rains a number of arrows down on the enemy.

"AAARRH!"

Most of them fell to the ground, defeated. The others ran away, realizing they couldn't win.

"What's with that bow?!"

Looks like my cover was blown.

I met Mald's eyes, and he nodded. He stepped forward and boomed, "Silence! Do you not see the bow in our master's hands?"

I raised my bow so that everyone could see it. The guards and the nobleman stood silent, dumbfounded.

"Surely you can see who this is. It is the revered Bow Hero, Itsuki Kawasumi, who stands before you."

After seeing how powerful my last attack had been, the men all lowered their heads to me.

They were all shocked—stunned—by my power. Of course they were.

"Now then, I will send word of this disturbance to the crown. I expect your punishment will be swift and severe."

"That cannot be! We've don't nothing wrong, and—"

"We already have all the proof we need. You can't wriggle out of this one."

"Hrm . . ."

The nobleman was trying to think of an excuse to get out of it. Mald kicked him and then started to punch him.

The nobleman had caused so much pain to so many people. A little beating was fair.

"Now let the girl go."

The nobleman rose on shaky legs, produced a knife, and ran at me with it.

He was actually pretty quick. I would guess that he was at level 65 or so.

He'd been rich, and that came with time to train and study and level up.

Watching him on his feet, I could see how he'd survived Mald's beating mostly without serious injury.

"So this is what it has come to. You pretend to be the Bow Hero?! I'll finish you!"

"You fool!"

Mald and the others had their weapons ready. They all rushed to land the final blow.

"Argh! You . . . ugh . . . I . . . die . . ."

The fool. He should have known not to challenge me.

"Ahhhh!"

The remaining guards all screamed and ran.

We were left alone in the courtyard with the defeated nobleman.

They really laid into him. It looked like he couldn't take anymore.

"I think that about wraps it up!"

I'd been trying to use that line when we finished a battle. It was starting to sound more natural. I saw Mald and the others smile.

"Fehh . . . Papa? Mama?"

We took the key from the nobleman and freed the daughter of the town's noble family. Her name was Rishia.

When we unlocked the door to her room, we found her crouched in a corner, shaking.

I couldn't immediately tell how old she was.

Based on some things her parents had said, I was guessing around 17. But she looked younger than that.

I could see why the nobleman had wanted to kidnap her so badly. She was a very cute girl.

"Wh . . . Who are you?"

"It's alright. I am a friend of your parents and I'm here to help you. We've taken care of that evil man, so please relax."

"Really?!"

"Yes. Now come on."

I approached her and held out my hand. After flinching

away, she took my hand in hers. She was still shaking.

I helped her to her feet and we left the mansion. I brought her straight to the inn that her parents were staying in.

"Papa! Mama!"

"Rishia!"

"I was so scared. But this man saved me!"

"We have just received word from the crown that the governor of these lands has been punished by the Bow Hero. It looks like we had someone looking out for us, Rishia.

"Fehhh! Is that true?!"

Rishia was very surprised. She regarded me with shock.

"Yes, I suppose there is no longer any need to hide my identity. It is true. I am the Bow Hero, Itsuki Kawasumi."

"Fehhhh!"

Rishia looked like she was about to scream.

And what was that whimpering sound she kept making?

"Now then, dry your eyes. It's time to live peacefully and joyfully with your family. Get a good night's rest," I said. With Rishia back in her parent's care, I decided to go take a rest myself.

The next morning, we were preparing for our departure in front of the inn when Rishia and her family came by.

"Oh, Master Bow Hero!"

"Shhhh!"

I held my finger to my lips and told her to be quiet.

How could I operate as a secret agent of justice if she was going to scream about it in the middle of the town?

Any bad guys would run away if they got word that I was near. I didn't want that to happen.

"We're terribly sorry!"

"Fehhh! I wanted to thank you for all you've done."

"Oh don't worry. It was nothing—but please keep it a secret."

"Yes, sir!"

Life was good! Nothing felt better than the swift administration of justice!

Huh? I noticed a strange monster pulling a carriage down the street.

I don't think I'd ever seen a monster like that in Dimension Wave.

It looked like a filolial, but different somehow.

"Now then, Mald, Rojeel, everyone, let's be on our way."

I forgot about the monster. We had other things to worry about. It was time to hit the road.

"Shall we go visit Mald's hometown next?"

"There's no need! There is no evil in my town!"

"Are you sure?"

"Yes! I know it very well!"

"What impressive people."

"Fehh . . . Yes. I wish I could be more like them!"

But I was so weak. What could I do? Nothing. I just let myself be kidnapped.

I wanted to be strong like the Bow Hero, like Master Itsuki. I wanted to save people. I wanted to be a champion of justice.

I wanted to help him.

"Papa, Mama. After all you've done for me, I'm sorry. I . . ."

I watched Master Itsuki and his party as they walked out of the town. My heart ached the further away they became.

"Rishia . . ."

"What's wrong?"

"I . . . I'm going with them."

I was surprised by my own conviction.

If I stayed with those people, I could grow stronger. I just knew that I could. I had to make it happen.

"The heroes are involved in very fierce battles."

"Are you sure you want that?"

"Yes. Even if the battle ends with my death, I won't regret it."

"You've always stuck to things once you've made up your mind—though that could take you awhile."

"Yes, and your father has always said that you should travel and see the world."

"Rishia, do what you want. But please don't forget how much we care for you."

Papa and Mama nodded and gave me a small satchel of money.

"I'm going! Mama! Papa! I'll do my best! Please don't forget about me!"

I waved to them, then turned and ran to catch up with Master Itsuki.

Eventually, though he looked a little concerned, he agreed to let me travel with him. However, he said how difficult it would be many times.

Mald told me that I would have a lot of work to do.

Duties as a new team member are taxing, but I'm not going to give up.

I wanted to be like Master Itsuki. I wanted to be a champion of justice for those in need, for those who cried themselves to sleep.

All that Itsuki Kawasumi, the Bow Hero, did for others, all his attempts to bring justice into the world, sprang from his need for approval.

Would a day come that he learned what justice truly was? Or would his sense of justice be his end?

Only time will tell.

But there is one thing we can know for certain.

Rishia Ivyred had not yet met with all that trouble, the

tricking, framing, and expulsion from Itsuki's party—all those terrible things had yet to happen.

He was thrilled. He thought he had been transported to an ideal, exciting world.

The *Records of the Four Holy Weapons* say that the Bow Hero is distinguished by his sense of justice.

What fate awaits those that proceed without understanding the difference between justice and self-righteousness?

He was not yet a true hero.

He was still occupied with fulfilling his own selfish desires. Soon, he would come face to face with a great obstacle.

The girl that he once saved vanished from the Bow Hero's story for a time.

Her story continued with the owner of the carriage that had passed them in the street, the Shield Hero.

They would not be able to stop the large waves that were yet to come.

Those waves of destruction will drown all that is, leaving only desolation behind.

The Rising of the Shield Hero Vol. 6
© Aneko Yusagi 2014
First published by KADOKAWA in 2014 in Japan.
English translation rights arranged by One Peace Books
under the license from KADOKAWA CORPORATION, Japan

ISBN: 978-1-935548-56-0

Written by Aneko Yusagi
Character Design by Minami Seira
English Edition Published by One Peace Books 2016

Printed in Canada

4 5 6 7 8 9 10

One Peace Books
43-32 22nd Street STE 204 Long Island City New York 11101
www.onepeacebooks.com